Endless

By Saundra Crum Akers

i

A Mysterious Ohio

WWW.SaundraCrumAkers.com

ISBN **978-1511527071**

DEDICATION

SPECIAL THANKS TO STEPHEN RAY GREER FOR THE THREE LINE RHYME IN CHAPTER 26.

ALSO TO MY CHILDREN AND GRANDCHILDREN WHO HAVE ENCOURAGED ME, AND TO THE STAFF OF ***OUR PLACE RESTAURANT*** WHO HAVE SUPPORTED MY WRITING EFFORTS.

THIS BOOK IS DEDICATED TO MY GHOST MYSTERY FOLLOWERS, INCLUDING, BUT NOT LIMITED TO:

JUDITH EILEEN SIMPKINS

ROSEMARY STEWART

DONNA MARIE JOHNSON

TINA WILSON

JEANETTE WILSON

MARIE PALMER

CINDY MONGOLD

THANK YOU FOR YOUR SUPPORT.

TABLE OF CONTENTS

Chapter One

On a farm near Urbana, Ohio, 1926

Cecile Montgomery went about her housework as if nothing was wrong. She could hear her husband ranting and raving to himself and to the kids about her, but surely he'd calm down soon. She didn't plan to back down from this fight. The issue was way too important. Her mind flittered around in her skull trying to find a way out, feeling trapped. She had to take the kids and leave this house right away; but where could she go? Her mother, Sarah, was dead, but her father, Henry Winston, was living. Henry had a store in town, but lived in the country about a mile out of Urbana, five or six miles from the Montgomery farm.

"Maybe I can take the kids and go there," she thought as she shoved another log into the cook-stove and then washed her hands in a wash basin that sat on a nearby stool. Using her wet hands she pushed a strand of dishwater blonde hair out of her eyes, then dried her hands on a towel that hung above the wash pan. In the old metal mirror above the basin she could see the strain around her soft blue eyes and the tiredness lining her once pretty face.

Sixteen year old Vanessa came into the kitchen and stood beside her mother.

"He's crazy," she said.

"He'll be alright," Cecile told her, patting her hand. "He gets like this but he calms down after a while."

"I don't know, Mom. This is different. He thinks you're going to leave. He was mumbling about it."

~ 1 ~

Cecile dried her hands and started to put flour and shortening into a bowl for biscuits. She whispered, "He's right. I want you and Harrison to start getting your things together so we can leave, but don't let him see what you're doing. Make sure he's not around while you pack. We'll leave once he goes to sleep tonight."

Vanessa gave her mom's shoulder a quick hug and left the room.

Later Harrison came in to tell her that his Dad was cleaning his gun and crying. "He's really off his rocker, Mom. What are we going to do?"

"Elton Montgomery is just full of himself. He won't do anything," Cecile said, "But stay away from him. Go out and chop some wood. Don't give him anything to complain about. Where's Vanessa?"

Harrison looked to see that his father wasn't around and then said, "She's getting stuff together for both of us like you said. I'll go outside and do the chores, like always and maybe he won't suspect anything."

"Good boy."

Cecile hugged her lanky fourteen year old son and gave him a smile. "That's good. We'll just go about our day as if nothing's happened. No need to set him off again."

But as she worked, Cecile couldn't help but go over the events of the day that had led to her husband's fit of rage. Early that morning, Elton had gone to town for some chicken feed and Cecile and the kids had begun their morning chores. Cecile noticed that Vanessa was hanging on her coattails about 9:30 am. It was if her daughter had something to say but didn't know how to say it.

"Let's take a break," Cecile said and she and her daughter went to the kitchen for a cup of tea.

"You're wanting to tell me something," Cecile said when they were seated.

"You might not understand," Vanessa whimpered.

"And yet I might... I was sixteen once."

"It's Dad," Vanessa said, eyes huge and tear filled. "He made an improper proposal to me. Please don't blame me. I didn't do anything. He just tried to touch me and he...said and did things."

This wasn't what Cecile had expected and she froze with her cup inches from her lips trying to assess what Vanessa had said. She'd expected that the problem might be about a boy that Vanessa fancied or something like that but certainly not a revelation about her own husband.

"When did this happen," Cecile thought she was doing good to keep her voice matter of fact.

"Last night when I was helping him put in the garden. We went to the shed to get some seed and while we were there, he grabbed me and...you know."

"Did he say why he was acting that way?"

Vanessa began to sob. "He said it was my fault because I'm starting to dress like a flapper and to act wild, but Mom, I'm not really. My dress is longer than any of the other girls. He came into my room one day when I had the phonograph on and was trying to do the Charleston. I guess that's what he means."

Cecile took her child in her arms. "None of that is any excuse for him to act this way. He's a lecher and worse, he's proposing incest, not to count adultery. Don't cry. We'll find a way to fix this. I'll confront him as soon as he comes home from town; it's not your fault. Just stay away from him until I figure out what to do."

When Elton returned Cecile had taken him outside, near the woodpile, and away from the children's ears to confront him. As predicted, he tried to weasel out of it at first saying that Vanessa was lying for some teenage reason of her own, then he said, "She's been acting like a whore doing those modern dances in her room and playing music all day."

"That doesn't matter," Cecile shouted. "She has a right to dance in her own room, naked if she wants, as long as she shuts doors and windows. It privacy. How did you come to see her anyway?"

Elton frowned and stuttered but finally admitted that he'd been working in the attic and there was a knot hole above Vanessa's room. He'd seen her playing dress-up with a flapper dress and dancing to music on the phonograph. I also walked in when she was doing that Charleston dance one time," he added.

"So you were spying. You're the guilty one; you're nothing but a window peeper," Cecile slapped Elton's face in a fit of rage, her disgust with him bubbling over in fury.

Elton grabbed her and shook her until her hair fell down and her teeth rattled.

"I won't have this. You will not hit me ever, or I'll kill you."

Cecile had turned violently, ripping away from his grasp; she ran away from him, leaving him stewing in the back yard. Shortly afterward she had heard him chopping wood.

Maybe he'll take out his anger on that wood and not on me.

He's hit me before but after today he'll never hurt me or my kids again.

We won't be here.

She had made up her mind to leave as soon as she knew what he'd done to their daughter. How could a father do such a thing? Even if it wasn't betrayal of his wife, which it was, how could he use his daughter this way? Elton disgusted her; hatred for her husband nearly choked Cecile so that she gasped for air. That had been two hours ago and Elton had been throwing fits ever since. Cecile looked up as Harrison came in the back door and let the screen slam loudly. He came close to his mother and whispered,

"Dad's got the 38 and he says he's going to kill you. I'm scared."

Harrison clung to his mother as if he'd never see her again. "Stay away from him Mom," he pleaded.

"Oh, I don't think he'll hurt me," Cecile said patting her son on his back and hugging him tight in return. "He'll calm down soon and try to make friends with me later. That won't happen though, he's broken what trust I had in him. I've got to get you kids out of here. He's dangerous one way or another."

"Please Mom, hide from him," Harrison begged.

Chapter Two

She had a hard time getting Harrison to leave the kitchen but Cecile knew that if Elton saw the kids gathering around her, excluding him, he would be even more furious with all of them. He'd think they were ganging up on him. The kids could get hurt. No sooner had Harrison gone out to slop the pigs than Vanessa was back in the room.

"What can I do Mom," she asked through lips that trembled.

Seeing that her daughter was shaking all over, Cecile asked her to go and pack some things for her.

"Your Dad will be expecting to see me packing my clothes if he suspects I'm going to leave. He won't think about you doing it for me. I'll just stay here in the kitchen cooking supper like always. It should confuse him. Use the old army bag my father gave me. He might check the suitcase."

Cecile treasured the comfort her children gave her but felt it might put them at risk to spend too much time together right now, angering Elton. It was contrary to her maternal instinct which bade her to gather her chicks under her wings and protect them. She looked at the Grandfather Clock and saw that it was already 5:00pm. The days were long and it would still be several hours until dark. Peeking out the window she saw that Elton had left the yard.

Maybe he's in the barn," she thought and then remembered the moonshine stored in a cabinet above the horse stall. "He might be drinking and working himself into a worse state. Hopefully he'll just go to sleep...then we can leave."

When the meal was ready, she instructed Harrison to go to the barn and tell his father that there was food on the table.

Harrison wasn't happy with the chore his mother had set for him, but he obediently went to the barn, and cautiously approached where his dad was sprawled in the hay drinking moonshine. Usually Elton abstained from liquor. He was a fine upstanding man in the community according to all the neighbors, but Harrison knew better. His father had a vicious temper when things didn't go his way. Still his outbursts were seldom and for the most part he was a stable father and citizen. Now Elton was grumbling to himself and Harrison hesitated to approach him. Deciding to listen to what his father was saying in order to gauge his intent, Harrison hid behind a stall and watched his father whisper into the moonshine bottle.

"She's not going to ruin my name in the neighborhood. I worked too hard; can't have her take it away" Elton mumbled, his words sloppy and indistinct.

Harrison stayed put.

"Not going to leave me either...kill her first...kill em all.

Won't get caught...say Cecile took kids and run away..."

Elton took another slurp from the moonshine jug.

"Neighbors goanna feel sorry for me." Elton took the gun by his side and sighted it on a cross beam of the barn.

And then Harrison saw his father start to sob uncontrollably. Scared he left the barn without approaching Elton. Back in the house he told his mother what his dad had said.

"We've got to get out of here. He'll kill us all."

"That's just the bottle talkin. What we're going to do is this. You and Vanessa eat up right fast and then go on over to the neighbors. Tell Ben Jones to call the sheriff or if he don't have a phone, go and get the law. You and Vanessa will stay at the Jones' until I come to get you. You hear?"

"We don't want to leave you Mom; go with us," Vanessa looked desperate.

"No...I got dishes to do. I'll be alright. Grab biscuits and ham and get on your way. Grab the bags you've packed and take mine too. I'll hold down the fort."

Cecile gave both her kids a long hug and a kiss on the cheek. "Go along now."

They went.

Cecile fixed a plate for Elton and set it in the warming part of the stove, then started clearing away the rest of the dishes on the table. The ham went into the ice box and the bread into a bread box. Although trembling inside, she focused on mundane things to help her keep her nerves under control. She knew that unless Elton had fallen asleep with a jug of moonshine, he would be in shortly and trouble was bound to start then. Eyeing a butcher knife, she wondered if she was going to have to protect herself from her husband of 18 years.

"Can't be a sheep and just lie down for the slaughter," she thought as she covered the knife with a dish towel but left it on the counter.

"Where's my supper. I see everybody done eat without me," Elton bellowed from the doorway.

Had he seen her hide the knife under the towel?

"Your supper is in the warmer, sit down I'll get it," Cecile said, not wanting to anger Elton any more at the moment.

Elton sat and she brought the food and put it on the table and then continued to wipe down the kitchen.

"What... you can't be bothered to sit down at the table with your husband/" Elton took an angry bite of ham, tearing off a big chunk, then continued with his mouth full. "Where's them kids?"

"I had some work for them to do before dark."

Cecile turned away and started to fill the sink with hot water from the stove. She'd already washed everything but she needed something to do. She began cleaning shelves in the pie safe.

"Vanessa's a liar. I didn't do nothing to her," Elton said.

Cecile said nothing.

"She's a little tramp, that's what she is. She can't wait to get out and rut with all the boys in the county."

Cecile tried to stay quiet but this was too much. "You have a beautiful and smart daughter... a decent upright girl; I won't have you tearing her down. She is not a liar. You're a pervert."

"And you're just jealous because Vanessa is younger and prettier," Elton charged.

Cecile turned and walked out of the kitchen, trying to control herself, before she grabbed the knife and gave Elton what he deserved. She had told herself not to react to anything he said but it was hard to keep that in mind given all of Elton's iniquities. Even Cecile's very practical mind was having difficulties with this.

Don't say anything...just wait until the sheriff gets here or until Elton falls asleep.

Then you leave, get the kids, and go to your dad. Make a new life without him.

Of course Elton wasn't going to leave it at that. He followed her into the living room where she'd grabbed a dust rag and was dusting the window sills. He grabbed her shoulder whipping her toward him. He had the 38 in his hand.

"Don't panic," Cecile warned herself. She said nothing, just stared at him.

"I'll kill you," Elton said, his voice slurred, but decisive.

Chapter Three

She couldn't help it; even with a gun at her throat, Cecile was outraged. "You've betrayed me and you've betrayed our daughter. You're worthless. I detest you." She threw herself into getting away from her husband. She didn't hear the blast that tore into her. She just silently slid to the floor.

Elton stood unsteadily looking at the woman on the floor and the blood that had sprayed over his clothes. He couldn't figure it out. He hadn't meant to pull the trigger but it happened. Why had she made him do it?

"Cecile," he wailed and grabbed up the rag doll that was his wife in his arms.

"I didn't mean it Cecile," he wailed into the emptiness of the house. His sobs rocked the room but Cecile lay inert in his arms, unmoving. Elton looked at the 38 which he had dropped on the floor. It had been sprayed with blood and was wet and slippery. Slowly he lay his wife on the couch and picked up the gun.

"I'm coming to be with you Cecile," he said and then a new blast shook the room as Elton turned the weapon on himself.

The Sheriff was too late for Elton but Cecile was still alive when he arrived. They got her to a hospital in Columbus but she was in grave condition. The neighbors, Ben and Nell Jones brought the two Montgomery children to the hospital later that night; both seemed be in shock, almost catatonic, as they sat in the waiting room hoping to see their mother. Cecile's father, Henry Winston, sat with the children but he was in almost as bad a condition as they were. Cecile was his only child. Elton's parents hadn't come to the hospital yet. They were probably making plans for their son's funeral, Dr. Grayson thought, as he approached Cecile's family to update them about her condition. After introducing himself, the doctor said,

"Cecile's in very bad condition and I won't lie to you. It's touch and go. She may become conscious long enough for you to talk to her soon. If she does, please don't ask a lot of questions. I'm even limiting the Sheriff as to how many questions he can ask. Trying to answer questions will only tire her and could lead to her death sooner. You need to prepare yourselves. She may not make it no matter what we do."

Doctor Grayson nodded to each of the family members and went back to Cecile's room. He motioned the Sheriff who had been standing beside her door to come in with him.

"I'm going to let you try to talk with the victim for five minutes. You have to restrict your questions to who shot her, and why. Don't go into detail, just confirm that her husband did it, as we already know he did from the evidence, and from the children's testimony. That way you can close your case."

The Sheriff nodded and stepped into the room.

Cecile didn't appear to be conscious. She looked as white as the sheets covering her and her breathing was ragged and incomplete. The Sheriff stepped up to her and lightly shook her shoulder. Cecile moaned but didn't open her eyes.

"Who did this to you? Who shot you Cecile?"

"El...El...Elton."

"Why?"

Cecile fluttered her eyes and opened them briefly. "Fight," she said.

"What was the fight about?"

"Improper with my daughter."

Cecile fell asleep again.

"That's all," Dr. Grayson said.

They walked back out of the room and the Sheriff went on his way. Dr. Grayson went back to the family and told them that they should let the patient sleep for about half an hour and then they could go in to see her for ten minutes. He gave them strict directions as to what to say and how to act while visiting. Half an hour later, her two children went into the room. Cecile was able to open her eyes briefly but kept falling back to sleep.

"I love you Mommy," Vanessa said, her eyes dripping gallons of tears in spite of the doctor's admonition not to upset her mother.

Vanessa was a classic beauty with long dark hair and bright blue eyes. Her hair was pulled back into a knot at the base of her head, showing off her long neck. Doctor Grayson noticed how dignified she was as she shook his hand while he murmured at the senselessness of this tragedy.

Harrison took his mother's hand and held it in his; he looked mournfully down at the woman who had given him life and who he loved. He was slender and wiry with his sisters coloring.

"It will be okay, Mom," he said.

Cecile tightened her hand on his before drifting away again for a couple of minutes. She woke again and mumbled, "Love you both."

A bit later Cecile asked, "Where's Elton?"

"He shot himself," Harrison said, ignoring the doctor's admonition not to upset his mom.

Cecile turned whiter and faded off again, but aroused herself to tell them, "Nest egg in teapot. Use it." Both children held her hands now and she started to cry.

"I love you both so, so much," she said in a whispery weak voice.

Both kids told her how much they loved her, then had to leave since their time was up.

The doctor made Henry Winston wait fifteen minutes so Cecile could rest before allowing the father in to see his daughter. He found her partially awake but white and worried.

"Elton dead," she asked.

"Yes; I'm glad of it."

Cecile reached for her father's hand. She was having trouble talking now and each thing she said was with great effort.

"Please...please...take care of my kids."

Henry leaned down to hug her. "You know I will, darling. You know I will," he said soothingly.

Cecile drifted away again and Henry stood there wondering what to do. He wished Elton Montgomery was still alive so he could shoot him again for what he'd done to his daughter.

"And to my granddaughter too," he thought. "Life's not fair."

A nurse bustled in and checked on Cecile. "She seems awful tired now. You'd better run along. She don't need any more company tonight," the nurse said.

Winston returned to the waiting room and got his two grandchildren, bundled them into his Model A, and drove them back to the farm.

"Don't worry," he said, "I'll be right here. I'm staying the night."

The kids just nodded, too distressed to do anything else.

At dawn the next morning the Sheriff was at the door. "I'm sorry to tell you this but Cecile died in the night," he said.

He was met with a flood of tears.

Chapter Four

Vanessa and Harrison were sitting together in a side room at the funeral parlor where their parents had been laid for viewing. Half the county had come to visiting hours; it was mostly out of curiosity because of the double shooting, the kids thought. They had gone away to be by themselves.

"I don't care what the adults decided," Harrison was saying, "I never wanted to see him again, and I'm sure Mom wouldn't want to have her funeral at the same time and place as his. He killed her!"

His voice was rising with hysteria, anger, and sadness. Vanessa was crying hopelessly.

"They said it was the money," she sobbed. "We don't have that much money and all that has to get sorted out. Having their funeral at the same time and burying them on our farm is the cheapest thing to do. Grandpa and Grandma think they're helping us by saving money. They'll just be here in the funeral home tonight and then they'll be at home in the parlor until they are buried. That will save money too."

"Grandpa Winston don't like it."

"No, but he did agree that they have to try to conserve all the money they can so we can get by until we're grown and can get jobs or something."

"I'm grown. I'll get a job."

"Better stay in school, Grandpa Winston says. You're only 14."

"At least they put Mom and Dad at separate ends of the room. I'm not even going to look at him if I can help it," Harrison said.

"Yeah, but they'll be buried side by side to save space in the family graveyard. We can't visit her without visiting him. I don' think Mom would like that at all." Vanessa sniffed and wiped her red eyes.

"His parents are upholding him in his evil-doing," Harrison accused bitterly.

"I know." Vanessa pulled her sweater over her eyes to hide the redness.

They sat quiet for a few minutes and then Harrison asked bitterly, "What do you think the Preacher is going to say about Dad. He's not going to say he was a bad man, I'll bet. He'll just gloss over what happened."

"It'll be hard for him; Preachers have to say good things, like about forgiveness and all that. He's probably praying for Dad's soul right now."

"Not me," Harrison said darkly. "Mom was the best woman in the world. She loved us and was good to us. She worked hard and took care of Dad too.

He killed her!

How could he kill her?"

Harrison let the sobs overtake him, as he leaned against his sister. The children clung together believing no one else could understand their pain.

"There, there," Mrs. Jones said.

Having missed the kids, she had tracked them to their refuge.

"It's going to be okay," she told them patting their backs.

Two days later the husband and wife were laid to rest in the graveyard that contained Cecile's mother and baby brother already, as well as some members of Elton's family. The cemetery was located near the old orchard about 500 feet from the house.

For the moment Henry Winston arranged to live with Vanessa and Harrison to help keep stability. Each morning Henry got them off to school and then went to Urbana to his store to work all day. He was worried sick as to how he was going to take care of the crops that Elton had managed to plant before his melt-down. There were also new crops that needed planted. The burdens of this tragedy were about to overwhelm Henry, but he knew he had to be strong for his grandchildren.

"I'm not a farmer," he told George and Ethel Montgomery, Elton's parents.

"Maybe we can get some neighbors to help out," George said. "I'll ask around."

"The kids need the money from the crops," Henry said.

Every evening Vanessa gathered wild flowers, which were plentiful at this time of year, and took them to her mother's grave. Harrison went with her some days. She talked to her mother but both children ignored the man who had destroyed their lives, the man who had killed their mother.

Sometimes Vanessa felt a coldness as if some evil force was studying her, stalking her even, but she knew this was just her imagination. Her father had done some terrible things but he wasn't really evil…at least not most of the time. Still she felt as if his disapproving eyes were on her. She limited the time spent at her mother's grave, because she felt uneasy and tormented.

"Someday I'm going to move Mom's grave away from him," Vanessa told Harrison. "I'll do it just as soon as I can afford to."

"I'll help pay for it," Harrison said, "Or we could have "him" put somewhere else."

"You're right. Mom should stay right here with us...send him away."

They never called their father Dad now. It was "He".

Neither of the kids were doing very well in school this year. It was just too hard to focus on the things the teacher asked of them when their lives were falling apart. Harrison wanted to quit school and get a job but all three grandparents opposed that.

"You can work in the summer helping us with the crops, but come the fall, you need to go back to school," Grandpa Winston said. "It's what your mom would want."

For that reason Harrison stayed in school...to please his mom.

Nell and Ben Jones, the neighbors to whom the children had fled for help, came to visit often. Nell frequently cooked up a stew or a dessert knowing that Henry wasn't a good cook. Vanessa cooked but she wasn't very good either. Sometimes the neighbors stayed to dinner sharing the food they'd brought with them.

One night everyone was at the table when the electric lights went out abruptly. It was nearly 9:00pm and there was still some light outside but it was dusky inside the house.

"There goes that light again. That's the third time it's happened this week," Henry said. "It's always the same thing. The fuse isn't working but as soon as I take it out and put it back in the lights come back on." He stood and reached for his flashlight.

"Maybe Elton didn't like something you said," Ben joked.

Henry scratched his forehead. "We were talking about him, weren't we," he asked.

"How about the other times when the light went out. Was you talking about him then?"

"You know I don't remember, but I'll pay attention next time." Henry winked at the kids.

The kids looked around the table at the adults, silent but thoughtful.

Later Vanessa asked Harrison what he thought. "Is his ghost around? What about Mom. Could she be trying to tell us something?"

"Ah...they were just joking. I don't believe in ghosts. Do you?"

Vanessa sighed. "I wish I could believe that Mom is still here watching over us, don't you?"

Harrison thought. "Yeah but if you get one you get em both. I don't want him!"

The next time the light went out it was just after Henry had said, "Your Dad left with crops in the field and more to be planted; he abandoned you with no way for you to plant or harvest this year's crops. I've talked to the neighbors. They want to help. They don't blame you kids, but they sure do blame Elton for what he's done."

Everyone in the room noted it when suddenly they were plunged into darkness.

Chapter Five

Vanessa was scared. She was sure it was her father who had thrown the room into darkness in retribution for what her Grandpa had said. Henry didn't comment. He just got the flashlight and went to fix the fuse.

"It's him," Vanessa whispered when the light came on and she could see her brother's wide eyes staring at her.

"It can't be. We're just imagining things. It's a short in the electrical system or something.

"It's not. It's him." Vanessa started to cry. "It's my fault; if I hadn't told Mom what he did none of this would have happened."

Awkwardly Harrison patted her hand. "You had to tell. It's not your fault. It's his."

Although he kept up a good front for the kids' sake, Henry Winston was uneasy. He didn't believe in ghosts...of course not. But it was creepy how those lights kept going out. He resolved to have the electric company look for a short in the system tomorrow. If it was a short it could cause a fire or something. Henry sighed and closed the door to the fuse box. He missed his daughter so much it hurt. He loved his grandkids but the responsibility for them, the farm, and his store was weighing heavily on him. Some days he felt that he couldn't do this one more day. His own farm needed some attention too. He hardly ever got over there anymore.

How am I ever going to do all of this?

The kids were good but clannish shutting him out. They seemed close to each other but aloof to the rest of the world. He didn't know how to reach them. In his own grief he felt alone because there was no one but himself and his grand children who knew just how precious Cecile had been. There was no way to make anyone understand the great loss her murder had been. Henry consoled himself with the thought that maybe Cecile was with her own mother now. He'd be able to join the both of them someday.

Returning to the kitchen he said, "I think we've got an electrical short. I'm going to contact the power company tomorrow."

The kids looked at each other and then at him.

"You don't think it could be a ghost then," Vanessa asked.

"No I don't; there's a rational reason for it. The wires must be too old and brittle. I'm going out to your mother's grave before dark. You two want to come with me?"

They did.

At the grave the three of them stood looking at the spot where Cecile had been laid. Flowers were still on her grave but now they were wilted and pale. Harrison cleaned the old flowers away while Vanessa laid some fresh cut flowers in their place.

"I'm thinking I'll plant a flower garden just for her," Henry said.

"That'll be nice. Can we help you?" Harrison sounded eager to do something for his mother.

"I'm expecting both of you to help, Henry said. "I don't have enough hours in the day as it is."

"Tell us what to do and we'll take care of it," Vanessa said.

They stood there a few more minutes and then slowly walked back to the house.

"Better get your homework done. I've got to work in the barn a while," Henry said, diverging from the path to the house to head toward the barn.

Dutifully they got out their books but then both sat at the kitchen table staring out the window toward where their parents lay. Grades had been suffering for both of them since the tragedy. Neither seemed to be able to concentrate.

"I still think Dad's here somewhere and he's watching us. I can feel his eyes on me and it's awful," Vanessa said. "It makes me nervous."

"How is he watching you...like a father checking up on you or like a man watching a woman," Harrison asked.

Vanessa turned sharply toward her brother. She hadn't thought about it that way and now she had to because of his question. She wanted to smack Harrison for that. She didn't say anything for a while.

"Don't you feel him," she asked instead.

"I suppose I do sometimes. But if Dad's spirit is here, wouldn't Mom's be here too?"

Vanessa shook her head. "I haven't felt her so far...just him, staring at me, accusing me of causing what happened."

"There's no way she'd leave us alone with him. If he's here, she is too." Harrison was adamant about that.

Vanessa voiced her biggest worry. "If his spirit is here, maybe he'll try to hurt us."

"I don't think he can. We're in different worlds now."

"But he might!"

Harrison shrugged and looked out the window again. "I guess we should just try not to make him mad then."

All night long Vanessa thought about the ramifications of having her father's spirit hanging around the house, spying on her. She was highly disturbed. Starting the next day she changed her style of dress from modern to dowdy. She just couldn't bear to think her father was watching her even lusting after her from the grave. Her dreams had been terrible during the rare moments when she had fallen asleep the night before. They had contained leering skeletons who were reaching for her with long boney fingers. She changed clothes in her closet and wore the most unattractive things she could find.

Harrison noticed the change in her dress immediately and asked her why she was wearing that old thing to school.

"I will if I want to," Vanessa replied.

She had put on make-up just before leaving the house and so even the frumpy clothes couldn't completely subdue her beauty. Harrison followed behind her as they walked, his face thoughtful. Finally the clouds cleared and he nodded to himself but didn't say anything. Vanessa had started down a self- protective path; day after day she withdrew more into herself, hiding in clothes her mother had worn. She found that it felt good to wear her mother's clothing because it seemed as if she was protected by her mother's arms. Her grandfather didn't say anything and after the first day neither did Harrison. Both of them seemed to understand what she was doing and why. Her grandfather did ask if she was okay a few times, disturbed by her withdrawal from friends and family.

"I'm fine Grandpa Winston," she said. "I'll get through this."

Henry nodded. Inside he whispered a prayer that Vanessa would recover from this awful time and live a normal life. He prayed for both his grandchildren, in fact.

Chapter Six

Two days after the shooting;
two months in the past.

Cecile felt herself rising from her bed but somehow her body didn't go with her. What a weird feeling. Looking back at the white hospital bed, where she'd been lying, she winced. Her son and daughter were standing beside a figure on the bed; they were crying, but she couldn't understand why. Her thoughts were muddled.

"What's wrong Harrison," she asked. She hadn't seen him cry for four years or more.

Harrison didn't look at her, he just bowed his head more deeply and sobbed as if he was heartbroken.

"It's okay," she said, but he showed no sign that he could hear her.

Peering again at the woman on the bed, Cecile finally realized that the body was hers, but looking down where she stood, she could see her feet. She was standing right here, her feet firmly on the tiled floor. She was not in that body on the bed; it was her as she had been, but not her in the present. How confusing. She brooded for some time as she watched the weeping children and her father stand by the bed and pat the hand of the body that had been hers.

Finally it made sense.

"I'm dead. They can't see me. But how can I be in two places at one time?"

Vanessa wasn't sobbing aloud, but a flood of tears was washing down her face. She was immobile as if struck to stone. Cecile put a hand on her daughter's shoulder but she couldn't get her attention. After a few minutes Cecile drifted down the hall. She couldn't stand to see her children hurt but she couldn't do anything about it. She found that she was able to travel all over the hospital but no one knew she was there. Traveling incognito was fun and she enjoyed it for a while. She didn't want to think.

Finally she had to though. Elton had shot her. Then he had shot himself. Why would he do that? He'd loved himself so much he'd been willing to sacrifice his daughter for his selfish wishes. He'd killed his wife to protect his reputation. So if he loved himself so much why would he kill himself? Maybe he thought he'd get locked up, talked about, and repudiated by the community. That would be worse than death to someone as egotistical as Elton Montgomery. Cecile shook her head in disbelief. The last thing she'd ever expected Elton to do was commit suicide.

She wandered from hospital room to hospital room visiting patients, then went to the nurse's station. Tucking herself onto a counter, Cecile sat down to listen to the gossip of the day. Julie Plankton, a woman from a farm near the Montgomery's, was going on about something so Cecile tuned in to her.

"I can't understand why they're doing it," Julie said. "If it was my family I wouldn't."

"I heard they were trying to save money for the kids," Betty Wakefield said.

Julie shook her short curly head of hair. "It's not right. I know if it was me and my husband shot me to death, I wouldn't want no double ceremony with him; nor to be laid beside him for all eternity."

Cecile's blood chilled.

They're talking about me and Elton.
Someone plans to have a double funeral for us.
They're going to bury us together!

Betty shook her head. "I don't guess it matters to her now. She was married to him for nearly twenty years but I don't suppose she'll know she's lying beside him for eternity. She's gone on to her reward and he's probably stoking the devils' furnace by now."

"But if she does know it must infuriate her."

Betty shrugged, her silver hair falling into weak blue eyes. "I just don't think it matters anymore."

"If I was one of her children I'd be upset, you bet," Julie said.

Agitated, Cecile pranced around the desk, wanting to throw something. But it wasn't these women's fault that her family planned a double funeral and burial. Maybe it was best for the kids if some money was saved. Somehow they had to survive and continue in school until they were old enough to fend for themselves. The family didn't have a lot of money.

Surely Dad didn't agree to this.

It sounds like something George and Ethel Montgomery would cook up.

But, If it helps the kids, and I don't have to see Elton again, I guess I can handle it.

She went back to her hospital room where a nurse's aide was washing the body on the bed getting her ready for the undertaker no doubt. Cecile felt a breath of gladness come over her to know that she wasn't in that body anymore. Her family had gone and she felt bereft all at once. They had left her alone and all she had remaining of her former life was a dead shell that would soon be buried.

~ 33 ~

What now?

People in the hall and waiting room were gossiping about the double shooting and wondering what would happen to the children now. Cecile couldn't stand it. She pushed at the door to the outside and was surprised that instead of it opening for her as usual, her hand went right through. Experimentally she tried to put the rest of her body through the barrier and found that she could walk through walls and doors. It turned out that she couldn't go very far though. Some invisible thread was holding her close to the hospital.

I want to go home!

I want my kids and my Dad.

Cecile started to cry...or was it the drizzle of rain that had suddenly started washing through her. The liquid seemed to be dripping through her as if she was a sieve or something full of holes. It didn't hurt or feel uncomfortable exactly, but it was unnerving. How was she ever going to get used to this state of nothingness where she had no solid form to depend on?

She huddled under a tree and watched the sick and injured, the visitors coming and going from the hospital. It seemed more peaceful out here where Cecile couldn't see the blue and lifeless body she'd lived in for so long. The sight of it sent waves of depression skittering through her.

"If it upsets me so much to see my own dead body, how will I feel when I see Elton's? I never want to see him again, living or dead. It's going to be hideous to have us buried together and to have to look at his evil face."

It never occurred to Cecile that if she could see Elton, he might be able to see her as well.

Chapter Seven

Cecile watched as they prepared her body and took it to a hearse which would convey her to a funeral home for one night and then to the farm where she had died. She would be laid out in the parlor where her mother had been two years ago, then the minister would come and preach a little. She and Elton would be carried to graves that had been dug in the old cemetery and that would be that. She had no idea what she'd do then. Why was she still here anyway?

She sat in an empty spot in the hearse watching the scenery go by as they drove and realizing that she'd probably never see it again. How could she be both here and there in that box? It was mind boggling. She listened to the two men in the hearse chat away as if this was an everyday occurrence. Of course it probably was for them. When the farm came in view she had a strong wave of nostalgia hit her. This was home. At least she would be resting at home and her children could visit her grave. That was something.

They carried her inside and she saw that there was another coffin in the room. Hers' was placed at one end of the long room and that must be Elton in the casket at the other end. She felt a wave of gladness that he was gone and could not harm her or her children any longer.

The best thing he ever did was kill himself.
Finally the rest of us can have some peace.

Cecile went to look at herself when they opened the casket. The face she saw was white and waxy. The eyes were closed as if she was asleep, her hands were crossed over her chest. The woman in that box looked like a manikin she had seen once when she and Elton had traveled to Cleveland. Nothing about her looked real.

Well, she's not real.

*The real **me** is right here.*

I outgrew that skin and shed it like a snake does.

Cecile cried silent tears when she saw Vanessa, Harrison, and her father weeping beside the casket. She wished she could tell them that the body they cried over wasn't her that she was right here, and was okay. Friends and family were coming into the parlor and going by the coffin to look at her remains and that bothered her. They would remember her this way forever and not the way she'd been before Elton's bullet had torn into her.

"Why did he do it," she asked herself.

Of course there was no answer.

The neighbors, Ben and Nell Jones went by the coffin, Nell shaking her head at the awfulness of it all. She hugged Vanessa and Harrison and then shook Henry Winston's hand and told him how sorry she was. Other people drifted in with pies and a ham which they gave to Elton's mother to put away in the ice box.

Cecile looked at Elton's parents and realized that they had lost a son just as her father had lost a daughter. However, it was hard for her to feel that sorry for them. Elton had done this thing to her and to her kids. He had also hurt his own parents by taking his life. Everything that happened was Elton's fault.

She watched as Ethel Montgomery went up to Henry Winston and shook his hand. "I'm sorry about this Henry," she said.

"I'm sorry for your loss," Henry mumbled politely.

That is all he said audibly but for some reason, Cecile heard his unspoken thought. "I wish your son was alive so I could kill him again."

That was exactly what Cecile had thought. If Elton was still alive she'd like to make him pay, and pay, and pay for the harm he'd done to her kids... her Dad, and to herself as well. She knew it wasn't right. She should forgive him his sins, but she just couldn't.

"Good thing that boy is outta my reach," she heard her father tell a friend of his a little later.

She cried some more thinking of the hurt her father was enduring. She wanted to hug him and tell him she was still around but no one seemed to be able to see her or feel her touch. She'd already tried that. People stood or sat in groups; Cecile noticed that her children had gone to a side room where they could be alone. She stood beside them for a while and then went back to her casket.

"I brought some milk from Quality Creamery on Court Street, and a pie from Daisy Bakery. That will help to feed people after the service," a woman from the Methodist Church was saying.

Henrietta Goth, the woman she spoke to was nodding her head rapidly, agreeing that the pie and milk would help. "I brought a small ham," she said. "It's in the ice box."

"I couldn't find the flowers I sent from the Bodkins florist. They said they'd have them out here by this afternoon," the first woman complained.

Cecile drifted away, not interested in ordinary gossip today.

"It's not like we never have any crime around here," a man she didn't know was saying. Last year that gang of six robbed the North Lewisburg bank of $ 9,000.00. But who would have predicted that Elton Montgomery would do such a thing?" The man who said this lifted a spittoon from beside him and spit a stream of tobacco into it. "He's supposed to be a pillar in the community and all."

"Did you see the obituaries in the Daily Citizen; neither one of them was more than a paragraph or so and didn't tell what happened. Here I got a copy." The tobacco chewing man wiped his hands on his red handkerchief and then pulled a paper out of his pocket. He handed the paper to his friend.

Cecile positioned herself behind the man and read:

Elton Montgomery, son of George and Ethel Montgomery will be laid to rest on the family farm at 2:00pm tomorrow. Funeral will be held at his home. He is the father of Vanessa and Harrison Montgomery and was the late husband of Cecile Winston Montgomery. .Reverend Roger Terrell of Urbana Methodist church will officiate.

In a separate obituary, she read:

Cecile Winston Montgomery, wife of Elton Montgomery, daughter of Henry and Sarah Winston, and mother of Vanessa and Harrison Montgomery will be laid to rest tomorrow on the family farm where she died. Visitation today from 2:00pm to 8:00pm. Service at 2:00pm tomorrow afternoon with burial in the family plot to follow. Reverend Roger Terrell will officiate.

Upset Cecile turned away. Her entire life had been reduced to four or five lines on a piece of paper. No one was telling the truth about what happened. She had been treated no better in print than the murdering man who had blasted her with a shotgun. As for Elton the biased newspaper was protecting him, it seemed. She was crying again as she turned away from the men and the newspaper aiming to look for her children. Instead she had an even bigger shock than the events of the last two days had presented. Standing near the end of the room beside the casket that was resting there was Elton Montgomery as big as life, and twice as frightening.

Chapter Eight

Cecile stood transfixed unable to react. The air she didn't need anyway, but still liked to breathe, whooshed out of her lungs; she felt icy all over. Elton seemed to be as surprised to see her as she was to see him.

They stood one at each end of the room, staring at each other.

Where did he come from?

Where has he been?

Why are we both still here?

Confusion muddied the scene around her and Cecile looked wildly for some place to hide. Maybe Elton couldn't hurt her now...but maybe he could.

The words her mind kept playing over and over were as follows:

"This is endless...endless...I will never get away from him. It's endless. Is there no escape?"

Cecile's form heaved with tears that could not be seen by the people in the room, and yet she felt as if she was making a spectacle of herself, so she tried to stop. Turning the other way, she attempted to ignore Elton's presence but then worried that he'd stab her in the back, she turned toward him again. Elton was glaring across the room at her, ignoring the people who had come to his funeral and the bad things they'd been saying about him. Cecile saw only anger and disgust, no sorrow for what he'd done, in her husband.

"Let us bow our heads in prayer the Reverend was saying.

Cecile bowed her head and prayed to God that he'd take her out of this place or that he'd bind Elton Montgomery and throw him into the fiery pit where he belonged. When she opened her eyes she saw that Elton was still where he had been; he was still glaring at her.

"Why would he be mad at me? He's the guilty one," she thought. "This is bewildering."

Throughout the room people were moving about and talking. The final service would be held tomorrow and then the two bodies would be laid to rest out under the old tree with other family members who had gone on before them. Suddenly Cecile wondered if the rest of the family had gone on or if, like she and Elton, they were still right here somewhere. She looked around her but saw only living people. She could tell the difference between spirits and the living by the slightly blue aura and translucent skin of the spirit. Her own arm held a bluish tinge and her finger nails looked whiter, not a healthy pink.

Maybe there are other spirits out in the cemetery, but they don't seem to be here.

She looked toward Elton. He had left the spot where he'd been standing and was listening to a group of men who had gathered to talk to Henry Winston, Cecile's father. They had moved out of the room with the caskets and into a kitchen area where there were refreshments. Although she didn't want to get any closer to Elton, Cecile wanted to hear what the men were saying so she moved that way a short distance. The conversation wasn't very interesting to Cecile, but seemed to be fascinating to Elton.

John Goodman was saying "The big four railroad has been elevated through Urbana and they're building a freight depot on Miami Street." "I hear there's going to be a passenger depot too," Bill Elliott said.

"Whatever that might be," John agreed.

"How about that White Swan Bar and Restaurant that Alva Strum is building at route 235 and route 36," a man Cecile didn't know asked.

"I don't know but they better hope there's no firebug loose after the fire we had in April, the one that destroyed all those businesses and houses on the north side of West Court Street, I mean. It destroyed the carriage factory and everything." John said.

"You think a fire bug did it," Bill Elliott asked.

"Don't know but seems like we've got a lot of fires around here; not much crime otherwise."

"Well this murder-suicide beats all. I'd never have suspected it," the man Cecile didn't know said.

"Nope. Elton seemed like he had his head screwed on right and then this happens," John said.

With a sudden whoosh a small rush of wind circled the room throwing napkins and paper cups into the air. Cecile saw the look of alarm that crossed the men's faces but more importantly, she saw Elton's face as he glared at his peers. As clearly as anything, Cecile knew that Elton had caused the rush of air. If he could do that, what else could he do? Conversation in the room had died down and Cecile saw that many suddenly had other places to be. People had begun to say their goodbyes. Among those staying, there were curious stares around the room, perhaps looking for the source of the mini whirlwind.

"Heavenly Father, please protect me," Cecile prayed, fearing what the night held for her once these people were all gone.

She kept her eyes closed for a long time, listening sporadically to the babble around her but mostly saying her prayers for protection. Finally she felt she had a communication from God.

"You will have a choice to stay or go," the voice inside her head said. "If you stay, he will not be able to harm you."

When she opened her eyes it was with a grateful spirit and some restored hope. The situation still felt endless but maybe there was some hope somewhere. God knew of her plight and he'd help her. She hoped the voice in her head hadn't been just her imagination.

Meanwhile Elton was having a little fun with the remaining guests. Drinks got spilled, food disappeared from plates then reappeared in their laps or on the men's best dress shirts. Ketchup and mustard ended up on tablecloths in the dining room and the funeral parlor began to look a shambles.

Wondering what powers she might possess herself, Cecile took up a plate and sailed it at Elton. It passed right through him and hit the wall where it shattered. After that the die-hards who had stayed past the initial manifestations, took their leave and the family was left with clean up duty. They had agreed to this in order to get a price reduction on the viewing.

Cecile felt bad watching the members of her family work so hard, but it would freak them out too much if she tried to help, so she didn't.

Chapter Nine

Cecile hid herself in a cabinet in her end of the room just before everyone left hoping that Elton would not know where she was. She had cried with her father and her children as they'd finally let down after everyone else had gone home, but she had not left her refuge. She was still afraid of Elton.

"Once someone shows me that under any circumstances they will be a danger to me, I'm through with that person," she thought. "There is no way I'd ever feel safe with Elton again. The good book says 'Can a man take fire into his bosom and expect not to be burned? I know better than that. That would be to test and tempt God and we are forbidden to do that."

She tried to settle down in the confines of the cabinet but she didn't like it any more than she wanted to be with her dead body in that restricting casket. Still she felt she had to hide from Elton. Clearly he wasn't through with killing her. He'd do it again if he could find a way. She wondered if the voice in her head had been God speaking to her or if it was just wishful thinking.

Sooner or later she'd find out.

She huddled inside hoping that Elton didn't know where she was. It broke her heart to see her children suffering and she could feel a knife twist in her gut with every word out of their mouths. Vanessa was obviously feeling guilty as if what had happened was her fault. It was harder to know exactly what Harrison was feeling. Both obviously blamed their father. She had noticed that neither of the children had stood beside Elton's coffin. His mother and father had huddled there to greet visitors while the children and her father had stood near Cecile's casket.

Elton's little demonstration at the wake had probably been for her benefit, she figured, or maybe he was just showing off. At any rate he had created a disturbance and had shown that he had some abilities on this side of life. Cecile determined that she would start testing her own abilities to see what she could do soon. So far she didn't know much about how to use the spirit body she was in, but Elton had had a head start while she lay in the hospital. He was picking up things and using skills Cecile wasn't aware of having yet. She might have to use any skills she possessed to defend herself from the man who had been her husband. She needed to learn things fast.

I don't feel like I need to sleep. What will I do all night?

I don't want to see Elton, but I don't want to hide in this cabinet either.

Maybe I'll stay here tonight and try to get a plan ready for tomorrow.

She settled down and tried to get comfortable,

The night was long but untroubled by Elton, her killer.

The next day at 1:00 in the afternoon people arrived for a last viewing of the couple. Cecile could see that her children were stressed and nearly at their ropes end. Her father wasn't doing well but he seemed better than the children. Elton's parents had their ups and downs. Both were defensive because it was clear that people were blaming Elton rather than mourning him. Cecile could feel the anxiety in the room, even in her altered state. Some were whispering about the strange wind that had played havoc in the parlor during last night's wake. Many seemed to attribute the disturbance to something supernatural and most blamed Elton.

He didn't fool anybody after all.

Cecile hovered around her daughter who was breaking into sobs every few minutes. It looked as if Vanessa might faint at the drop of a hat although she was usually not the fainting type. Harrison was clearly upset too. Cecile knew he was fighting tears because he thought it wasn't manly to weep. She also knew that in privacy, Harrison would cry his heart out tonight.

"You going to bury them under that old tree out there," a man was asking Henry Winston, Cecile's father.

"I guess," Henry said shrugging. "That's where they dug the graves. I didn't tell them to do it."

"It's just that that tree looks so eerie with one of its' broken limbs looking like an arm pointing up and the other pointing down as if it's choosing Heaven for some and Hades for others." Ben Jones said.

Henry shrugged again; this tragedy had been almost too much for him. "I know; it's a strange sight. Funny how lightening zapped it just right to make it look that way. The rest of the tree looks like any other tree."

Cecile thought about the tree they were discussing. Harrison had stood in front of it one day with his left arm crooked upward and his right crooked down, posing the way the tree was. Elton had laughed at his son's antics that day, but if he was buried on the side that pointed down, what would he think then? Vanessa had taken a picture of Harrison. Cecile didn't suppose the children would find that picture funny once their parents were laid beneath the lightening fractured old tree. She tried to think...

"Is that tree an oak? If not what kind is it," she wondered.

She was scared about what would happen when her body was placed under the sod. Right now the casket was open and she could see herself lying there, cold and rigid but open to the air. Being a bit claustrophobic, she feared having that lid closed down on her, even though she was aware that she no longer needed the air to exist.

Will I be forced back into that body for eternity?
That would be a fate worse than anything.

She trembled while wet tears dripped through her body and landed on the rug beneath her.

Elton was back beside his casket this morning. She wondered if he was limited to that area of the room or if he could approach her. Curious about what she could do, she moved experimentally around the room, although not going near Elton. Nothing seemed to be confining her to one place. That would probably mean that Elton could go where he pleased too.

He's probably waiting for all this to be over and then he'll make his move against me.

Elton is not a forgiving man.

Everyone was talking in hushed tones as if louder voices could wake the dead and that was the last thing they wanted to do. Elton's shenanigans last night may have caused a lot of uneasiness and misgivings among their friends and acquaintances. The Reverend started to speak and all voices hushed as he mentioned pertinent dates and events in the lives of Elton Montgomery and told about the family he left behind. He then did the same for Cecile. Eventually he bowed his head and said,

"Let us pray."

Ignoring the words the minister was saying, Cecile prayed her own prayer for protection.

"Please protect me from the man who murdered me once and may try to do it again. And please help my children," she said. "Amen."

Chapter Ten

The couple were laid into graves side by side under the old tree. Someone had decreed that Elton was to be buried on the side where the arm of the tree pointed downward and Cecile on the side where the arm pointed up. No one admitted to giving those directions but that is where the grave-diggers buried them. Ironic perhaps, because Cecile knew that they were both right here and neither of them had gone either up or down as was traditionally believed.

Elton wasn't visible to her though. Maybe he had returned to his body. As for Cecile, she stood as far away from the grave as she could while still seeing what was going on. She cried with her father and her children, she followed them back to the house where someone had laid out casseroles and baked goods contributed by friends and family. She wept for joy because she was able to move around and hadn't been imprisoned in that box for eternity.

That joy was dampened a bit when Elton showed up for the food.

Well, not really for the food because when he tried to eat it, he caused a commotion as people saw a ham sandwich balanced in air, moving around like a small flying saucer. Many left at that point and whispers started all over again.

Cecile went back outside and drifted to her grave, smiling a little at the prophetic tree that stood above their resting place. That tree did make an apt statement; she like it and felt validated by it. Thinking about the prayers she had sent God's way and how she felt he'd answered her, telling her she'd have a choice whether to move on or not, she smiled. If she chose not to move on she would have protection from Elton and he would not be able to harm her.

I *probably imagined that; but look there, what is that bright light over my grave?*

Cecile stared at the light. Its shaft of radiance angled downward, missing Elton's plot but centering squarely on hers. She wondered if that could be the light a friend had told her of after nearly dying when a tree fell on her. The friend had said, "I knew that all I had to do was walk into that light and I'd be with God."

Voices distracted Cecile. Her children Vanessa and Harrison were coming toward her grave. Cecile stood behind the tree although by now she knew they could not see her. She stared at the light which was beginning to dim, her mind wavering as to whether she should go to the light or not. There was a strong pull toward the radiant vision and she hesitated, looking back at her children. Even when she looked away from it she felt the light drawing her toward it. It was hard to resist.

All at once Elton was behind the children and she could see maliciousness streaking his face like a disease. He was looking at the light over her grave. Was he jealous? Looking her squarely in the eye, he reached for Vanessa and caressed her neck letting his hand slide down her chest, smiling a horrible smile of cruelty. He was trying to hurt his wife, not his daughter. Cecile knew that, but she couldn't bear what he was doing to Vanessa. Even though Vanessa could not feel his touch and he could probably not feel her, it was awful that he'd use his children in this way, just to hurt her. His lecherous eyes and hands touching her sweet daughter did just what Elton wanted. He was terrorizing and intimidating her.

Cecile silently told the light, "I can't go now. I have to protect my daughter from this horrible man, from her own father." She only prayed that she was right and Elton would not be able to harm her, that she could in fact protect her children. Even if Elton could hurt her, she had no choice. She had to protect the children. He'd just showed her that there were many other ways he could hurt her and he was willing to do whatever it took to punish her.

Hurt her he could...just not physically, she hoped.

Life hadn't been easy and death wasn't going to be a picnic either.

Just as when Cecile had put her arms around her children, they had not appeared to feel her presence, Vanessa didn't seem to feel her father's touch. Cecile had not been able to actually touch the children earlier. Still what Elton had done was obscene. Cecile wondered how she was ever going to get away from this endless marriage. The tie continued to bind her, even after death.

Whatever happened to "Till Death Us Do Part?"

Cecile fervently wished that death really had parted her from her husband!

She drifted back inside the house after having watched Harrison and Vanessa at the graves, hearing and feeling their despair. What was going to happen to her babies she wondered. She felt she had to stay here to protect both of them, but particularly Vanessa from their father. She had made that decision opting to let the light leave without her. For a moment the temptation to abandon this life and move on into the light had been compelling and she'd almost done it. Only

Elton's well timed actions had deterred her from that. Maybe that had been his intention...that she have a reason to stay on the farm and not leave for whatever place God had prepared for her. He'd made it clear that last day that he didn't want her to leave him.

"I hope I'll get another chance someday," she thought, feeling a sense of overwhelming loss.

Cecile felt a sense of despair. Moving on would have been the best thing for her but staying here to protect her children was her duty and Cecile held duty in high honor. Even though Elton's incestuous actions toward Vanessa just now were mostly meant to disturb his wife, still Cecile knew there was a possible threat after what Vanessa had told her. She wasn't sure what Elton could do to his daughter now, but she had to be around to alleviate any danger. Furiously she went over the situation in her mind.

Come to think of it, Elton always did like to do things he knew would hurt and disturb me.

He has a cruel streak a mile wide; but he fooled a lot of people...until he became a murderer.

From the conversations at our funeral, most people are on to him now.

It's funny that one thing he was upset about was having his reputation ruined.

I didn't have to do it; he did it to himself.

I saw a newspaper; it said the argument started because Vanessa reported an improper advance by her father. Elton didn't protect his precious reputation in the end, did he?

She drifted back inside the house after having watched Harrison and Vanessa at the graves, hearing and feeling their despair. What can I do to help my babies she wondered. Neither of them deserve this. Although she believed strongly in God and God's fairness and ability to run this world properly, she just didn't understand why he'd chosen to let things happen this way.

Chapter Eleven

It had been two months and Cecile had never said a word to Elton nor had he said a word to her. They had been in the same room as their family many times and she had witnessed Elton throwing around his hot air when someone said something he didn't like. He had cut off the electric lights time after time to annoy her father and had interfered in various ways with things the kids were doing. Sometimes this was just a way to entertain himself, she suspected, and many times it was just to annoy Cecile. He liked to upset his wife in any way that presented itself to his twisted mind. Clearly he was still furious that she had challenged him. Their used and cast-away bodies lay side by side under the old tree in the cemetery, but the essence of both Elton and Cecile remained in the house with the living, monitoring the comings and goings on the other side.

Cecile found herself pondering why Elton was still here. There were other dead bodies in the cemetery out there but no other spirits. If there were, she'd have seen them. She knew why she was here. She had to protect her children from Elton. The light had come for her but she couldn't go. Why was he still here? And then she realized... the light hadn't come for Elton. It had only shone on her grave, not his.

If the light comes for the innocent, what is supposed to come for a murderer?

That was certainly something to think about. And if something was coming for Elton, she wondered where that "something" was, and why was Elton still causing trouble on earth.

They were in the house at dinner time again, the best time to see all the family and to find out what was going on. Cecile was sitting by the sideboard and Elton was standing belligerently at the end of the table, as if challenging everyone to deny him. Cecile could see that the family was nervous since this was the place and time of day when most unusual occurrences in the house happened. No one spoke of it but her father looked around himself furtively, and the children had become almost silent as they ate the evening meal. It broke Cecile's heart to see what was happening to her family. Both her children had become withdrawn and didn't even talk to each other that much anymore. Her father seemed overwhelmed by the kids, the house, the farm, his store in town, and his own homestead...not to mention antics of vengeful ghosts. He seemed frailer to her and much more nervous than she'd ever known him to be.

Neighbors had come for two days straight to help tend the crops in June but now everyone was wondering how they were going to get the rest of the work done and how the crops would get harvested. Cecile had been considering ways in which she could help with some of the work but in her altered state she didn't know what she could do. Also, how could she help with cleaning or cooking, planting or harvesting, without spooking everyone in the house?

She had been experimenting with objects, picking them up and putting them in different places just to see what was possible. She found that she could touch and feel objects now. She had not touched a person to see if they were able to feel her touch yet. Of course Elton had played with the electricity and a few other things as well. If he could do all that, then he could do some work around here to help out couldn't he? She looked around the room. Vanessa sat dejectedly at the corner of the table, hardly looking at her food. Her hair was no longer shiny and beautiful, but appeared dry and brittle.

Such a shame; she's a beautiful girl.

Harrison was picking at his green beans, putting them on his fork then letting them fall off. He was keeping his eyes down as if he was afraid of what he'd see if he looked up. Maybe Elton's shenanigans had made him afraid. Cecile shot a furious look at her husband, then looked away. She didn't want to acknowledge his presence.

"Good job with the fried chicken," Henry told Vanessa, although he had only eaten one small piece.

"Thanks."

"I think your Mom had some good cookbooks if you want to try some of her recipes," Henry said.

"Okay, when I have time."

They lapsed to silence again."

School was out but the children had been working hard on the farm. Vanessa had taken over household duties and Harrison was doing what he could with the animals and the farm work.

"I talked to your Montgomery grandparents this morning; they said they could come here and stay for a couple of months so I can catch up with the store and all," Henry said.

Both kids looked at their grandfather.

"Don't go," Vanessa said.

"It wouldn't be for good...just for a couple of months so I can catch up."

Her father looked so tired it made Cecile want to cry. Across the way, Elton clapped his hands to let her know that he wanted her father out of the way. She didn't know why because he hadn't seemed too fond of his own parents in the past. Maybe he just wanted a change, or maybe he was just trying to annoy her. She ignored him.

"Why don't we all go to your house and stay for a while? That way we can work on your house and with all of us working on it, we'll get a lot of your work done. We could go to school from there just as easy," Vanessa said.

"Yeah, there's not as much to do here until we're ready to harvest the crops. We could drive over during the day while you're at the store and feed the animals," Harrison chimed in.

Cecile noticed that both kids were looking around the room as if expecting a manifestation of their father's anger. She had no doubt that they both knew Elton was still around and that was one reason they wanted to leave the farm. Henry appeared to be thinking this over seriously. Finally he said,

"It will just be for a couple of months. I'll come back and help harvest the crops and take them to market for you. This will give you a chance to spend time with your other grandparents. I'm sure George and Ethel will be thrilled to spend some time with you and see what you're doing."

Harrison blurted out, "I don't want to spend time with them," as he stood up and stumbled out of the room.

Cecile heard the door slam as her son banged his way out of the house. Then she heard him yell out in pain. She jumped up to go to him, noticed that Elton was no longer in the room, and sped right through the wall. Harrison was sitting on the ground rubbing his jaw which was already swelling. Cecile ran to him and saw his wide eyes rolling rapidly in fear. She touched his shoulder but couldn't feel the cloth of his shirt. Harrison couldn't seem to feel her touch either, and did not react. By now Henry was outside with Vanessa right behind him,

"What happened?" Henry asked.

"I don't know," Harrison said, "Something hit me. It felt like a sledgehammer."

There was no denying the lump that was forming and the redness around it. Vanessa helped her brother to his feet. "Let's get you inside and put some cold water on that," she said.

"Did you hit the doorframe on your way out," Henry asked. He was looking bewildered.

"No," Harrison said.

Henry and Vanessa stood looking at the red lump forming on Harrison's cheek. As they went back inside, Harrison confided to Vanessa.

"This feels just like it used to when Dad fisted me in the face."

They were both silent for a beat as Vanessa looked the area over.

"Looks like it used to too," she finally commented.

Chapter Twelve

Meanwhile, outside the farmhouse, things had finally come to a showdown. Cecile lost it when she saw what Elton had done to Harrison. Everything pointed to an invisible (to Harrison) fist to the face, although she hadn't exactly seen it. Apparently Elton was able to touch the kids, to hit them. Cecile grabbed a 2 by 4 and swung it into him throwing her husband into the bushes. To her surprise, the board connected and Elton had just laid down in the brush and made no effort to get up. She couldn't believe it; the board had connected with her husband and knocked him off his feet. She didn't know how much pain, he'd felt but he had not got up to challenge her.

Cecile continued to stand brandishing the weapon while her father, daughter, and son had their discussion. She even heard Harrison's whisper about how this wound felt like those his father had given him in the past. Cecile had wondered about things that had happened when she was alive, bruises on Harrison's face and body that he explained away as having got into a fight at school. Harrison never wanted to confide it her although she had given him opportunities.

He must have been afraid to tell me because Elton would just punish him more.

I wish I'd known what I know now, and protected my children better.

When everyone had gone inside and Elton began to get to his feet, Cecile whacked him with the 2 by 4 again, called him a "vicious, low, snake in the grass, viper" and strode away. In her anger, she had forgotten to be afraid.

Elton did not pursue her; Cecile knew it wasn't over though. He was just biding his time.

It surprised her that she'd been able to actually hit him with the 2 by 4, but then Elton had been able to hit Harrison with his fist. Had the rules changed suddenly? It had been as if her abilities had slowly been evolving and she could do things now that she couldn't before. If so why had she not been able to feel Harrison's shoulder and he not feel her touch? Since the beginning she hadn't been able to feel the children's shoulders when she hugged them, and they didn't feel her arms around them or her hand on their shoulder. Maybe that had changed or Elton had learned to do something she had not. However, if she could feel them, they would be able to feel her touch too. Look at that bruise Elton had put on Harrison's face. Elton had a very heavy and painful touch.

Cecile vowed to stay closer to both her children in the future. Although she tried it was so hard to be everywhere at once. After what Elton had done to Harrison, she was terrified about what he might do to him next time and to his daughter...especially if he could actually touch her! She envisioned rape along with other awful things.

From now on I stay in Vanessa's room during the night. Since I don't have to sleep I can keep watch on her when she's the most vulnerable.

Cecile didn't forget to say her prayers. In life she had been quietly religious although she never had time to go to church; she believed that God was with her all the time and if she couldn't get to church, knowing her mind and heart, God would not condemn her. Now caught in this strange situation where she was on earth but not on earth in the usual sense, she was unsure what to do but she still talked to God. Now she was praying for guidance as to how to protect her children from their father.

I don't even know why Elton hit Harrison.

Was it because he said he didn't want Elton's parents around?

Elton didn't get along that well with his parents; so why?

Cecile let herself drift back into the house where Vanessa was doing supper dishes and Henry was totaling up some bills from his store. Wondering where Harrison was she searched the house but didn't find him. Finally she located him by searching the barn. He should be feeding the horses and the two cows needed milked but instead Harrison was buried in hay in the hayloft, staring out an open window at the evening sky.

Wishing she could talk to and comfort her son, Cecile went to him and just sat looking into that beloved face. Softly she reached out and instead of her hand going through his shoulder as it had before, she felt the solid rough texture of his work shirt. Harrison felt her touch too. He sat up abruptly and looked hurriedly around the hayloft. Cecile wanted to hug him and reassure him but she didn't. It would surely terrify him. Maybe later if he got used to a touch, it wouldn't scare him too badly to embrace him. Wouldn't that be great if she could at least hug her children once again? A lot of comfort can be communicated by touch.

She had no idea why things had changed and her hands no longer passed through solid flesh but in some ways she was glad. In other ways it terrified her because apparently the same thing had happened to Elton. He had been able to fist Harrison and leave welts and bruises.

At least I was able to hit Elton with that 2 by 4.

But why didn't he fight back? He just stared at me but didn't try to hurt me.

When he was alive, he'd have been all over me for defying him.

Has something else changed?

Cecile was conflicted as she tried to assimilate the new rules and understand them. She had been given no rulebook for this in-between life and it was very confusing. Meanwhile, Harrison had arisen from his hay bed and climbed down the ladder where he'd begun to pitch hay into the feed troughs for the animals. The pitchfork seemed poised to defend himself if he was attacked again. Suddenly Cecile wondered what would happen if Harrison used that pitchfork to defend himself against Elton. If Elton could physically connect with Harrison, could Harrison stab Elton with the pitchfork? If so, what would that do to Elton? He was already dead but maybe it would hurt him or limit his movement somehow; the 2 by 4 had knocked him down after all.

Interesting question.

Later that evening Cecile hung around the living room where the family was gathered before bedtime listening to the news on the radio. Someone on the local radio station was discussing a murder that had occurred the previous year in 1925. A man named Bert Hi-warden had been executed for the murder of two women. His actions had resulted in nine children being orphaned and one man being committed to the Insane Asylum, the commentator said.

"Now his body is hidden underground in Oakdale Cemetery's potter's field," the man on the radio continued. "He can't hurt anyone any longer, and no woman will have to look into his treacherous eyes."

"Don't bet on that,"

Cecile wondered if Bert Hi-warden like Elton Montgomery was still somewhere in another dimension preying on women. She looked around the room and was shocked. Everyone in the house appeared to have heard her voice. They were staring around the room and at each other. The room was alive with fear.

"Who said that," Vanessa asked in a timid voice.

"Sounded like Mom," Harrison said.

Henry was trying to keep the kids from panic. That was clear by his hand on Vanessa's shoulder. Finally he said,

"Well, we've been thinking your Dad was still here. Stands to reason your mother might be too. It's nothing to be afraid of. They can't hurt you."

Harrison fingered his swollen cheek. "I'm not so sure about that," he said.

"Oh no," Cecile thought. Another rule she had relied on had changed. She could not only touch the living, but they could hear her words as well. Would they eventually be able to see her too?

I've got to be really careful now so I don't scare everyone to death.

Chapter Thirteen

Elton's parents moved in and Henry Winston moved out September 1st.

Ethel Montgomery set about getting used to the house and kitchen and George went to tour the barn and outbuildings. Cecile followed George since she trusted him the least of the two. She wished her father could have stayed with the kids but realized that he had been badly overextend over the past months. He had told the children that he'd move back in with them in November or December and let the Montgomery's celebrate the holidays in their own home, if possible. The children seemed anxious to get past the next few months. Although they weren't really comfortable with Henry yet, they had expressed doubts to each other about Elton's parents and what life would be like with them.

Cecile trotted along behind George Montgomery who was looking through harness in the barn, and carrying it to a new location which he apparently thought would make it easier to access. He was a thin man about 5 foot 11 inches tall with a balding pate surrounded by stringy light brown hair. His eyes were a washed out blue as if they'd been laundered a few times too many. His eyes weren't attractive like faded denims though. George's eyes were small and mean. She had an idea that's where Elton had found his own cruelty.

Elton...Cecile wondered at his behavior since his death. He had not spoken to her, nor had he tried to retaliate when she'd belted him with a 2 by 4. That wasn't normal for Elton. Had God rendered him unable to harm her, as she had prayed for? If so, then why had God let him hurt her children? That hurt Cecile more than if Elton had struck her. She didn't understand.

She also wondered where Elton was. He was out of sight for long periods every day although he usually showed up at suppertime to monitor the family. Cecile had watched vigilantly over her daughter but Elton had never showed up at night. Frequently Cecile passed through the wall between her children's rooms to check on Harrison also, but Elton had not made an appearance in either room any night so far.

What's he up to?

George's behavior was boring so Cecile traveled back to the kitchen where Vanessa was trying to show her grandmother where things were. Ethel was short and round, her body type in strong contrast to her husband. They must be like Jack Sprat and his wife in the nursery rhyme, with George not able to eat fat and Ethel not able to eat lean, Cecile had decided long ago.

Ethel's long gray-brown hair was twisted into a knot on the back of her head. Her face was wrinkled and her eyes had lost most of the sparkle they had once had, although there was still a hint hiding in there on occasion. She was in her element in the kitchen loving to cook as well as eat. This was something George highly approved of so, Ethel did a lot of it.

"I'm sorry about what Elton did to your mother," Ethel was saying.

Cecile suspected she'd never say such a thing if George was present.

'He did a lot of bad things; that's just one," Vanessa replied, then turned away to carry a pan of dishwater out the door to empty it.

"He's my son and I love him," Ethel said. "I don't know what got into him."

From outside the door, Cecile heard a splash as the water landed on the ground but Vanessa didn't reply to her grandmother's words.

"I wasn't a bad mother to him," Ethel said as Vanessa came inside. "He wasn't really a bad man. He just lost his way."

Vanessa said "Hmmm" She put clean water in the pan and started washing onions and turnips from the garden.

"Mom didn't do anything to him. He was the one who did bad things," Vanessa said after a while as she cut up the vegetables.

Ethel started to say something then Cecile saw her literally clamp her own hand over her mouth to stop the flow. She took a piece of chicken and carefully floured it before putting it into a skillet of grease.

"You don't believe me do you," Vanessa said. "I heard you tell people at the funeral that the papers got it wrong and Dad didn't do anything to me."

Ethel wiped her hands on a dish towel. "I think you misunderstood him," she said.

Vanessa scowled at her grandmother. "I know what he did and I didn't misunderstand."

Ethel didn't say anything. She started washing potatoes and peeling them. As she peeled and sliced the potatoes, Cecile could see that Ethel was disturbed. Clearly she wanted to defend her son but Ethel also loved her granddaughter. The expression on her face betrayed the push and pull of these opposite emotions. Reaching over, Cecile put a comforting hand on Ethel's shoulder before she realized her mistake. Ethel dropped the potato she was peeling with a plop and jumped away from the sideboard where she was working.

"What's that," she screeched.

Vanessa looked up from her work and stared at her grandmother. "What do you mean?"

"Something touched me, but nothing's there."

"Maybe it was Dad; we think he's still here."

The look Ethel gave Vanessa was the kind you'd give someone who had just blatantly lied to you. Vanessa stared back defiantly. Ethel finally asked, "What do you mean, your Dad is still here?"

"We think his ghost is around. This touch you felt, was it like someone comforting you or did it hurt you?"

Ethel thought. "It didn't hurt me."

"Lucky you then. He hit Harrison in the mouth with his fist."

Ethel's breath whooshed out of her…"What are you saying? Are you telling me that a ghost or whatever it was attacked your brother? Elton wouldn't do that."

"Elton, as you call him, hit Harrison all the time when he was alive…why not when he's dead."

Ethel frowned. "Don't call your father by his given name. It's not proper."

Vanessa snorted. "It's as proper as him doing what he's done to us when he was living and now he's hurt Harrison even after he's dead."

"There's no such thing as ghosts. I don't believe a word of this." Ethel lifted her hands in a grand gesture of throwing in the towel.

"Then what was it that touched you just now?"

Ethel just shook her head; she had no answers.

Chapter Fourteen

School started again in September and during the day it was quiet around the farmhouse. George spent time in the fields and at his own place during the morning and early afternoon. Ethel worked around the house and usually fed the chickens twice a day. Often she took a nap in the early afternoon. The liveliest time of day was as it had been from the beginning, the supper hour. Cecile's father no longer dropped by the house as he had his own farm work to do and his business to attend to. Cecile couldn't figure out where Elton went during the day but she never saw him. Sometimes she wandered out to the graves where her body and his lay. She searched around her mother's grave, hoping to see her mother's sweet face again, but no one was there. If none of the other spirits of people buried in this place were still on earth, why was she? Why was Elton?

Often she stared for a long time at the old tree above their resting place. The uplifted "hand" on the right of the tree as she faced it, even looked like it had fingers when the light was just right. The one above Elton pointed downward as if predicting his ultimate fate.

The hand above me is pointing to heaven and eventually I hope to go there.

I can't right now; my kids need to be protected.

I do wish Elton would make his trip downward though; that would free me.

I wouldn't have to stay earth bound because I'd know he couldn't do anything to the kids.

Cecile sometimes followed George as he worked around the farm. His manner was bitter and his demeanor was as if he felt he was being picked on. She had heard him tell Ethel that he resented having to be over here when all his work at home was getting behind.

"Kids are more trouble than they're worth," he said, "Look at what our son did to us and to his wife and kids. I wish we'd never had Elton, then we wouldn't be in this fix."

Cecile knew Elton's father was mad at Elton but it didn't appear to be because he'd killed his wife and committed suicide. It wasn't because he might have molested or tried to molest his daughter and had beaten his son. He was mad at Elton because he'd brought wide-spread scandal to the family and because now George and his wife had to step in and help with Elton's children since Elton had left them orphans.

She wrinkled her nose as she looked at George's weather-beaten face and gnarled hands where they rested on the pitchfork. He was mucking out the barn and Cecile could smell the pungent smell of cow manure mixed with Georges' sweat and other barn odors. Cecile had left the barn to Elton when they were both alive and now she looked around it curiously wondering just what Elton had done when he spent so many hours out here. Of course there was plenty of work to be done and laziness was not one of Elton's faults.

In one of the corners of the barn sat an old reclining chair and a radio resting on a bale of hay. She supposed Elton had taken time to rest in the chair and listen to the news around noon each day. There was also an old stove which he used to warm the barn during extremely cold weather. Sometimes her husband came to the house and got a plate of food which he took back to the barn with him. Above the radio was a cabinet that was attached to the wall. She wondered what was in it. Probably horse liniment and things like that she supposed...and moonshine. Elton didn't drink much but resented it that the government said he couldn't. He'd been buying illegal moonshine ever since.

She turned toward George who was swearing under his breath, apparently because he'd run into a warren of cobwebs and they had attached themselves to his face. But maybe it wasn't just cobwebs like George apparently thought, because Elton was standing beside his father.

Had he done something to George?

At least this time Elton was showing himself in daylight. Maybe he wasn't a werewolf or vampire after all She watched as Elton deliberately pulled a cobweb, complete with surprised spider, from its spot atop an old stable opening and swiped it over George's face. George jumped back, staggered and nearly fell as he struggled to bat the spider off his skin. He looked around as if trying to see how he'd encountered a spider web when he wasn't even moving. He had not walked into it. George didn't seem to be scared, just confused.

Cecile figured Elton hadn't liked some of the things his father had been saying to Ethel concerning him. He was focused on small tortures at the moment. However, Cecile knew well enough that Elton was prone to escalate his campaigns against others once he had started. She was surprised that he appeared to be leaving Vanessa alone even though his daughter had told on him. Cecile hoped that didn't mean he was working on something awful to make her pay.

Watching out for my kids will have to be my main goal in life...or as it happens, death.

George had started to fork hay into the cow's feed box now. Elton stared across at Cecile and grinned. He grabbed an armful of loose hay and threw it over George's head where it fell like a dry waterfall over him. Spluttering and coughing, George seemed confused once again as to what had happened and how.

With sudden insight, Cecile realized that Elton was performing for her benefit at the moment. He might not even be angry with his father. He just wanted her to see what he was doing, either to get a rise out of her or to make her admire him. Hard to tell which. Perhaps he was sorry for what he'd done to her, maybe he was once again the young man who had clowned for her attention. It didn't matter. She was through with Elton Montgomery forever.

She turned abruptly and exited through the wall, moving toward the house.

George could fend for himself, and Elton could go...well the tree was pointing the direction. She wished he would take the hint.

Chapter Fifteen

Life went on. Seasons passed, holidays were endured and a new year, the year of 1927, was begun. 1926 had been a traumatic year for the family, and for the community. Among other things, Sherriff Jacob (Jake) Bosler was killed on a downtown street in Urbana while trying to talk a mental patient down from upstairs. The man had threatened to kill any police who came up the stairs, but the sheriff was a former co-worker of the man and believed that he could talk him down. When the sheriff climbed the stairs, he was shot and killed. Jacob's wife Anna then finished out her husband's term as sheriff. She was the first and only female sheriff in Champaign County, Ohio.

Amazingly Cecile was able to keep up with local happenings better now that she was dead than when she'd been alive. When she was alive she had far too much work to do to sit and read the paper or listen to the radio. Now she found it hard to fill the hours of each day. By reading the newspaper and hearing news on the radio, she knew when City Bakery opened on North Main St. She knew that James Downey, a professional baseball player had returned to Urbana and was planning to purchase Arch Pool Hall, and that Lakewood Beach Swimming Club was designated to open in July 1927.

She garnered this information through conversations among the family and a few friends who visited them, and through the local newspaper which was read by both her own father and by Elton's. Often she was reading over their shoulders as they enjoyed the morning paper. Sometimes

Cecile wished she could go to town and see all the changes but doubted that she'd be able to travel so far away from her grave. She was afraid to try.

Meanwhile, she saw continued strain in her children and it broke her heart. One day, not long after the murder/suicide, Vanessa had taken a washtub filled with water, set it on rocks and built a fire under it. When Harrison questioned what she was doing she said she needed to go into proper mourning and didn't have the clothes for it. Vanessa proceeded to bring out almost all her clothing and dip each item into black dye which she had added to the hot water. She was still wearing these outlandish clothes, which made Cecile very sad.

Harrison was different now also. He had started eating less although he'd originally had a huge appetite. He spoke very little, and seemed to enjoy life not at all. He didn't even appear to care about going to local parties or socials. Worse, he seemed to be afraid of his own shadow after Elton had hit him. Cecile could imagine how scary it must be for Harrison to have been attacked out of a clear sky with no warning and to be unable to see his attacker.

The adults had all tried in their own way to help the children but they were out of touch. In mid-December, Henry Winston, had returned to the house freeing up the Montgomery's who seemed glad to go. Henry was planning to stay until April and then he'd leave in time to plant crops at his own place. It was late February now. George and Ethel would return April 1st.

It was probably hard for the children to have their grandparents rotating in and out in this manner but at least they weren't alone and they got to spend time with their family. Cecile was grateful for that. She watched over Harrison as he did his chores. At that time of day Vanessa was usually with the current adult in the house helping to prepare supper. She flinched with Harrison as he jumped at shadows or sudden sounds. Sometimes she saw Elton flitting around Harrison, disturbing the air or items in the barn, just to make Harrison startle.

She would kill the man if he wasn't already dead! At least she thought she would. Although she believed killing Elton would condemn her to be with him for eternity, both of them stoking the Devils stove.

Sometimes Vanessa seemed to sense her mother's presence and she visited her mother's grave two or three times a week. Bravely Vanessa always turned her back to Elton's grave and communed only with her mother. Cecile fretted as to what Vanessa would do if she knew her father was still here, above ground, and still a threat to her. She wished she could tell her daughter but hesitated to try because she wasn't sure if that would result in good or bad consequences.

Right now she was shadowing Harrison as he slopped the hogs and fed the cows. Elton was up to his tricks again and she had seen him weaving in front of Harrison as if daring him to notice that his father was watching his every move. At least Elton hadn't found a way to make himself visible to the living, or he'd surely be doing that too. Anything to punish and intimidate.

That's a thought...can we make ourselves visible to the living? If so...how?

At first we couldn't touch people, but now we can...so maybe...

~ 79 ~

What good would it do to be visible? It might comfort the kids, or it might scare them to death.

Cecile decided that she'd try to figure out how to become visible at will but she wouldn't practice on the kids. They were too young. If she was able to appear to someone, it would be an adult who, she hoped, could handle it better.

Harrison looked tired tonight. Since she checked on him during the nights, she knew he hadn't been sleeping well although school and the work at home had him fatigued. Maybe he thought his father's ghost might visit him in his sleep. Maybe he just hadn't been able to accept the role of an orphan. It would be hard to lose both your parents at once, especially in the way it had happened.

Harrison needed a friend, someone to go fishing with or to ride his bike with, someone to pull him out of his solitary state. It wasn't good for him to be this way. She prayed for a friend for Harrison each night, saying her prayers in death just as she had always done in life. She hoped that God could still hear her from this state of limbo in which she was stuck; surely he could...surely he had already. Had he not assured her that Elton would not be able to hurt her, and had Elton not stayed away from her, never even speaking to her? Yes! God could find her and help her still, and he could help her children as well.

She wasn't prepared for the answer he was about to give though.

Chapter Sixteen

Harrison brought a new friend to supper on a Friday night. No one knew the stranger was coming, but he was with Harrison when the teenager came in from doing his chores.

"This is my grandfather Henry Winston," Harrison told the man, "And this is my friend Reuben Shoup," he said to his grandfather.

Cecile shuddered. "This is not what I meant," she whispered to God.

Reuben looked like he was around forty years old. His face was leathered by the sun and his eyes looked as if he was prone to allergies due to their watery nature. He was medium height and slender. His clothes were none too clean although Harrison had announced that they'd both washed up outside with water from the rain barrel. Reuben's face was lined with a multitude of wrinkles and Cecile wondered if he was a drunk. He was one of the ugliest men Cecile had ever seen.

Henry, who was not sure how to handle this new friend of his grandson's, made a seat for Reuben and handed him a plate and silverware.

"We ain't fancy around here," Henry said. "Just dig in and enjoy."

Reuben didn't seem shy about doing that and he was soon on his second plate of potatoes, green beans and fried chicken, showing a hearty appetite.

"How did you and Harrison come to meet," Henry asked the newcomer.

"We was both fishing down at the fishing hole."

"I guess you live around here somewhere then," Henry said.

"Yeah." Reuben didn't say any more.

"Where abouts do you live?"

"Oh I got me a shack in the next thicket over. I'm living on the old Eubanks farm."

Cecile thought Reuben seemed a bit slow and she could smell liquor on him. What was her son doing with this man anyway? He wasn't their type of people and he was way too old to be a friend to her son who wasn't even 16 yet. Reuben was sure to teach Harrison bad habits if the friendship went anywhere.

Maybe Harrison's trying to replace the father he never really had

Elton mostly ignored him or bullied him.

Suddenly she noticed Elton sidling around the newcomer giving him a once over. His nose was wrinkled up in distaste. She wondered what her husband would do next. She didn't want Harrison embarrassed in front of his friend no matter that this man was not a good friend for him to have. Elton reached out and pulled Reuben's hair on the right side of his head. Reuben turned toward the ghost, his hand clutching at his scalp. Elton chortled silently, hamming it up.

"What's wrong," Harrison asked.

"I don't know. Something was on my head or pulled my hair but I don't know what."

"Probably the ghost," Henry said.

"Ghost?"

"Yep, we have a ghost. We think it might be Harrison's Dad but we aren't sure what it is."

Reuben looked around the table to see if Henry was joking. Vanessa shrugged and looked down at the table, Harrison just nodded his head in agreement with his grandfather.

"What does this ghost do?"

Henry thought as he took a big bite of fried potatoes. "Mostly innocent things like messing with the electric lights, but it hit Harrison in the face once before. It bruised his face but good. You don't want to make it mad."

Reuben looked around the room apprehensively. "I didn't see a thing," he said.

"What do you do? Do you have a job," Henry asked Reuben.

Reuben sniffed as if he smelled something foul. "I do some work for farmers. Otherwise I've got my garden, fish in the creek, and squirrels and rabbits in the woods."

"We might need some extra help at planting time," Henry said. "Check with me."

Reuben nodded his head and took a large sip of creamed coffee.

Elton was mouthing something and looking across the room toward Cecile. She couldn't tell what he was saying. Abruptly, he thumped Harrison on the head; Cecile suspected that was to wake Harrison up to knowledge of the type of friend he was associating with. The thump wasn't hard and Cecile didn't know it was coming to prevent it. Now she moved toward Elton and Harrison only to have her husband almost rush away to the other side of the room.

What's wrong with him; this isn't like Elton at all but he acts like he's afraid of me for some reason.

She went to her son who was looking confused and scared. Reuben was peering fearfully around the room again, and Henry was trying to figure out what was going on. Cecile laid a comforting hand on Harrison's shoulder only to have him shy away from her as if traumatized.

She removed her hand.

"I've got to get back home now," Reuben said, standing and heading swiftly for the door. "Thanks for the grub."

"Nice to meet you," Vanessa said, speaking for the first time.

"Likewise Ma'am," Reuben pulled the cap off his head and doffed it in her direction.

"At least he has some manners after all," Cecile thought.

"Wait," Harrison was on his feet running swiftly out the door following Reuben. "I'll walk with you a spell," he said.

Cecile followed the two of them curiously. She wasn't sure how far she could go, but this would be a good test. How far did Harrison plan to walk with Reuben?

"Something's in your house for sure; you know that don't you?"

Reuben was staring at Harrison.

"I know... I think it's my Dad. He knocked me around a bit when he was alive."

"You come to eat at my house next time. I'll fix us up some catfish or something."

"Okay, thanks."

"I heard in town that your Dad killed your Mom and then his self. I don't want to bring up bad things but if he's around your house, I'd just as soon steer clear of him."

"I know. Yes...he had a temper. Are you going fishing tomorrow," Harrison asked, changing the subject.

He doesn't want to lose the only friend he has, now that he has one.

How sad is that?

"Later in the evening when the sun goes down," Reuben was saying in answer to Harrison's question. "Too hot in the day and fish stay down at the bottom anyway."

"Okay, I'll see you then. It would be good to get some fish for Vanessa to fry up. She's actually getting to be a good cook."

"Does your sister always act like that, all quiet and sad? Does she always wear black?"

"Only since my parents died."

"She needs to get on with life," Reuben said.

"I know." Harrison nodded his head sadly.

Cecile had been aware of Vanessa's withdrawal, of course, but she hadn't know that Harrison was aware too. That made her even sadder. And this stranger who'd met Vanessa for the first time today, knew right away that something was wrong.

She racked her brain to think of how to help Vanessa, but nothing came to her. She vowed to watch her daughter more closely. Maybe in time she'd think of something that would help. Her mind turned to Reuben Shoup and the unwanted answer to her prayer. She had prayed that God would send a friend to help Harrison, but Reuben Shoup??? He was not what she'd prayed for. Had God misunderstood? He'd answered her prayer but certainly not in the way she'd hoped. Should she thank God or pray for him to remove Reuben from her son's life?

Just another dilemma.

Chapter Seventeen

For the next few days, Cecile was her daughter's shadow as she went about the house, as she slept...no matter what she did. Vanessa didn't talk to anyone much. When Ethel had been with the kids, Vanessa had spoken occasionally to her grandmother but almost never to Henry or George. Cecile wondered if her daughter was turned off men forever because of things that happened with her father. She knew that Vanessa was carrying a huge load of guilt believing that what had happened occurred because she had told her mother, Cecile, about what her father had done. Perhaps she was right; but what else could Vanessa have done? Cecile wished there was some way to comfort her daughter without scaring her to death.

Meanwhile Harrison was spending every evening with Reuben Shoup, sometimes at home but most often at Reuben's shack over the hill. Cecile had been surprised and pleased to find that she was able to follow her son all the way to Reuben's place and also to the fishing hole where the two of them liked to spend their time.

At least Harrison has a friend of sorts.

Vanessa has no one and I'm worried about her.

Vanessa had previously been friends with girls from church and school. They had visited her and she them. However, no one came to visit anymore and Vanessa didn't seem inclined to go anywhere. Mostly she spent time in her room, or cleaning, puttering around the house, or reading. Her taste in books had changed too and now she read a lot of dark literature that she got from the school library. She didn't even go to church these days.

Although Cecile spent most of her time with Vanessa, who she perceived as needing her more, she would usually check out Harrison when Vanessa was helping her grandparent to fix supper. At that time, Vanessa was with an adult and Cecile didn't think that Elton would harm her in any way when there were witnesses.

Drifting through the trees, following the path to the fishing hole, Cecile worried about her children endlessly. She didn't like Reuben's influence on her son. He usually had alcohol with him, even when fishing, and she was afraid he'd offer some to Harrison. He had not done this yet as far as she could tell. It wasn't that Reuben drank a large amount at a time and he never seemed to be drunk. He just carried the alcohol with him and had a nip of it from time to time.

Mostly the two friends chatted about man stuff, fishing, animals of various kinds, hunting, and farming. All of that seemed innocent enough. She noticed that Reuben chewed tobacco as well as drinking alcohol. He had a plug of twisted long green tobacco that he called Mickey Twist. She didn't know if that was a brand name or what. She'd heard him say that he bought the tobacco at the store. He offered Harrison a chew one evening but her son refused and that made her proud.

As for the alcohol, Reuben had some kind of corn brew he'd made himself. Prohibition had come in some years ago and was still in force although Cecile doubted that it would last. Too many men loved their liquor, and it was a man's world out there. Most made up some home brew from time to time, and those that didn't knew someone who did. Reuben was a doer. She'd give him that, but did he know what he was doing or was his mixture poison. She certainly hoped Harrison would never try it. The movement to ban liquor had originated with the dry crusaders and the anti-saloon league. Cecile didn't care for the stuff but had never been a part of the effort to ban it. She realized that banning something often makes it more popular.

She was sitting on a grassy bank above the fishing hole watching the fishermen when she saw Elton on her right about ten feet away. Not being able to stop the impulse, Cecile jumped, startled. Elton grinned at her discomfiture. It was then he spoke to her for the first time since they had been on the underside of the grass.

"Nice friend your son has."

Cecile stood and moved away from her husband.

"You can't get away from me," Elton said. "Our marriage is endless. Even death didn't part us. I told you I wouldn't let you leave, and I haven't. I never will."

Cecile had decided that she'd never speak to Elton again but she was fighting a strong urge to put him in his place Then despair slid over her like a heavy cloth falling from the sky. It was all so hopeless. Hadn't she herself lamented the endlessness of this situation?

"Harrison...what about Harrison."

Cecile moved back toward the house hoping Elton would follow her to continue his taunts. Anything to get him away from her son and his friend. She didn't trust what Elton might do to them. Elton followed her, grinning his nasty grin, and dogging her steps. Cecile had successfully led him away from her son. At least something had gone right. She ignored Elton, refusing to look his way. Elton continued to stay his distance. Cecile wondered if he was able to come closer or if he was being blocked. She hoped and prayed he could not come closer; had she really heard a voice telling her that he wouldn't be able to approach her, to hurt her? It was all murky now, just a far memory.

At the house she stood beside Vanessa while Elton looked over her father's shoulder. Henry was making a Mulligan Stew, which Elton had liked when he was alive. She bet he'd love to have a bowl of that stew now. Vanessa was humming a little under her breath today, something so unusual for her daughter that Cecile paused in wonder. Was her child pulling out of the deep depression she'd been under? Cecile prayed that it was so. Across the room, Elton had waited for Henry to turn his back then he lifted a ladle of hot soup and adjusted it to pour over Henry's shoulder. Without thinking of the consequences, Cecile screamed,

"Watch out Dad!"

Henry wheeled toward her voice, and the blazing hot mixture fell to the floor, missing his shoulder. Henry stared at it. He looked at where Elton had stood as he lifted the ladle, then at the spot where Cecile's voice had come from. Then he froze as if unable to move, staring at the stew on the floor.

Vanessa was in shock too.

"What was that? It sounded like Mom," she said.

Henry blinked. "Yeah to me too." He looked down at the soup on the floor. "How did that get there," he asked.

Vanessa only stared at him shaking her head in fear and wonder.

Chapter Eighteen

Cecile wasn't sure what Elton had meant to do. He might have just been torturing her by making her think he was going to burn her father, or he might have actually intended harm to Henry. Either way, she'd blown it by crying out. Everyone had heard her. Now her father was scared...she could tell, and Vanessa seemed to be in a deep fog locked inside her head. She had drawn into herself even further than before, moping around the kitchen as if scared of her own reflection.

Cecile couldn't blame her daughter.

Vanessa couldn't know what happened after death, especially what had happened to her mother and father, and she had every reason to be scared of voices coming out of nowhere. Cecile had watched Vanessa slide deeper into depression for many months now. She couldn't remember when her daughter had last laughed. Now fear seemed to be activating some of Vanessa's senses that had been dormant for a long while.

What can I do; what will help and not make everything worse?

Henry was stirring the stew while trying to keep his back to the wall. She knew he had no idea how close he'd come to having the hot stew hit his neck and shoulder, but he had seen the results of the upturned ladle on the kitchen floor. There was no normal interpretation as to how that had got there. He had also heard his daughter's voice warning him. He seemed to be afraid to turn his back while doing his work. Vanessa was chopping up vegetables for a salad and seemed to be clinging to the knife obsessively as a tool to protect herself.

The family was hurting and Elton was the cause. Desperately Cecile sought a way out of this mess...some way to protect her family.

Harrison came into the house nosily; he brought Reuben Shoup with him. Harrison had a string of three fish and Reuben was carrying a bucket with four more.

"Looks like we're too late for fish tonight," Reuben said, "But I'll leave some for you to have tomorrow."

"Put them in the icebox after you clean them," Henry said curtly

That's when Harrison noticed the atmosphere in the room. His grandfather's curtness was unusual, not like Henry at all.

"What's wrong," he asked his sister.

"Walk out to the woodpile with me," Vanessa said.

She glanced around the room as she took off her apron. The three of them, Vanessa, Harrison, and Reuben, went outside with Cecile floating along behind them. Vanessa stopped beside the woodpile and looked curiously at her brother. "Have you heard any voices around here...I mean like Mom's voice or Dad's," she asked him.

"Not really; have you?"

"Not till tonight," Vanessa said, shuddering.

"What happened?"

Vanessa described hearing her mother's voice cry out, warning Henry just before a ladle of hot stew hit the floor beside him.

"It's Mom. I know it's her. What does it mean?"

Harrison looked pale and strained as he said "Well if Mom's ghost is here, she won't hurt us. You say she warned Grandpa?"

"Yeah, but what or who was trying to hurt Grandpa? Something poured that hot soup out right where he was standing. It wanted to burn him."

Reuben, who had been ignored, butted into the conversation. "I hear your Pappy was a mean man. It was probably him trying to hurt Henry. You'd better watch out, he could hurt you too."

"Don't scare my sister," Harrison said, smacking Reuben on the arm.

"I'm just saying...you'd better both be careful." Reuben rubbed at his shoulder as if in pain.

"Oh quit it; I didn't hurt you," Harrison said impatiently.

"Seriously; you two best be careful. Something weird is going on in this house," Reuben said. "You can both hang out at my shack if you need to get away."

Vanessa looked at Reuben suspiciously but mumbled a thanks. Harrison just smiled and nodded his head at his friend. Reuben scratched at his face where a beard was growing, "If it's your folks haunting the place, what kind of people are they? What might they do?"

"My Mom would protect us from our Dad if she could," Vanessa said.

"That's probably what happened tonight," Reuben said knowingly. "Ghosts have a life too you know. Don't be scared because your Ma yelled out to save her father. That shows she's still the same kind of person she always was. Be glad she's here to protect you."

"I miss her a lot," Vanessa said, tears drip dripping down her cheek.

"Me too," Harrison mumbled.

'You should...she's your Ma. I miss my Ma every day," Reuben said.

"I'd better go back in and help Grandpa wash the dishes," Vanessa said, turning back toward the house.

"I've still got cows and horses to feed. Come along with me if you want Reuben." Harrison headed toward the outbuildings.

Cecile watched her son and his friend go off toward the barn. She went to the kitchen to see how her father and Vanessa were doing. She found Henry elbow deep in dish water while Vanessa flipped a dishtowel mercilessly across plates and other dishes, drying them. Neither of them were talking, but tension was evident.

Finally Vanessa walked over to her grandfather and put her arm around him.

"I'm sorry Grandpa. I know you almost got burned and that scares me, but in a way I'm happy because I heard Mom's voice again. I think she's here watching over us like a guardian angel or something. She kept you from getting hurt. That's the good side of this."

Henry patted Vanessa's shoulder. "That's right," he said. "We did hear her didn't we? That means she's really here as a ghost or guardian angel, or a little of both; doesn't matter. Your Mama isn't gone forever."

Wiping tears from their eyes grandfather and granddaughter stood together surveying the room

"We love you Mom," Vanessa said

"You're still my little girl," Henry said, his tears breaking into a sob.

Cecile was crying herself but she didn't know what to do, so she didn't reply. A while ago they had been scared to death. If she spoke to them again, would they be scared again? Right now they acted like they wanted her to communicate with them, but if she did, it might be bad.

She remained silent.

After a minute Henry left to check on Harrison in the barn and Vanessa went to her room. Cecile followed her daughter. Elton had disappeared right after the hot soup incident but he was around somewhere and instinct told Cecile that right now Vanessa was the most vulnerable to his evil. Vanessa pulled a journal from under a floorboard in her closet and sat down at the small desk in her room to write in it. Cecile was surprised. She had never known that Vanessa had a journal.

Watching over her daughter's shoulder she saw that Vanessa had written:

"Tonight was scary but good. I think my Mom's here. I heard her voice. I'm also beginning to like Reuben a lot better than I did when Harrison first brought him around. He may live like a hermit and be poor as dirt but he has some common sense at least."

Chapter Nineteen

Time went on and suddenly it was a nice warm Saturday in early May. Vanessa and Harrison had both begun to hang out with Reuben on Saturdays and some evenings. He was different but Cecile grudgingly realized that without a Reuben in their lives, every day was boring drudgery on the farm. Neither of her children went anywhere for social activities, except for hanging out with Reuben and listening to his ideas and stories. He represented their only social outlet.

She had to admit that Reuben was unique. He had next to nothing but he was generous with the kids. Sometimes he made baskets and one day he helped Vanessa make a small basket for herself. She seemed inordinately proud of her accomplishment. Today he had a large washtub full of water suspended on rocks with a fire underneath it. He had strips of wood that he had harvested from the woods lying nearby. These strips of wood he called basket splits and he wove baskets from them.

"What are you doing?" Vanessa asked.

"I'm going to dye these basket splits different colors so I can make some new baskets. I'll sell them to Taylor's store and use the money to buy things I can't kill or grow. Things I need."

Harrison said. "One of these days they'll make baskets in factories with machines of some kind. What will you do then?"

Reuben tested the water in the tub and picked up a packet of red dye.

"I'll cross that bridge when it happens. I've heard of a factory that made baskets, but it shut down, I think." he said. "Maybe I'll just learn to make and sell something new that they aren't making with machines."

"So you'll just try to stay one step ahead of new inventions?"

"That's right. Think ahead I always say."

Harrison poked some more wood into the fire under the washtub. "What colors are you going to dye those splits?"

"Red, white, and blue. I like patriotic colors; don't you?"

"Yep; I see you have some green dye too."

"I do but I'm not going to use it this time. This batch will be patriotic for July 4th."

"Do you ever put things on the baskets to decorate them?" Vanessa asked. "I mean flowers or little charms or something?"

"No but that's something you can do with your basket. I have an old broken gourd over there. You could cut it into chips, paint them, and then glue them to your basket or you could sew some silk flowers or the like and decorate it."

"Maybe."

Vanessa continued to stare at the fire under the washtub, her mind seemingly occupied with something else. Cecile worried. All the spark in Vanessa's life seemed to have gone out and she had no idea what could be done about it.

"What are you doing this afternoon," Reuben was asking the two kids.

"I'm supposed to muck out the barn. That's what Grandpa wants," Harrison said.

"How about you," Reuben nodded at Vanessa.

"I'm going to pick some flowers and take them to Mom's grave."

"What kind?"

"I don't know. Violets and some spring flowers like Sweet Williams are growing in the woods. I'll find whatever I can. I don't guess she'll be able to see them anyway."

"I've got a pot of beans cooking Come back later and we'll have some bean soup if you want," Reuben said.

Cecile could smell the scent of the wood smoke on the cool air and even in her altered state she felt the smoke begin to irritate her eyes. It was blowing directly on her. She shifted and then saw that Elton had joined them and was looking at his children balefully. She supposed he didn't approve of them keeping company with Reuben and thought they ought to be home working on something useful. He had been blowing the smoke her direction on purpose using a small bellows that used to stay in the barn. She could see the bellows clearly but could Reuben and the kids? She looked around. No one seemed to be noticing anything. Elton took the bellows and hid it behind a tree. Perhaps he too was wondering if it was visible.

Harrison took a long branch and stirred the fire causing the smoke to shift toward Vanessa. She spluttered and moved to the other side of the fire. Reuben had placed cut tree stumps around the fire and these stumps were what her children were sitting on.

"Anyone want coffee," Reuben asked pouring some dark brew from an old granite coffee pot into a tin cup and looking around at the brother and sister.

"I will," Harrison said.

Reuben produced another tin cup and filled it for Harrison.

"You?" He waved the pot toward Vanessa.

"No thanks."

He replaced the pot on a stone grill where it had been steeping and sat on a log to sip at his steaming hot cup of brown liquid.

"Where'd you get the tin cups," Vanessa asked.

"They come in feed for animals. It's to measure the feed out, I guess, but they come in handy for drinking. I keep one down by the spring so I can get a drink when I want. It's nice cold water that way. It gets too warm after it sits around in a bucket for a while."

"I suppose," she said unenthusiastically.

Cecile glared at Elton, furious that his actions had caused her daughter to fall into this overwhelming despair. Elton was also gazing at his daughter. Afraid that he might be thinking of a way to harm her, Cecile wanted to grab a hot branch and poke his eyes out. However, she wasn't going to act on that impulse. She didn't even know if it was possible to hurt Elton now that he was already dead.

Reuben stood up. "Well I'd better get started. These basket splits are not going to dye themselves." He took a strip of wood and dipped it into the tub of water where he had put two or three packets of red dye. When he had if fully dyed, he hung it over a bush and started working with another.

"I thought you were going to make some blue and some white too," Harrison said.

"I am but I have to empty the tub and clean it out, boil some more water and put in a different color dye. I need more red because people like the red. Some will be red and white, some red, white, and blue; I might even make one that is all red. Bet it would sell."

Behind his back Elton was standing mimicking Reuben's every word and movement silently. Cecile wanted to leave the area but if she did, what would Elton do? She stood her ground, watching, always watching over her children.

Chapter Twenty

Reuben marched around the washtub of boiling water, tin coffee cup in hand. He sniffed at the wood smoke that permeated this little clearing and sorted out the distinct smell of burned coffee that was mixed in with it. Striding to the coffee pot he took it off the fire and dumped it on some weeds growing at the edge of his space. The fire crackled as he stared at the plant he had just boiled. It was wilting before his eyes, cowering down into the ground as if in terrible pain.

Smacking his own face for his stupid thoughts, Reuben turned and got back to work. The kids were gone now and he was glad. Maybe they couldn't feel a ghostly presence but he could. He knew the father, a man he'd never met in life was present at his little shack this morning and he didn't like it. Elton Montgomery had been here. Why? Reuben rubbed his arms as they chilled suddenly. It felt to him as if the ghost was still with him but surely Elton would have left when his kids did.

Pop! A log sputtered and exploded with a fiery cascade. Reuben couldn't help it. He jumped and crouched, ready to defend himself. Seeing nothing, he sat down on the stump where Harrison had been sitting. It was sawed unevenly and very uncomfortable to sit on. He got back up and wandered to the coffee pot where he began to get it ready for a new batch of coffee. The spring air was tangy, damp, and cold. Reuben pulled on an old flannel shirt, then stirred the fire. The children were gone but he could still feel a disturbing presence...although no living person was inhabiting his little world.

It was Reuben's impression that someone, probably Elton's wife was helping to control Elton's behavior. Still it was upsetting. Instead of one ghost, Reuben suspected there were two or maybe more. He peered into the trees looking for the presence that he knew was here somewhere watching him. The feeling was so strong he should be able to see what was causing it but he couldn't.

Going into his dark cabin, Reuben felt around until he found his flask of moonshine. Since alcohol was now prohibited, he had to make do with whatever farmer's batch of home brew he could find or what he could make himself. He wasn't that good at making moonshine, but could in a pinch. He made wine from berries and such during the summer months also. This batch, his own homemade brew, was bitter and he didn't care for it much. Still, he wanted something to settle his nerves.

"Why don't you come on out and let me see you," he asked the trees, loudly.

They didn't answer, nor did any ghostly form present itself.

Reuben took a gulp of the home brew and wrinkled his face in distaste. He needed another supplier but people around here were careful of the revenuers. The man he'd bought this bottle from had hid his supply in the hog's slop bucket to keep it from the revenue agent who had come to his door.

Maybe that's why this bottle of white lightening tastes like slop!

Cecile sat on a nearby log trying to read Reuben's body language. Elton had not left when the kids did, so neither had she. When Reuben had gone inside his shack to get a flask of alcohol, Elton had gone in right behind him but had never come back out.

What's he doing in there?
Reuben deserves some privacy.
What's he looking for anyway?

Cecile bowed her head in despair. The problems with Elton were endless. Death had not stopped her problems. She did seem to have some protections from her husband now; either that or he was trying to lull her into letting down her guard. Too bad that "till death do us part" line hadn't been true. It would have been great if death had parted her from Elton Montgomery! As it was, every day was a day of stress and worry because of him.

She sometimes wanted to speak to Elton, to yell at him, to tell him just what she thought of a father and husband such as he'd turned out to be. She didn't say a word though, nor did he speak to her. It wasn't that she was giving him the silent treatment. She literally had <u>nothing</u> to say to him. Elton must feel the same. He almost never said a word unless he was trying to get her goat.

But I can talk; I yelled out to warn my Dad. Everyone heard me too.

Reuben was standing by the fire pulling the old flannel shirt closer to his shoulders looking around suspiciously, she thought.

"Why is Elton hanging out here," she asked herself.

She decided to go see what he was doing in Reuben's house. Creeping slowly through the door, she spotted Elton lying on Reuben's cot, hands behind his head, staring at her.

What in tarnation was he doing?

She wasn't going to ask.

If he's staying here; I'm leaving. Reuben can take care of himself.

Cecile drifted down the path to the old farmhouse where she'd lived so many years and where she had died. It didn't feel like home in the same way it used to. It was as if her time here had passed and she belonged somewhere else.

But I can't leave my kids to the mercy of their father.

He has no mercy; he doesn't worry about their wellbeing like I do.

Elton's parents were at the house again. Cecile's father had left to try to catch up on his work at home and in the store. George and Ethel had moved back in. Vanessa and Harrison seemed to prefer Cecile's father to Elton's, she believed, but they didn't say so. They were good kids. They just tried to get by the best they could. Ethel was dragging around the kitchen with a cup of lemonade in one hand and a butter and honey biscuit in the other. George was sitting at the table smoking a pipe and looking at a magazine.

"I thought you were going to plant corn in the south field today," Ethel said.

"A spooky thing happened. That's what I'm sitting here studying over," George said.

"What are you talking about?"

"I went out to the barn this morning and Old Ben, the best draft horse we got was laying in his stall as if he was all tuckered out. I got him to his feet wondering if he was sick or what and gave him some feed. Right in the middle of eating it he lay down again. I finally had to go hitch up Tom to plow the field."

"Is the horse sick or what?"

"I think he was just tired, best I can figure."

"What would make him tired? Was he dreaming of racing all night." Ethel gave a scornful smile.

"You just wait; you don't have the whole story...I hitched up Tom and got out the plow and headed to the south field just like I planned. Guess what I found when I got there?"

"I don't want to play your guessing games old man. What was it?"

"The field was already plowed and seeded."

Ethel exploded out of the corner where she'd been standing.

"What? No: you're joshing me."

"I'm telling you, that field was plowed and seeded, and I think someone used Old Ben to do it."

"How; they'd have had to work in the dark...to work all night."

"Exactly; that's what I'm studying over."

"Could it have been one of the neighbors trying to help us out but not wanting us to know who did it?"

"I doubt it; we've got good neighbors, but not that good. They have their own plowing and planting to do."

"So what are you thinking," Ethel asked; she sat down in a chair across from him.

The old man sighed. "What if our son is still here and decided to do some work for us and the kids," he finally asked.

Ethel stared into her cup of lemonade. Finally she said, "I wish I could see our boy again. I know he made a big mistake but I'll always love him."

Watching from the corner, Cecile felt unexpected sympathy for her mother in law. It was hard to lose your child she knew, even if he was a monster.

"Could Elton have actually hitched up Old Ben and ploughed and planted all night as a present for his father? Maybe he's getting bored with lying around and doing nothing. Is that why he was lying on Reuben's bed? He's tired." Cecile thought. "It's funny but I still get tired sometimes although I think it's a mental thing and not physical."

She began to examine her situation in a different light.

Chapter Twenty One

For the first time in all the months since her death, Cecile wanted to ask Elton how that field had been ploughed and planted. Curiosity was tickling her brain. It was her first real desire to speak to her husband since he had murdered her, except to yell at him.

What did that mean?

Were her feelings shifting: was she forgiving him?

"I certainly will not," she thought. "I won't speak to him either unless it's absolutely necessary."

Even though she didn't plan to ask him what had happened, she vowed to keep a closer eye on Elton. Usually he just wandered away and she was glad not to have to be in his presence. She hadn't been all that curious as to what he was doing or where he was...just defensive of her kids.

Would Elton actually do a good deed?

Could he really hitch up and command a horse in his state?

Could he hold the plow upright and plow a field?

Maybe he would do that if he was bored or wanted to test out his abilities after death.

He'd do it just to see what the living family members would say and do, if nothing else.

All of this set her to wondering if she could also be useful to her family once again. If she could do some chores around the house for instance it might relieve some of the burden on her children and on their grandparents. She decided that she'd try something small and see how that went.

I won't do anything in a hurry. I'll just watch and wait for something and then try to help someone out. I'll see what happens.

The idea soon captivated Cecile. When she was a child she had been fascinated by a fairy tale where the little elves came at night and helped a shoemaker. There had also been another story where children were going about doing good things for their parents and other people around them, but doing it in secret and not taking credit for it. She had liked that story also.

She didn't think Elton had that same romantic overview of the world. If he ploughed the field for his father it would be to see his family's reaction...to see what everyone would say about it. It would be a game to ease his boredom and get something going. Would they believe a ghost did it and be afraid or would they think kindly neighbors did it? What would happen? That would be Elton's motivation. He'd be entertained by the living and that would relieve some of the sameness of this in-between world.

Still, Cecile hated to copy Elton's behavior by doing her own good deeds, even for a good cause. She planned to think things through first and to see what happened after Elton's escapade, providing that it was Elton's doing, before taking any actions herself. She had drifted out of the kitchen and house as she contemplated what George had said but now she went back to seek further insight into how Elton's parents were interpreting what had happened.

"Are you going to tell the kids," Ethel was asking.

"I don't know. If I don't say anything they'll think I did that ploughing and seeding. They won't know the difference."

"But what if something else happens…something you can't explain? It will scare them I know."

"Exactly. Meanwhile, I'm getting a day off today and I need the rest," George said.

"You're still behind. You should be using this day to catch up on some other things."

"Maybe my son, the ghost, will do it for me."

"You could plough the garden for me so I can start some vegetables growing." Ethel stood in front of her husband, hands on hips, showing annoyance at him for his apparent laziness.

"Maybe I will, after my siesta," George said. He got up, walked to the living room and laid himself down on the davenport. "Good night," he called to his wife, who harrumphed in reply.

Cecile had mixed feelings. George did have a lot of work and he was being lazy today. However, he had been going at a busy pace and maybe he truly needed some extra rest to recharge. She figured that Ethel might be a little jealous. None of her work had been done for her.

"Maybe I'll help you out one of these days," Cecile silently told Ethel.

Her biggest concern was for her kids. If they realized things were getting done without them or their grandparents doing it, how would they react?

Would they lay back and become lazy saying "Let the ghost do it?"

Would they be scared into a catatonic state, or to the point they couldn't do anything even if they wanted?

Would they run crying to a doctor thinking they were insane?

It was all so uncertain and Cecile wished Elton had not opened this can of worms.

Maybe Elton didn't do anything.

But then who ploughed and planted that field?

I don't think we have any neighbors that helpful; they'd have had to work in the dark.

Elton can see in the dark; he could see to do it.

One of the things that Cecile liked best about her ghostly state was the fact that she had good night vision. It wasn't really clear like it was in daytime, but she could see well enough...much better than when she was alive. Since she didn't have to sleep, the nights were long and boring. She contented herself with gliding around checking on her loved ones, watching them sleep, protecting them with her presence.

Maybe I'll check on Elton to see what he's doing tonight. As long as I can see where he is, he won't be doing anything to harm anyone. I'll keep my eye on him instead of Vanessa and Harrison.

But how do I even find him? He disappears like smoke.

Cecile looked at George sprawled out on the couch snoring. She drifted into Harrison's bedroom where Ethel was putting away clothes she had just brought in from the line. Each piece was folded neatly and put into the dresser drawers. A stack of black items showed that she still had Vanessa's things to put away. Vanessa was still dressing only in black mourning clothes.

"I have to admit that Ethel and George take good care of the kids," Cecile thought.

She'd heard the couple speak to each other when they were alone and knew that they preferred to believe that Elton had been driven to kill his wife and himself because she, Cecile, had nagged him into it. To their credit they didn't say anything to the children against their mother, however.

Some parents uphold their children no matter what they do.

That attitude creates the Elton Montgomery's of the world...

You love your kids no matter what, but you don't uphold them in wrongdoing.

It makes monsters of them.

Chapter Twenty Two

Cecile tried to keep up with Elton when evening came but he eluded her and she couldn't find him. She left her post with the kids and searched the barn and fields but didn't see a sign of him anywhere. Even though she was watchful all night, she didn't locate him. Morning showed its face with a pink slit on the horizon and a yellow sun peeking over the hill. Cecile thought it would be a beautiful Saturday. George was already out doing work in the barn and Harrison was eating breakfast preparing to join his grandfather for morning chores. Ethel was frying eggs for Vanessa and making coffee for George who was due to come in for his breakfast soon.

"I want a cup of coffee," Vanessa said suddenly.

Ethel turned around waving the pancake turner she'd been using on the eggs in front of her. "You don't drink coffee."

"I know but today I want to. I don't feel so good. Maybe I'll feel better if I drink a cup."

Ethel didn't say anything, she just poured a cup of coffee and put it in front of Vanessa.

Cecile, who was watching this tableau, had mixed feelings about her daughter drinking coffee. Given the state of her depression, coffee might pep her up a bit and make her more alert and active, less depressed. However, some thought caffeine was bad for the heart and Cecile had always believed this was true. That's why she had never drank it herself. Recently Harrison had begun to drink coffee when he was with Reuben. She had not noticed him doing it at home though.

Lots of good my health consciousness did me!

I'm dead at a young age anyway.

Of course there's no way to plan for being murdered.

She stopped thinking and concentrated on watching and listening.

"I'm going fishing with Reuben after my work is done," Harrison told Vanessa. "You could come with us if you had a mind to."

Vanessa fiddled with her empty cup. "Maybe I will," she said surprising everyone.

"Great," Harrison said and Cecile saw a spark of happiness in his eyes.

That's when she fully realized how much Harrison had been concerned about his sister. He was inviting her to go fishing with him in an effort to pull her out of her moody mindset. In the past he'd never even have thought to invite his sister to go fishing.

"I'll get a pole together for you, Sis," he said enthusiastically, "I'll do it just as soon as I finish feeding the chickens, hogs, and cows. The horses are already out to pasture. Grandpa let them out."

That's when Cecile noted that Elton was standing over Vanessa, smirking and shaking his head. She knew he was sexist and didn't think girls were cut out for even the simplest sports. Also, he was probably pantomiming his disrespect for women in general to annoy his wife. Cecile turned and trailed after Harrison as he went to the barn to feed the animals. In the corner of her eye, she saw that Elton was following them.

Good. He won't be doing anything to Vanessa while my back is turned.

Cecile watched from one side of the barn and Elton watched from the other as Harrison slopped the pigs, then pulled weeds growing outside the barn door, put them into a basket, carried the basket inside the barn, and gave the weeds to the pigs. The scruffy animals squealed and pushed each other to get to the best morsels. He then moved on to feed the chickens which he also gave some weeds to supplement the corn he scattered for them. This time he used a small hand sickle to cut the weeds which he put in a large bucket and then hauled to the chicken pen. George had already milked the cows. Now Harrison forked hay from the hayloft to reward the cows for the morning's milk. He then cut more plants and brought those to the cows.

"My boy's doing a good job," Cecile thought proudly.

Across the room on the other side of the barn, Elton seemed bent on doing something to get attention. He was looking around the barn restlessly, walking around peeping into corners and crevices. Suddenly he spied a pitchfork stuck in a bale of hay. He pulled it out and hefted it to his shoulder in a throwing position.

"No," Cecile screamed.

Elton tossed the pitchfork impaling it on a bale of hay to Harrison's right.

Harrison's body stiffened as he saw the pitchfork, detected the whoosh of its passage through the air, and heard his mother's scream. He was shaking all over. Cecile wanted to hug him to her and protect him always from the beast his father had become. Elton stood smirking at her as she moved toward her son, placed a comforting hand on his shoulder and then withdrew it at Harrison's panicked look. Elton moved to the hayloft, hefted a bale of hay, and threw it down into the manger, baling string and all. Harrison leaped back, looked around in a panic, and grabbing the pitchfork, he exited the barn on a run. Cecile glared at Elton who shrugged and moved to the bale of hay, took up a knife and cut the string, then scattered the hay into the trough in spite of the cows frightened mooing and thrashing.

"Why?" Cecile screamed the words into the empty barn.

Elton smirked and evaporated into the hayloft.

No doubt about it; he's trying to torture me.

He missed Harrison by a mile. He just wanted to provoke me and scare Harrison.

Ignoring Elton, Cecile raced out the barn door in pursuit of her son. He had gone to the house and was in the kitchen now trying to tell his grandparents what had happened. George and Ethel were looking at each other covertly, remembering what Harrison's other grandparent had described to them.

"Tell me again; a pitchfork just flew through the air and landed on a bale of hay beside you, and then another bale of hay came falling out of the haymow into the trough in front of you...is that right," George asked.

"How far from you did the pitchfork land," Ethel asked. She was wringing her hands in agitation.

"Not really close," Harrison admitted.

"Did you see anyone or anything that could have caused this to happen," George asked.

"No but I heard my Mom scream. I know it was her. She said 'No!'"

Again George and Ethel looked at each other.

"I'm not lying and I'm not crazy. I almost got stuck by that pitchfork and hit by that bale of hay and I know my mother yelled to warn me."

"It's okay; we know you're telling us the truth. At least you're not hurt, and if it was your mom who yelled, aren't you glad she's here watching over you?" Ethel rubbed Harrison's shoulders trying to release the rigid cast of his posture.

"It wasn't my Mom who tried to hurt me; I think it was my Dad, your darling son," Harrison said, pulling away and bolting for the kitchen door.

Chapter Twenty Three

Harrison raced into the yard where Vanessa was hanging up a load of washing. She took one look at him and dropped the clothespins that were in her mouth and ran to him.

"What's wrong?"

Harrison told her in a voice squeaky, high, and breathless. The strain he was under obvious to Cecile and apparently to Vanessa as well.

"Let's go fishing right now; you always say it relaxes you. I only have three more things to hang. In just a minute we can go. Why don't you get our poles while I do this?"

Harrison nodded as if glad to have something to do. He headed toward the shed where the cane poles were hanging on the wall. Cecile stayed with Vanessa watching her as the girl hung up the last of the clothing, then tucked the clothespin bag inside the basket and took it to the screened porch where she left it under a roof in case of rain.

Vanessa donned an old pair of Harrison's pants and a long sleeved shirt although the weather was warm. She then went to the shed to help her brother string a line on the extra fishing pole. George didn't fish much but sometimes Henry did when he was taking care of his grandchildren. However, he'd taken his pole home with him. That left only a bare cane pole sitting in the corner waiting for someone to string it.

"I don't have to fish if you don't want to go to all that trouble," Vanessa said. "I can just watch."

"No, it's okay; I don't mind. Watching wouldn't be any fun."

Cecile knew that Vanessa didn't care much for fishing and it was surprising that she was going at all. She thought Vanessa was doing it to help her brother who she knew was having a hard time.

"I heard Mom," Harrison said. "She's here; she really is; I know it!"

"I think she is too," Vanessa said, but it's scary to hear someone you can't see.

"We shouldn't be afraid of Mom should we?"

"No, but what about Dad? He's done bad things and he killed Mom. He might hurt us too. What if he wants us to be dead like him?"

Vanessa had a tear running down her right cheek and her brother spied it. He took his thumb and wiped it away, gave his sister a brief hug, then turned back to the fishing tackle.

Cecile was touched at how much her children seemed to care for each other.

I must have done something right.

She followed them down the worn path to the fishing hole they'd always used. When they got to the spot, Harrison began to overturn rocks looking for fishing worms and Vanessa carefully laid out both poles on the bank. When he found a couple of worms Harrison put them in a tin can filled with damp earth and went in search of more. Vanessa sat staring sightlessly out at the peaceful creek, slapping at flies absently, her tears dripping.

Cecile didn't understand what was upsetting her daughter so much. Harrison was scared and Vanessa could see it, but why was this upsetting Vanessa more than it appeared to be affecting Harrison? Vanessa reached down into the water and cupped some of it to wash her face. The cold of the water lessened some of the redness around her eyes but not all of it. The ground was damp from last night's rain and Vanessa perched on a high, sharp rock which was at least dry.

"I didn't find many worms. I should have gone out last night after the rain to get night crawlers," Harrison said, returning with his can of worms.

"We'll remember next time," Vanessa said.

"What you all doing," a voice from behind a tree said. The kids looked up to see Reuben Shoup standing there with his fishing gear in hand.

"Goanna do a little fishing," Harrison mumbled.

"I heered you say you didn't have very many worms. I just happen to have some nice fat ones I found last night. I'll share with you." Reuben took a squirmy night crawler out of his can and began to put it on Harrison's hook.

"Thanks," Harrison said.

Reuben nodded at Vanessa. "Going to try your hand at fishing are you?"

"Yeah...I thought I'd try. I'm not so good at it."

"Well if you cast that pole over there under the bank you'll probably get a big un."

Vanessa squished the worm Reuben handed her over the hook and threw the line out where he said. In no time she had a nibble and eventually pulled in a large sunfish. It wasn't a trophy but it made her face light up.

Meanwhile Harrison was grimly trying to fish but fishing seemed to have lost its magic.

"Let me put another one of these fat worms on your hook for you; I'll bet those catfish have eaten all your bait off the hook," Reuben said eyeing Harrison shrewdly. "It's one of the biggest fattest night crawlers I've ever found. I'm sure this one will do the trick."

Harrison passively sat as Reuben put the worm on his hook, then cast the line as far out into the creek as he could. Vanessa, encouraged by the fish she had caught baited her hook and threw out her line again. It was almost immediately that the bobber dipped into the water as another fish struck on her bait. Then they could see movement as the fish took the bait and tried to swim away with it. Excited, Vanessa jerked on her pole swinging fish, line, and sinker into a startled Reuben's face.

Whomp! The fish hit him just under his left eye.

The look on his face was priceless and Cecile tried to keep her chuckling to herself. Both the kids seemed shocked at what had happened, but when Reuben started to laugh they joined him.

"I'm just so irresistible that this fish wanted to kiss me," Reuben laughed putting Vanessa at ease.

"I'm sorry; I didn't mean to hit you. I just got excited."

"Well, I would too if I'd caught this one. It will make a good fish stew. You can have it for dinner." After putting the fish Vanessa had caught into a bucket of water, Reuben reached into his can of worms and put one on her hook then threw the line back to her.

"Thanks."

"Watch out I got one," Harrison yelled out suddenly. He yanked his line toward him then groaned when he saw that he had a turtle on the line instead of a fish.

"That's good. Your grandma can make turtle soup," Reuben said. "Pull it in."

"I hear those things will bite you and if they do they won't let go until it thunders," Harrison said, letting his pole go slack.

"Here,"

Reuben had gone to grab Harrison's pole and began to pull in the turtle which was hissing at them. Vanessa stopped fishing to watch the drama unfold. Eventually Reuben landed the turtle.

"If your grandma don't want to make turtle soup, give it to me. I will."

"You can have the thing," Harrison said. "I don't want to deal with it."

Come on over and try the soup though," Reuben said.

"Okay; I will."

From her perch on the bank, Cecile smiled, happier than she'd been since she was murdered. Her children were having fun. Harrison had a friend and even Vanessa was enjoying the day.

"Thank you so much," she whispered to God, afraid if she spoke louder others would hear.

Chapter Twenty Four

It was several days later when Cecile caught Elton working in a small area behind the barn. She had heard his mother say the area needed tilled so she could plant a garden there. Elton must have heard her request too. He was working the horse as if he were alive again. The horse sniffed and snorted, apparently spooked by this invisible master who was putting it through its paces. Cecile stayed behind a tree and watched for a long time, thinking...

Elton can definitely affect and manipulate the world of the living.

That is scary because he could hurt or kill a living person.

Right now what he's doing helps the family but how long will that last?

She had planned to do a chore sometime to help one of her family members but had become distracted and so had never attempted it. Drifting away from where Elton was working the poor scared horse to a lather, she headed to the house and kitchen.

What would happen if just before everyone gets up I make coffee, fry some bacon and potatoes? Will it make everyone happy or scare them to death?

Better do something less intrusive to start with, but what?

She began to search the kitchen for something that she could do that would be helpful but not dramatic. Ethel had wiped down the kitchen before going to bed. The floor had been swept and mopped. It was a Monday night and washing had been done, but no ironing. Tuesday was ironing day. She decided to use the old sad iron to iron the family's clothing for this week.

If I can.

If Elton can do what he's doing; I should be able to.

She carried the iron to the stove and started heating it. Cecile found it hard to manipulate the heavy iron but not impossible. Meanwhile, she sprinkled down the basket of clothes that Ethel had set aside rolling each garment into a ball to allow the moisture to penetrate the material.

The clock said it was 1:00 am. She could hear snores from the various bedrooms. No one was about to disturb her, or to see an iron floating in midair, then sliding over clothing on the ironing board.

If Elton can be helpful, so can I.

Taking a pot holder she lifted the iron but didn't feel the heat very much. Some of her senses seemed dulled in this state of afterlife. She began to iron one of Harrison's shirts. She'd picked his shirt because this was her first attempt and she didn't know how it would go. Harrison wasn't particular as Vanessa would have been. She had noticed a supply of coat hangers beside the laundry basket and when she ironed the shirt, she hung it on a hanger and the hanger on a short clothesline erected for that purpose. Stopping, she surveyed her work and found it passable.

"Yeah!"

For the next two hours Cecile struggled with the ironing and finally she had a line of ironed clothing hanging against the wall and an empty basket. Somehow this had made her incredibly tired. In her ghostly state, Cecile didn't get tired much nor did she sleep. However, she wanted to at least take a twilight nap now...to rest her eyes and mind.

Vaporizing into Vanessa's room, slipping through the wall, she pulled an extra blanket carefully from the closet and lay down on the floor beside her daughter. At that point she allowed herself to drift away in her mind to a restful place. It wasn't exactly sleep...just a sort of twilight sleep. By morning when Vanessa started to stir Cecile had managed to rest her mind enough to notice that she felt much better than at any time since her death.

I always knew work was good for you.

She moved from her spot on the floor as her daughter began to stretch and move around on the bed above her. Quickly she shoved the blanket she'd been lying on under the bed, then moved under there herself as her daughter swung her legs to the floor. Cecile lay still as Vanessa moved around the bed spreading the covers back to a facsimile of a made bed. Then Vanessa took a pair of black pants and a red and black flannel shirt that had somehow avoided the dye bath and put those on. She followed Vanessa to the kitchen where her daughter began to help Ethel fix breakfast by cutting up boiled potatoes, cooked with the jackets on, and placing them in a skillet for frying.

"Did you sleep good?" Ethel asked her granddaughter.

"Okay," Vanessa mumbled.

"We've got to use up some of that summer squash and those tomatoes today. I thought I'd make some sauce to go over spaghetti." Ethel said.

"Okay."

"Or we could do chili; but it's a little hot for chili."

"Just so we don't waste them," Vanessa said, knowing what her grandmother was aiming for.

Her grandmother grunted, "Can't afford to waste anything, that's for sure. Hard times a 'coming."

"Reuben says we are headed for a depression before long; I don't know how he figures."

"He's not so bright but he could be right about that; things don't look good to me either."

Vanessa moved from frying potatoes to chopping up an onion and some banana peppers to go into the potato dish. Ethel got some eggs out of the icebox and began to break them into a skillet, she put in some milk and seasoning and tossed the eggs, scrambling them. Cecile noticed that Ethel was using the pan that held bacon grease. The bacon was dripping onto a clean cloth which covered a plate.

She sat back watching and wondering just how long it would take for the women to notice that the laundry had been ironed. Both women were already dressed and so neither would be seeking ironed clothes to put on. Still it was ironing day and Vanessa and Ethel usually switched off from week to week. One week Ethel ironed, the next Vanessa. Cecile had no idea whose week it was. George came in from outside and slid into a chair at the table. Ethel put a cup of hot coffee in front of him.

"You can start planting in that garden area anytime you want," he told Ethel. "It's ploughed."

Ethel's hand flew to her mouth as she looked at her husband with questions sparkling in her eyes. George ignored her questioning look after gazing at Vanessa for a minute. Ethel didn't pursue it.

"Well at least George isn't taking the credit for what someone else did. He's going to tell Ethel," Cecile thought. "And they'll just be surer than ever that the problems between Elton and me were my fault, because they have such a nice helpful son." Disgust sniffed at her nose, wrinkling it and her upper lip.

"The summer's half over. It's too late to plant anything," Ethel complained.

"You can plant things that don't take long to grow like onions and the like," George told her. "You said the other day that you wanted that area ploughed and it is."

"Should have been done a month or two ago,"

Ethel didn't want to let it go. 'No doubt her agitation that the ghost of her dead son may have done the ploughing had her scared and on edge. She was taking it out on George,' Cecile surmised.

"If you wanted it done two months ago you should have said it two months ago," George accused.

"You were too busy then. I knew you couldn't get to it."

"Well, things get done when they get done." George picked up the morning paper and began to read.

Chapter Twenty Five

Cecile hung around Ethel and Vanessa waiting to see who would first notice the ironed clothing. They took their time. Once breakfast was over, they washed and dried dishes together and then snapped some green beans which Ethel put on the wood range to slow cook for dinner. After that Ethel sat down with a cup of coffee and called a friend on the party line while Vanessa took a book and headed outside to a shade tree. She carried a glass of lemonade with her which she set on a stump beside her chair.

Finally Ethel went out to look at the ploughed patch of earth while Vanessa went back inside to do the ironing. Cecile was right behind her daughter when she heard the gasp of awe, panic, and fear that came out her daughter's mouth. Vanessa stood staring at the empty basket and the neat row of ironed clothing hanging beside it. The ironing board had been put back into the cabinet so having a line of ironed clothing seemed miraculous. However, Vanessa seemed to be having a hard time. She was gasping for breath. Although the windows were open and there was a breeze, the day was already hot. Cecile watched her daughter uneasily, worried.

Vanessa stumbled to a kitchen chair which was in view of the row of ironed clothing and sat staring at the line as if in a stupor. She was mumbling to herself but Cecile could not hear what she was saying. Standing suddenly, Vanessa ran out the door calling for Harrison frantically as if frightened out of her mind. Harrison was in the barn forking hay down from the hayloft to the cows below.

"What's wrong," he called down to his sister.

Vanessa plopped onto a bale of hay and put her face in her hands trying to catch her breath. Harrison began to climb down from the hayloft. Once down, he sat beside her quietly, waiting.

"It's my day to iron but someone ironed all the clothes," Vanessa finally said.

The look on Harrison's face was priceless, Cecile thought. He looked surprised, questioning, stunned; it was as if he couldn't understand what the problem was.

"Grandma probably did it," he said, placing a comforting hand on Vanessa's shoulder.

"No; she wouldn't. It's my day to do it and Grandma always takes her day off. She wouldn't do my work for me."

"So...what are you thinking?"

"Something else did it."

"Who?"

"You may think I'm crazy but I think it was Mom. I looked at how it was done. It's just the way she always ironed things."

"I wish Mom was here to do it, but you know she can't be," Harrison said, his voice sad and resigned. "She might be here, but she couldn't do something like that."

"You said yourself that you heard her voice. I did too that one time. I think she's here watching over us. I think she tried to help me out by doing one of my chores."

"Then that should make you happy."

"No..." Vanessa's voice rose on a wailing note. "I'm scared. What if she is here but she's different, she's...a ghost? What if Dad is here too? Ghosts who can iron clothes could kill you just as easily."

"Mom would never hurt us. If she ironed clothes for you that shows she wants to help."

"Maybe…"

They sat together in the hot air, sweating and thinking. Vanessa was still shaking in spite of hot dusty air swirling around her.

"I'll tell you something if you won't repeat it," Harrison said finally.

"What?"

"I heard Grandpa and Grandma talking. They didn't know I was there so don't tell them. Grandpa said that someone had ploughed the field for him during the night. He thought it was Dad's spirit that did it."

Vanessa shivered and her arms goose pimpled in spite of the heat. She was looking into every crevice of the barn now frightened of seeing ghosts.

"I hope Dad's not around spying on us," she whispered and buried her face in Harrison's shirt.

Harrison hugged her for a minute and then pushed her away. "If he is here, I don't think he'll hurt us…at least no more than he did when he was alive. I know Mom won't hurt us if she's here."

"Do you think Dad hit you in the face that time?"

Harrison stopped breathing. Catching a breath finally he said, "I'd almost forgotten about that. Dad might have done it. It's something he would have done when he was alive. He was always hitting me when I didn't do things the way he wanted me to."

"And how about me," Vanessa said in a tiny frightened voice. "I'll be afraid to take a bath or change clothes. He might be watching me. He might do bad things to me."

Harrison gazed at her worriedly. "That's why Mom is here," he finally said. "She stayed here to protect us...to protect you from him. It will be okay."

Vanessa continued to sit face in hands sobbing silently. Harrison's eyes darted around the barn like restless butterflies that didn't know where to land. From time to time he looked at his sister.

"It will be alright," he said again patting her shoulder.

Finally Vanessa looked up through red eyes and asked him. "Are you sure that Mom is here to help us? I appreciate it if she did the ironing but I don't understand what is going on. You're right that she would stay to protect us if Dad was still here, but this is so strange and scary."

Cecile, who had been watching her children, had a hard time keeping herself from speaking to them. She wanted to tell them that it was all right and that as long as she knew of any threat to either of them she wasn't going to go anywhere.

It was about then that she noticed Elton standing behind her, but at a distance. She jumped, unable to control her own anxiety at his sudden approach. He wasn't paying attention to her at the moment though. His gaze was fixed on their children. She tried to place the look on his face, to interpret it but she didn't understand. He almost looked sad at what he'd heard. And then he was looking at Cecile, his expression hateful once again.

Walking to a washtub in one of the horse stalls, he took a large stick and struck the metal with it causing a loud sound that vibrated from wall to wall of the old structure. He grinned at the frightened looks on his children's faces and the furious look Cecile gave him.

Smiling jauntily, Elton strode away, passing through the wall.

Chapter Twenty Six

Reuben saw his friends were upset when they got to the fishing hole where he was stringing a line onto a cane pole he'd cut downstream a ways. He didn't say much except to acknowledge their presence and watch out of the corner of his eye as they played at getting their poles ready for fishing, having no heart in it.

"I got some good bean soup on the fire back at my place," he finally said. "After we fish a while lets go have some. I got cornbread too…a big old cornpone I made myself in a skillet on top of the stove."

"My Mom used to do it that way," Vanessa said.

Everyone was silent again.

After a bit, Harrison asked Reuben, "You been out here very long?"

"No. Don't need any fish for supper this time. I got bean soup."

"At least beans are cheap," Vanessa said.

"Yep; there's been times I lived on beans and taters for a month. I've fixed beans all kind of ways. I've fixed em, with noodles in em, soup bones, and even with onions and potatoes cooked in the beans, just to get variety. I even write poems about them."

"Poems? What kind of poems?"

"Well the one I just made goes like this:

Beans a- cookin' in the pot,
Boy did they hit the spot!
Now I feel like a gastro-naut."

"Wow…that's a good one," Harrison said. Vanessa smiled but didn't say anything.

"I like biscuits better than cornbread," Harrison mentioned, playing with his fishing line which had become tangled in roots under the bank.

"Well, I fix those too when I can get some good cold milk to pour over them; buttermilk's even better. Cornbread's good that way too."

Cecile sent mental blessings Reuben's direction. She knew he was trying to distract her kids and get them to think of something besides their fears. Her mind swirled with indecision. She wanted to talk to her children and from past experience knew that they would be able to hear her. Would that drive them insane or make others think they were insane? People get locked up in mental hospitals when they hear voices.

What would I say? Would I tell them that Elton is here and that I've stayed to protect them?

Can I protect them? I don't even know if I can.

Is it better for them if I just leave them alone?

Cecile tuned back into the conversation. Reuben was asking Vanessa what she planned to do with her life once she was out of school.

"I'm going to leave this place," Vanessa said.

Harrison looked at his sister, his expression shocked. "What do you mean? We've got to run this farm."

"I don't have to. We can sell it."

"But Mom...and Dad are buried here. We can't leave them. Who'd take care of their graves?"

"I'd come back and take care of the graves a couple of times a year if I had to...if the new owners wouldn't mind." Vanessa's voice was stubborn and defensive.

"Why do you want to leave the farm...scared?" Reuben's question was gentle.

Vanessa hung her head and kicked at a rock on the bank. "I guess I am."

"That's understandable after what you and Harrison have been through."

"I'm scared too but this is my home. I don't want to sell it," Harrison said, his face miserable.

Reuben looked thoughtful but continued on with his work in silence for a bit. Finally he said, "Well: if it was me and I thought there were ghosts around I'd try to talk to them and ask them what they want. If your Mom's around she's probably just looking over you like a guardian angel or something. I don't know about your Dad, but maybe you could reason with him too."

"We never could reason with Dad," Harrison said.

"Surely he loved you," Reuben suggested.

"I doubt it; I'm afraid of him too," Vanessa said.

Reuben nodded. "I read about it in the paper," he said.

Cecile remembered that the paper had said that the fight between her and Elton that had led to her murder and his suicide was because their sixteen year old daughter had accused her father of having made an indecent proposal to her. Vanessa had colored a tile red and was looking at the ground as if unable to lift her head. Harrison glanced at her and then said,

"Do you think that bean soups ready now? I'm getting powerfully hungry."

"Should be; let's go see," Reuben jumped to his feet apparently glad of a subject change, realizing he'd said something wrong.

Vanessa stood too but took her time pulling her pole out of the water and securing the hook before following slowly behind her brother and his friend.

At Reuben's yard, she sat in an old chair and watched without spirit or enthusiasm as Reuben got bowls and ladled bean soup into them. She saw that he'd tacked up the poem he'd just recited to them in a notch above the coffee pot.

His yard is more like a campsite than a yard, Cecile thought. He did a lot of living outdoors and it didn't look like he used the inside much unless it was raining or too cold to be outside. He had built a lean-to, under which he had his coffee pot and fixings, along with other things he regularly used. It was also a place to get out of the rain and still stay outside. She wondered if he slept in the house or out here under the stars. Maybe under the stars in good weather like an old cowboy.

Looking around she saw an old metal mirror nailed to a tree and on a stool under it, Reuben had a wash basin and shaving supplies. An old mustache cup held soap and a brush. A straight razor lay nearby. Yes he certainly did most things out of doors.

"Tell me about your Dad," Reuben said suddenly causing Vanessa to choke on the hot soup she'd just spooned into her mouth and Harrison to spill some of his on the ground. Neither of the children answered Reuben right away. Reuben waited, cutting slabs of cornbread for each of them as he looked silently from one to the other.

"He was hard to deal with," Harrison mumbled.

"He liked everything to be his way," Vanessa agreed, her eyes shuttered and downcast.

"How did he get along with your mother before they had that last fight," Reuben asked.

Harrison looked at Reuben as if to judge why his friend was being so nosy, then he said. "Mom usually went along with him unless they disagreed about one of us. Then she'd stand up for us. When she stood her ground, Dad would usually either back down or he'd hide what he did. He'd beat me when he had a mind to but he made it clear that if I told her I'd get another beating."

"Mom loved us...Dad, who knows what he thought," Vanessa said. "He sure didn't worry about leaving us orphans."

"Maybe it's the same way it's always been then," Reuben speculated. "Your Mom's right there protecting you from your Dad. Try not to make your Dad mad at you if you can help it but if you do...well, your Mom will be able to handle him."

"She wasn't able to handle him that last day," Harrison said. "She misjudged what he'd do. I warned her he had a gun but she said something like 'he's just full of hot air' and went about her plans. She was wrong."

"Like I said," Reuben repeated. "Don't make him mad if you can help it; maybe he'll leave you alone. He must love you at least a little."

"That's why I want out of here," Vanessa said, her eyes bleak. "I'm scared to death; I can't even sleep good at night."

Reuben patted her awkwardly on her shoulder. "Your Mom is watching over you. Try to remember that."

Chapter Twenty Seven

Trailing behind Harrison and Vanessa as they walked down the path toward the farmhouse where they lived, Cecile wanted to cry. In fact water seemed to coalesce in the air around her eyes and drip to the ground as she traveled. After they had left Reuben's place, Vanessa had admitted to Harrison one of the reasons she was afraid of her father's ghost.

"Because if he could plow a field, using things of this world, he could probably rape me," she said. "He's mad at me for telling and he wants to punish me."

Harrison looked shocked. "Do you think he'd do something so horrible?"

"I don't know but he had started down that track. I was afraid of what he'd do to me so I told Mom...and it got her killed." Vanessa sniffled trying to retain her balance.

Harrison stiffened and stared at his sister as Vanessa let go a sound so unearthly it confounded him. Her wail was eerie and heartbreaking. Vanessa had started to shake and sob so violently that Harrison helped her to a log and sat down beside her hugging her to him.

"It's alright; Mom won't let him hurt you," he said.

"I know she'll help me if she can; but can she," Vanessa sputtered, her breath coming in large gasps, her voice almost unintelligible.

"Yes; that's the question I want answered too," Cecile thought. "I've never tried to stop Elton from doing anything since I died."

I have to practice to see what I can do.

Next time Elton is doing something he shouldn't, I need to test my power.

An opportunity to test her power came a few days later when everyone was at the dinner table. Cecile's father was present also and Harrison had invited Reuben. From her seat on the sideboard, Cecile watched as Elton joined the party. He hovered on the other side of the room, his glance her way was mocking and evil. George, Ethel, and Henry were working out details for Henry to move back into the house so they could go home for a while and attend to their own affairs, that's why they were at dinner tonight also.

"I can move in this weekend. That will give you a chance to go home, harvest your crops, put up some food, and get ready for winter," Henry said.

Cecile looked at the calendar on the wall beside her. September 4, 1927. She had been dead for over a year now, but she was still trapped here on earth trying to protect her children from Elton. She briefly wondered if the light would ever come back for her. Cecile has been thinking about what Vanessa had confided to her brother. Poor child. She was carrying around a load of undeserved guilt for what her father had done.

It's Elton's fault all the way.
He made improper actions toward his daughter.
He shot me to death; He killed himself.
My kids are paying a heavy price for the sins of the father.
It's not fair!

She glared across the kitchen toward her husband, the perpetrator of all the evil that had befallen her family. He glared back challengingly.

~ 144 ~

"I've already made some jams and jellies for the kids," Ethel said. "I've also canned some beans and tomatoes which I'm going to leave here. I've plenty more to do at my own house. I need you to come and help me with that Vanessa. You can work with me on weekends when there's no school."

"Yes Grandma," Vanessa said.

Cecile could see that her daughter was still frightened and despondent. It would be good for her to get out of this house even if it was to work at her grandmother's place. Work builds character, she had always found.

"I can use your help getting ready for winter," George told Harrison. He turned to Henry, "I know you'll need some help from the kids too but they can help you in the evenings after school."

"They need a little time to enjoy life," Reuben said, "Maybe they can fish some and stock the icebox with fish."

"We can always use some meat," Henry agreed. "Gosh...I might even go fishing with you all myself sometime."

Elton had been standing behind Reuben but now he moved behind Henry while he stared at Cecile across the room. Cecile stood and for the first time in over a year approached her husband intent on stopping him from any mischief he might have in mind. She stared him in his eyes hoping he wouldn't know that she was shaking inside.

Why am I still here if not to protect my family?

Elton stared back but as she approached him, then he began to look uncertain, then nervous. He whirled with a flourish when she got a few feet away and bolted through the wall, leaving Cecile confused. Elton had never backed down from a fight, nor from her, in all the time she had known him...well, at least not that he allowed her to see. He always just changed his mind or took things in a new direction so she wasn't to know she had won. The kids were the only issue she ever fought him on and that was so important to her, she wouldn't back down

What did I do?

I challenged him with my eyes but I didn't do anything.

Why did he leave?

She felt a new strength and euphoria. Elton had backed down from her; at least he appeared to have left to avoid her. She wondered what she'd have done if she'd actually got close to him.

Would she have done anything?

Could she have done anything to him?

Cecile was aware of her own body and to some degree she could use it still, as with the ironing she had done. Could Elton feel pain? Could she herself feel pain? She had felt no pain since her death except for emotional pain. Now she wondered what she could actually do to Elton and what he could actually do to her in their altered state. Remembering when he'd hit Harrison and she'd clobbered him with the 2 by 4, she realized that there were things she could do to him, but he could also do these things to her most likely. She had knocked him down with that 2 by 4 but had it actually hurt him? The answer to that question was unknown.

I had the impression that God was protecting me from Elton. Is he doing that by keeping him at a distance? Elton acted as if he couldn't let me get close to him...or was he afraid of me for some reason? Is there something I could do if I did get close?

But how would that work? She had no clue. Elton could approach the living. He'd been able to harness and use a horse to plow. Was there some kind of boundary between her and Elton that couldn't be crossed? She had felt no barrier between them except the barriers in her mind. It was all very confusing.

It's a puzzle to ponder on during the long hours of the night.

Cecile was glad her father was moving back into the house to be with the kids. She loved her father although they had had problems communicating. Henry was a man of few words and strong convictions. However with Elton being the way he was, she worried because her father had been one of his targets in the past.

"I'll have to keep an eye on Dad as well as my children."

She reflected on the fact that this incident, instead of showing her what power she had to protect her children, left her more confused than ever as to what she could do to stop Elton. She was still uncertain as to how things worked on this side of the veil.

Maybe I should follow Elton instead of keeping an eye on the kids.

That's the last thing he expects me to do.

He thinks I'm afraid of him...

Of course; I am afraid of him.

After all he shot me to death just to have his own way.

I won't let him hurt my loved ones; I need to learn what I can do to stop him.

I need a plan.

Chapter Twenty Eight

Floating along behind Elton, Cecile watched as her wayward husband wandered around the farm in the moonlight, checking on things.

He wants to be sure Dad and Harrison are keeping things up to his standard.

Henry had settled in as if he'd never been away, taking over chores that George had been performing. There was no one to do Ethel's work, however, except Vanessa. Cecile was debating whether to take over Ethel's job to provide relief to her father and daughter but was hesitant given previous reactions from the family when they suspected a spirit might be around.

Maybe I can talk to Dad when the kids are at school and offer to help him.

Would it scare him into a heart attack?

Her thoughts going up and down, seesawing, Cecile could not decide what to do. She decided that she'd just play it by ear.

I'll do the ironing. Dad never pays attention to that, but Vanessa might... Vanessa will.

It's possible she'll think my Dad did it though.

Maybe I can eventually work with Dad to keep things running in the house.

The kids won't have to know.

It upsets them.

Acting on that thought she returned to the house leaving Elton to wander aimlessly around in the night. She began work with the iron, taking great care to be quiet so as not to wake anyone. Suddenly Elton appeared on the other side of the room. He smiled as he reached over and pulled a crock off the sideboard and let it fall to the floor with a crash. His face was full of glee at the problem he was sure to cause by such a loud crash coming in the middle of the night.

Cecile jumped and started to put the ironing away as fast as possible. She had most of it hidden just as Henry walked carefully into the room and stood looking around. He spotted the broken crock on the floor then looked at the spot where it had been setting. He scratched his head, then his arm, and finally his chin. It was obvious that Henry was trying to think of a way the crock could have fallen all by itself. Now the kids were in the kitchen clutching blankets around them, directing sleepy eyes at their grandfather. Vanessa's eyes noted the garment that Cecile had been ironing and her eyes got big. She didn't say a word though.

"What happened," Harrison asked Henry?

"Someone left this crock too close to the edge of the sideboard and it fell off."

"How did it fall off all by itself?"

"I don't know," Henry said irritably. "Maybe a mouse pushed it off...or maybe we have a rat running around in here somewhere.

Vanessa shuddered, then turned and ran out of the room. Harrison hesitated and then went back to his room too. Across the kitchen, Elton was doing an exaggerated laugh holding his belly and pretending to guffaw. It made Cecile sick to look at him. She turned her back on him and left the kitchen going to Vanessa's room. Her daughter was covered head to toe. Even her face was buried in the covers. Still her shaking was visible. She couldn't help it. Cecile bent over and touched her daughter's head.

"It's okay. Mama is here," she whispered.

The shaking intensified as Vanessa curled her body into a ball. Too late Cecile realized that she had terrified her daughter instead of comforting her.

"I'm sorry. I didn't mean to scare you. I love you," Cecile said to the blob on the bed, then vaporized through the wall. Elton was on the other side but moved away as she came into the hallway. His gaze was mocking; apparently he realized what she'd done.

Elton said nothing.

Cecile said nothing.

She moved away from him going toward Harrison's room. Gliding through the wall she checked on her son but left quickly for fear that Elton would go into Vanessa's room. He wasn't in his daughter's room however, when she checked; and gliding around the house, Cecile was unable to find him.

Good...he's gone back out to prowl the farm in the moonlight.

Cecile sat on a kitchen chair, weary from all the stress. For a long time she sat looking out the window watching the moon shine on an eerie landscape. Elton was out there somewhere and that made her feel shaky and scared. Finally she got up and began to iron again.

Vanessa was too upset to go to school the following day. She spent the day lying in bed tracing patterns of wall paper with her eyes, staring into space, and napping. Cecile hovered near her for hours but was afraid to make her presence known given the result she'd had the night before. Henry checked on his granddaughter several times offering her lunch which she refused and asking her what was wrong with her.

"I just feel sick," she mumbled.

Her grandfather left her alone.

Cecile was at a loss. She had tried to tell her daughter that she was here and that she'd protect her but instead of reassuring her, Vanessa had been violently traumatized. Should she try to talk to her father when the kids were out of the house? Would he go off the deep end too? That question was still up in the air too.

About an hour before supper time Vanessa came out of her room and silently began to help her grandfather cut vegetables for a salad. Henry glanced her way but decided to avoid rocking the boat apparently, and said nothing. Cecile watched as Vanessa walked to the area where the ironed clothes were hanging and inspected them. She stood looking at the empty basket for a long time but still she said nothing.

"What else needs done," she asked her Grandpa.

"You could snap some green beans if you want," he said.

Harrison and Reuben clomped into the mud room where they took off their boots before showing off their catch of fish.

"Clean em outside," Henry said. "Put them in the icebox and we'll have them tomorrow."

The two fishermen hauled the fish outside where they began to clean them on an old wooden table beside the shed. Noticing Elton was hanging out with them, Cecile stayed to watch. Elton moved behind Reuben and began to imitate his moves in a mocking way. Reuben seemed to be unaware.

All at once, Elton shoved the elbow of Reuben's knife hand sending the knife skidding into Reuben's left hand. Reuben screamed and looked around him angrily at nothingness. Cecile believed he had felt the push from Elton. She advanced on them and once again Elton left the scene.

"What am I doing that scares him away," she wondered. "If I knew what it was, I'd do it more often; maybe he'd go away for good."

Chapter Twenty Nine

Reuben ran to the pan of water they'd been putting the fish in and stuck his bleeding hand into the cool liquid. He held his right hand over the cut to stop the bleeding.

"I'll go get some tea," Harrison said. "I've heard it will stop bleeding."

Cecile watched as Reuben continued to bleed turning the water first pink and then red. Harrison returned with some loose tea. Reuben was using his free hand to remove the fish and place it on the newspaper he had laid down. Harrison took Reuben's hand out of the water and plastered loose tea over the wound. To Cecile's surprise the blood flow diminished quickly. Maybe Harrison should be a doctor, she speculated. He had been really cool in this emergency and seemed to have a talent for healing. She watched as Harrison wrapped a white muslin cloth around the cut, padding the area of the wound which was still seeping blood.

"What happened," Harrison asked Reuben. "How did you cut your hand?"

Reuben frowned, his brows drawing into a straight line across his weathered face. He looked at the bandaged hand and then around the area where they had been working.

"Someone or something pushed my knife hand," he said finally.

Harrison winced as if receiving a blow himself. He knelt beside his friend and took his hand looking to see if blood was seeping through the bandage. "I'm so sorry; if my Dad did it, I apologize for him...I just don't know what to do anymore."

Cecile could see that Harrison was ready to weep. Apparently Reuben saw it too.

"It's all right," he said. "Just a small wound; I heal up pretty good."

Cecile left them alone. She was so angry and confused she knew if she didn't leave she'd be blurting out some kind of apology herself. That wouldn't do. Look at the damage she'd done every time she'd spoken aloud in the past. Inside the house, Henry and Vanessa seemed oblivious as to what was going on outside. They were getting food ready to go on the table. Cecile sat on a chair in the corner watching and listening to their conversation.

"You didn't iron that basket of clothes did you," Henry asked.

Vanessa hung her head. "No."

"Who did it?"

"I don't know. Mom I think. The ironing was done when I woke up, that's all I know."

Henry rubbed his chin leaving streaks of flour on it. "When I went to feed the cows this morning, they already had hay," he said.

Vanessa looked at him curiously. "How did that happen?"

"I don't think your brother or his friend Reuben did it so, who does that leave?"

"Not my Dad...he didn't like you very much, did he?"

"No...but what helps me to run the farm helps you kids, don't it?"

Vanessa shrugged and seemed to draw further into herself. Cecile wondered if she had confided in anyone that her mother had spoken to her during the night, leaving her more distressed than before. That question was soon answered.

~ 156 ~

"Can you sit down a minute Grandpa? I need to tell you something and I can't think how to do it with you moving all over the place."

Henry nodded and sat on a chair.

"I heard Mom talk to me last night. She knew I was upset. I saw someone had been doing the ironing when I came into the kitchen and it scared me. I went to my room and covered up my head. I was crying. Then I felt her touch me and she said, 'It's okay, Mama is here.' I was upset and didn't say anything so she said, 'I didn't mean to scare you. I love you'. I was terrified out of my mind and she knew it so she left. I never even said 'I love you too' to her."

Vanessa was sobbing now and Henry reached to comfort her.

"I wish I could hear her voice again," he said.

"Wouldn't it scare you," Vanessa mumbled.

"Yes, it would scare me but it would still be nice to hear."

From her chair in the corner, Cecile smiled the first real smile since her death. "We are going to have a long conversation tomorrow when the kids go to school," she thought. "I'm going to take you at your word Dad, and we are going to have a nice chat."

The next day, Cecile could hardly wait to have her father alone so she could speak to him. Of course, as things go, nothing is easy. A neighbor man stopped by to chat with Henry when he was in the barn feeding and milking the cows. The long winded neighbor stayed on and on, talking as Henry mucked out the stable, sent cows out to pasture and did other chores. Finally the man left just before time for Henry to fix lunch.

Cecile followed her father to the house and kitchen where he opened the icebox and got out some milk, ham and biscuits for lunch. She was about to speak to him when Elton appeared on the other side of the room. Angry at having another delay, Cecile strode toward him, passed through the table and found herself in the spot where Elton had been. Elton had waited until she was traveling through the table, a feat that took a little concentration, and vanished before she got to him.

He's still running away from me; whatever is he doing that for?

Turning back toward her father, she saw that Henry was seated at the table looking out the window. He had biscuits and ham with a glass of milk in front of him but wasn't eating. He was just staring out the window. When she looked, she saw Elton waving a tree branch back and forth in front of the window. Knowing that her father would see only a disembodied branch waving back and forth and not the ghostly man waving it, she spoke.

"Don't be scared Dad. Elton is just up to his usual tricks. It's okay."

Henry shuddered but stayed in his seat. He turned his head to look toward her voice but she could tell that he saw nothing.

"Cecile...is that really you?"

His voice was trembling with fear mixed with excitement and longing.

"I'm here Dad; unfortunately Elton is too. Don't worry. For some reason he doesn't seem to be able to hurt me. He can hurt people who are still alive, it seems, so be careful."

"Was it him who hit Harrison in the face?'

"Yes. I didn't know how to stop him that time."

"Can you stop him now?"

"I don't know. He seems to be avoiding me. If I go toward him, he leaves the area. I don't know what that's all about but I'm using it."

Suddenly the effort to communicate left Cecile weak and dizzy. "Tired...got to go," she said before she fell into a hazy never world.

"Cecile," her father called. "Don't go."

But she was already gone having drifted into a twilight sleep of sorts. She heard her father from far off but she floated away, leaving his voice behind.

Chapter Thirty

Although Cecile wasn't there to see it, Henry had perked up after having heard his daughter's voice. "She may be dead, but she isn't gone," he thought in amazement. When the kids came in from school he sat them down and told them what he had heard.

"Your Mom's still here looking over us," he said.

"I told you so," Vanessa said, looking at Harrison.

"Why hasn't she talked to me then," Harrison asked petulantly.

Henry let his gaze rest on his grandson for a moment, then said, "I think she's been afraid of speaking to us for fear she'll scare us. She told me she was afraid I'd have a heart attack."

Vanessa was nodding her head. "Yes, I was too scared to take the covers off my head when she talked to me. At least I know I'm not crazy now that other people are hearing her too."

Henry looked at the two youngsters planning how to say what he needed to. "Your Mom says that your Dad is here too," he told them.

"I knew it!" Harrison's reaction was loud and spontaneous. "He hit me didn't he?"

"I'm afraid he did. I'm sorry." Henry said.

"How about other ghosts. I mean there are several people in the cemetery. Are there any other ghosts around here?"

Henry seemed surprised. "No, your Mom didn't say anything about any other spirits. Maybe she and Elton got stuck here because of how they died or something."

"I don't know if this makes me feel better or worse," Harrison muttered.

"That's why your Mother didn't want to let you know she was around. She knew it would be hard on you."

The conversation went on for some time but there was no conclusion. They didn't know when or if Cecile would be back to speak to them again. Everyone was fearful of Elton and unhappy to know that he was hanging around watching them. It even felt spooky to have their mother always watching; it was as if they had no privacy at all.

When Cecile came out of her in between state, she boldly went to look for Elton. He was nowhere to be found. She searched the barns and sheds, and traveled the fields but no Elton. Although she was afraid of him, she had some things to say to the father of her children. She planned to tell him to move on to wherever he was supposed to go and to leave his family alone. That was the least he could do, to try to compensate for the damage he had done to everyone.

But she couldn't find him.

Was he hiding from her?

Why?

After a while she gave up. Maybe he'd figured it out on his own...the fact that he was doing a lot of damage to everyone. Maybe he'd decided to do the right thing without being told.

Wouldn't that be wonderful? My murderer, the man who has tortured and scared my children, gone...no more need to worry about him.

It would be great but Cecile didn't believe that had happened. Elton was just laying up somewhere plotting.

A few days later she still had not seen Elton. Maybe he was trying to lull her into a false sense of security by hiding out. Then when she least expected it, he'd spring out and cause trouble.

It was mid-day and the children were in school. Henry was in the kitchen preparing his lunch and Cecile was sitting in her favorite spot where she could look out the window while watching over her father as he worked. She felt close to him at these times, especially when he fixed something to eat and sat at the table dreaming about better times, or losing himself in his memories, as she suspected he was doing.

Seeing that his attention was fixed on something outside the window, she followed his gaze and saw a woman and a girl child coming up the lane. They were on foot and both looked tired. The woman had a faded beauty with light brown hair, blue eyes and a small figure. The girl looked like a miniature version of her mother. There was a haggard simplicity about the two of them that tugged at Cecile's heart.

Abruptly she saw Elton appear by the gate and attempt to block the progress of the strange woman and child. By now they were at the front gate, trying to open it. Elton held the gate shut as the woman tried over and over to push it open. Cecile could see the woman struggling with the gate, gazing at the latch which was in the open position, and trying again. Anxious to see what was going on Cecile wafted through the wall even as her father opened and exited the door and started toward the front yard and the unknown women. Elton looked as if he were in agony. Belligerence had left him it seemed; he tried to motion Cecile away as he mouthed the, unusual for him, word,

"Please."

Cecile hesitated but her father did not.

"Hello," Henry said to the woman. "Don't know what got into that gate. It doesn't usually stick like that."

"Hi," the woman said, relief spreading over her face.

Henry opened the gate, ushered the travelers into the yard with a flourish, and asked the woman, "How can I help you?"

"We're looking for Elton Montgomery. Is this the right place?" the woman asked.

"Well, yes and no," Henry said, eyeing the two travelers carefully, taking in their ragged appearance and tired eyes. "Come on in and have a cup of hot cocoa or coffee with me and we'll talk about it." Henry added.

Cecile looked for Elton to see how he was taking Henry's invitation. Obviously he didn't want these people inside the house. Elton had disappeared.

"Thanks,"

The woman pushed the girl in front of her and they headed toward the house.

"I'm Henry Winston."

"You can call me Rosa," the woman said. "This is Louise." She indicated the girl, who smiled a tired hello and nodded at Henry.

Henry seated them at the table and made hot cocoa for everyone. The day was cool and expected to be much colder by evening according to the radio. It was mid-November but colder than usual.

"I hate to give you the bad news but Elton Montgomery died nearly two years ago," Henry said once everyone was settled with the cocoa.

The woman's face collapsed as if her last hope was gone. The girl who appeared to be twelve or thirteen years old looked concerned as well. In fact tears popped into the girl's eyes as if a fountain had been engaged.

"Oh no," Rosa said.

"What are we going to do Mama," the girl asked, ignoring Henry, her eyes pleaded for assurances from her mother.

"I don't know. We'll talk about it later," Rosa said, glancing Henry's way.

"How about his wife...he had a wife didn't he," Rosa asked Henry.

Henry nodded his head, "Yes...Cecile. She was my daughter but she's dead also."

The woman looked at him as if he was lying to her... "But how? Why are they both dead? Where are their children?"

"Did you know Cecile?" Henry looked perplexed. He didn't answer her question.

From her position across the room, Cecile shook her head. She didn't know this woman at all. How did the woman know her? Rosa began to cry. Large sobs shook her as her daughter cried with her and yet found the strength to try to comfort her mother.

"He was our last hope," Rosa spluttered in explanation.

"How did you know Elton," Henry asked, his suspicions alerted.

"He was my papa, okay," Louisa blurted out defiantly before her mother could speak. "We've lost our house and everything. We needed Papa's help and here he's gone and died on us. We don't have a home anymore and now my Papa can't help us either. What are we going to do?"

Shocked at this revelation, Cecile could only gasp, her own tears drifting eerily through her limbs and collecting on the floor.

No wonder Elton didn't want to let them in the gate.

Chapter Thirty One

Henry demonstrated his shock by staring at the woman and girl who were sitting there in his daughter's kitchen. They were shamelessly telling him that his son-in-law had fathered a child with the woman Rosa while married to Cecile. His gaze fastened on the girl looking for traces of Elton in her features, seeing none.

"How old are you," he asked Louise.

"Thirteen next month."

"Did Elton know about this girl," he asked Rosa.

"Yes...he helped us out at first but then he stopped. I didn't know he was married until after I was pregnant...if you are wondering. He said he was a bachelor."

"Where are you from?"

"North of Urbana. I had a little house there after my parents died; I took in washing and ironing, did some house cleaning, had a garden and all. to get by. I met Elton at the Urbana Fair and he told me his pack of lies. I fell hook, line, and sinker. Only after I told him I was pregnant did he say that he had a wife and kids."

"Did you know Elton," Henry asked Louise.

The girl looked down, apparently aware of the delicacy of the situation. "I remember him from a few years ago but we haven't seen him for a long time."

"So Elton treated you like a daughter; he visited you and helped raise you?" Henry looked skeptically at the young girl, then at her mother.

Rosa nodded. "Even though I broke up with him after I found out he had a wife, Elton kept coming around...said he wanted to see his daughter grow up. Then he stopped coming about three years ago. We had a sort of falling out. I never heard from him again. I wondered if his wife found out about Louise or something, but I never tried to find him to ask. The only reason I'm here now is we're in trouble. I lost the house and we don't have any money to live on. Since Louise is his daughter, I hoped Elton would help, but I guess that's out of the question."

Rosa sank back on the chair looking desolate and woebegone. Louise was crying, her face hidden as she lay her head on the table in front of her.

Cecile was still in a state of shocked limbo, much like her father appeared to be. Elton had been cheating on her way back when Harrison was a baby. He'd had a daughter, this girl Louis, and had continued to visit with her and her mother for years. The betrayal of her husband and his double life floored her. Of course she knew that Elton was selfish and headstrong. He came and went as he pleased so finding time to visit his other family wouldn't have been hard for him to do. She felt sick in the place where her stomach used to be. Elton had tried to block Rosa and Louise from coming into the yard and then had pleaded with Cecile to go away when that hadn't worked.

He doesn't want me to know the extent of his betrayal; he's ashamed.

He cheated on me with this woman; he had a child with her.

He tried to abuse his own daughter; what else has he done that I don't know about?

Would he have tried to have sex with Louise too once she was older?

Her stomach was uneasy and Cecile wanted to leave the kitchen and forget about the new revelations. The kids were due home from school in the next half hour or so and she thought her father should get rid of the woman and her daughter.

But Louise is a half-sister to Vanessa and Harrison.

They have a right to know about her and to meet her, don't they?

The thought made her tremble. If this was their half-sister, the children had a right to meet her. After all she was their flesh and blood and it wasn't her fault that she had a louse for a father any more than it was Vanessa and Harrison's fault. Still she wanted to stop time and to think about it before she robbed her children of any trust they still had in their father. She wanted to do that for her children's sake...not their father's.

She tuned back into the conversation.

"We're going to have to go now. Sorry we bothered you," Rosa said. "It's going to be awfully cold and we've got to get back to town and try to find a place to sleep tonight."

"I thought you said you didn't have any money," Henry said.

"We don't...I've been wondering if the Sherriff will let us sleep at the jail overnight until we find an answer to our problems."

On the spur of the moment Henry made a decision. "Louise is a half-sister to my grandchildren. We can't send you back out there with no place to go on a cold night. You can stay here at least tonight and that will allow you to meet your brother and sister," he said to Louise.

Louise looked at her mother afraid to believe their good fortune. Even one night where it was warm and where they didn't have to worry for a few hours would be a relief. Rosa was looking surprised and grateful as she riveted on Henry's eyes to see if he meant it.

"That is so nice of you," Rosa said. "Thank you. It would be dark before we got to town if we were walking there now. This means a lot." She hung her head and whispered, "I know Elton's wife was your daughter. That makes what you're doing for us doubly special."

"I don't know where we'll put you but we'll think of something," Henry mumbled.

Cecile couldn't believe what her Dad had done. It wasn't like him to take people he didn't know into his house. What if they were lying and Louise wasn't Elton's child after all? What if this woman was a flim-flam artist out to swindle the family out of money? She had to hold back to keep from protesting loudly her father's poor judgment.

Elton knew who they were and didn't want Henry to talk to them. He'd motioned Cecile to move away from them. He knew them. She is probably his daughter like they said.

It popped into Cecile's head to wonder what George and Ethel would think about having a granddaughter they had never met. Did they know about her? Would Elton have confided in his parents? She thought not. Henry was making some more hot cocoa. "I've something else to tell you before the kids get home," he said.

"I need to let you know how my daughter and Elton died."

Cecile watched closely as her father described the murder suicide from his point of view. He went on to explain what had started the fight that ended up in tragedy. Louise drew into herself seeming appalled by her father's actions. Her mother didn't seem to be as surprised as her daughter seemed to be.

"Elton always had a temper and a sense of entitlement," she said. "He thought he should have anything he wanted, right or wrong."

Cecil was starting to warm a little to the woman who had been her competition. She liked the way she made no excuses for either herself or for Elton. She was sure that George and Ethel would excuse this as well as Elton's other actions. They would deem it Cecile's fault...that somehow she had driven him to his behaviors.

Cecile snorted her disgust at that.

Everyone in the room jumped then looked warily around, wondering what the noise had been

Cecile wafted out into the yard and went to watch for the kids. Nothing was to be gained by staying around these newcomers.

Chapter Thirty Two

Cecile wanted to boycott the family dinner because it hurt her too much to look at Rosa and Louise, however, her curiosity got the better of her. It cut into her heart to realize that while she was slaving to be a good wife to Elton, he was out tomcatting around with other women.

How many other women?

Will any more show up here?

Harrison and Vanessa had arrived to find the visitors sitting comfortably in the living room talking to their grandfather as if he'd known them forever. He had asked the children to sit down with them and then encouraged Rosa to tell them her story. Of course the kids had been dumfounded at this new revelation. Cecile had expected that. Neither had said much, too stunned to speak perhaps.

"I've invited them to spend the night," Henry said. "Tomorrow is Saturday. We'll have your other grandparents over to meet Louise. She is their granddaughter after all."

"But where will they sleep," Vanessa asked suspiciously.

"Afraid the women will have to bunk in your room with you for now. We can get out that roll-away bed." Henry explained.

"That's not goanna work. My room's too small."

Vanessa stood up and left the room.

"She's just upset; she'll come around," Henry said.

Cecile followed Vanessa; so did Harrison after mumbling that he was going to check on his sister.

Vanessa grabbed her coat and headed toward the barn with Harrison running to keep up with her.

"It'll be okay," he said to his sister. "We knew Dad did some bad things. This is just another of his chickens coming home to roost."

"Doesn't mean we have to feed his chickens and give them a place to roost," Vanessa said bitterly.

After a few minutes she asked "Why did Grandpa invite them to stay?"

"He told me that they are destitute and have lost everything including the house they lived in. They are almost hobo's I guess. Anyway they needed a warm place to stay overnight so he let them stay here. I suppose he'll send them on their way tomorrow."

"I don't think he will; Grandpa's got a good heart and he'll feel sorry for them."

Harrison nodded, was silent and then said, "She is our sister whether we like it or not."

"She's no sister of mine," Vanessa exploded.

"You won't like to hear this but I think Louise looks a little bit like you," Harrison said, moving away in case his sister wanted to strike him for saying so.

"Does not. We aren't a thing alike. Dad must have been fooling around with that Rosa when you were a baby. How does that make you feel?"

Harrison brooded a while, saying nothing.

"It's not Louise's fault," he finally said.

"No. It's Dad's and Rosa's, but we can't accept her as a sister and leave her mother out...and now Grandpa thinks I should share my room with the two of them. I'd rather die!"

"What if I sleep in the hayloft and give my room to them or to you tonight? If it's only one night that should work."

Vanessa looked at Harrison measuring him for sincerity. "It's too cold out here but thanks."

She stared up into the hayloft for a few minutes, thinking.

"I suppose I can stand the two of them for one night. If it's more than one night we'll have to figure something else out," she finally said.

Returning to the house, Vanessa quietly started to prepare her room for visitors.

In the middle of the night there was a mighty crash that jarred the house. Vanessa, Rosa, and Louise looked up to see a tree limb protruding from the ceiling. They jumped out of bed and ran into the hallway. Harrison and Henry were rushing toward them from the other end of the house.

"What is it," Henry asked befuddled by sleep.

"There's a tree sticking out of the ceiling. I guess that tree outside my window decided to fall," Vanessa said.

"But why? That tree ain't dead," Harrison said sidling around the others to look into the bedroom.

"Sure enough a tree branch was poking through the lathe and plaster on the ceiling pointing its wooden fingers at the occupants of the room.

"This is weird," Rosa said.

"I think this house is spooky," Louise added, loud-whispering to her mother.

"Well it's your wonderful father who's doing it," Vanessa said in a huff. "He's not happy you're here and he's making a statement."

"He's your father too since you mention it," Louise said haughtily "Are you saying he's a ghost and that he can pull trees out by their roots and all? That's just crazy."

Henry shushed the two girls. "Elton is around here still," he admitted, "And so is my daughter. He's done things around here before and we have heard Cecile speak to us."

"You're all crazy," Louise huffed but she looked uneasy to Cecile who was watching.

"It's okay," Rosa said. "We'd better try to get some rest. Morning will come before we know it. At least it's not raining so we shouldn't get wet before daylight. In the morning we can see what happened."

"Rosa has a good point. There's nothing we can do about it right now. Wait until daylight." Henry said.

Everyone went back to their rooms and settled into their beds. Cecile hovered near Vanessa thinking that Elton's revenge might be centered on the women in this room. She had been in the room when the tree fell, had swiftly moved through the roof and saw Elton vanishing into a foggy mist.

He had caused the tree to fall; *what was he trying to do?*

Did he intend to hurt someone or to scare the women away?

I know he doesn't want them here because he doesn't want us to know what he's done.

Well too late; we know.

Rosa was staring at the hole in the ceiling apparently afraid to close her eyes. Vanessa had curled onto her side and was trying to go back to sleep, and Louise was glaring fearfully around the room in the dim light. Cecile almost felt sorry for Rosa and Louise. She knew Elton was capable of having lied to Rosa She wondered if Rosa was telling the truth when she said that she'd ended the relationship when Elton finally told her he was married with kids. If she had, then she'd acted responsibly and that sin too was squarely on Elton Montgomery's shoulders!

It was an hour later when the tapping on the wall started. Cecile sped through the wall only to see Elton vanishing once again.

He's trying so hard to make them leave, to scare them to death... it almost makes me want them to stay a while just to see why he wants rid of them so badly.

Cecile went back into the room and laid a hand on Vanessa's trembling shoulder. The other women were sitting bolt upright in bed and it was clear that nobody was going to sleep another wink tonight. Vanessa jumped at her touch but when Cecile kept the hand where it was, she relaxed a little. Apparently it was better to have a ghostly mother's hand on your shoulder than a virulent father on the loose bent on mischief. Cecile hoped Vanessa felt protected from harm.

Cecile checked on Harrison and her father. Both were wide awake also. She watched as Henry got up, looked at the clock which said 5:00AM, then trod a heavy step to the kitchen to make coffee. Apparently the long night was over and everyone was going to start a day full of questions.

Chapter Thirty Three

To say that everyone was grumpy that morning would be to understate the facts. No one in this troubled house had been blessed with good sleep and although she didn't really in the way she used to, Cecile was as grumpy as the rest. She hadn't seen hide nor hair of Elton since he'd played his little tricks during the night. Vanessa was in a mood and Harrison was angry, she could tell. Her father wasn't speaking to anyone and the two guests seemed uneasy and frightened.

Why did Elton disrupt everyone's sleep?

He must be trying to drive Rosa and Louise away; make life too unpleasant here.

Starting to feel sympathy for her husband's mistress and daughter, Cecile considered what she could do. Since Elton wanted them gone, to be perverse, Cecile thought it might be okay if they stayed a while.

Harrison had gone to invite his Montgomery grandparents to brunch at Henry's direction.

"Don't tell them anything about Rosa and Louise," Henry had instructed. "Just ask them to come. Tell them we need to discuss something."

At 10:30, George and Ethel arrived at the house. Henry sat them down and introduced them to Rosa and Louise, and once again instructed Rosa to explain how they were involved in the family. Ethel sat white-faced, mouth pursed, as she listened. George didn't seem to know how to react. He appeared to be stunned. In unison both looked at Louise who was apparently their granddaughter.

"Why don't you tell us about yourself," Ethel suggested to the girl. "Did you know Elton?"

"Yes; until he quit coming to see us."

"Did you call him Dad?"

"No Ma'am," Louise mumbled. "He didn't want me to."

"Why not," George interrupted.

"Said he didn't want people talkin' and all."

Cecile couldn't help it...she harrumphed aloud, startling everyone.

Realizing what she'd done, she shrunk back behind a cabinet hoping her outburst would go unheard. It didn't; everyone was looking nervously around the room.

Finally Henry said, "I might as well tell you...we have good reason to think Elton is still around here...and my daughter too. I guess you suspect that from what happened during the night. You'll have to get used to unusual happenings."

The women looked at Henry trying to gauge what he was saying but he fell silent. Ethel jumped in to ask the women some more questions and Cecile took a deep but unneeded breath in relief. Finally Henry interrupted the flow of general conversation.

"Why don't you and Vanessa take our guests out to see the barn, the horses, and cattle; let them have a little tour?" he said to Harrison.

Knowing that his grandfather was trying to get rid of them so the adults could talk, Harrison got up, went to get coats for everyone and ushered the women out the door, heading toward the barn. Vanessa followed but her steps were reluctant. Cecile stayed to see what her father and her in-laws were up to. Henry got to the point rapidly.

"I'm thinking about offering a place here for Rosa and Louise to stay this winter. Two women, on their own without a home, are bound to fall into trouble out on the road what with all the hobos traveling about. In the spring they can figure out a place to go. Right now if they aren't raped, robbed, or killed, they might freeze to death out there."

The Montgomery's stared at Henry in shock and surprise.

"You'd do that for the woman who cheated with your daughter's husband? Why?" George was not just astounded, but distrustful.

"I just explained. I can't leave two women to fend for themselves out there. You should be happy that I'm willing to help your granddaughter."

"I am, but I don't understand it. I wouldn't if I was in your shoes."

"I know." Henry's simple reply said it all.

Cecile cheered inwardly at how easily her father had shown the shortcomings of the Montgomery family. Her father was a good man, willing to do the right thing as he saw it. They were not.

"But we'd have to live with them too when we're here with Harrison and Vanessa," Ethel said.

"That's right; that's why I'm discussing this with you without just deciding on my own. Are you willing to do that?"

"I don't know," Ethel said.

"Two women won't be any help to me," George said. "They might help out in the kitchen but I need help in the barn and fields. What are they going to do to earn their keep? Even the animals have to earn their way or we don't keep them around...times are hard. The horses plow, the cows give milk, the chickens lay eggs, and the cats keep mice and rats out of the barn. What are those two going to do for us?"

Henry scratched his head wearily, "I don't know. We can come up with some chores that we are asking them to do before they come back in if you've a mind to. No need if you are saying 'No' to this idea."

"It would give Vanessa a little break if they help with cooking and cleaning for a while. It would give her a chance to focus on her homework more. Her grades have not been up to par for a long time. Give me a break too," Ethel said.

"No help to me," George grumbled.

"There's no reason that Louise can't feed the chickens and things like that," Henry suggested. "She could help with the flowers and the garden in the spring. We can adjust chores as we go along."

"I guess..." George was reluctant.

"Just for about three or four winter months and then we can figure out what to do with them when it gets warm," Henry said.

They could hear the children and Rosa returning to the house so Henry asked hastily, "Do we have a plan? We can offer. If they don't like it they can refuse."

"Okay, I guess," Ethel said, doubt clouding her voice.

"I recon," George mumbled just at the others came into the room.

"Vanessa, you, Rosa, Louise, and you too Harrison. Breakfast is your job today...all of you. George, Ethel and I are working on a list," Henry said to the surprised faces in front of him.

He got out paper and pencil, gave one each to Ethel, to George, and kept one for himself. He had written 'suggested chores for Rosa and Louise' on each piece of paper near the top. Harrison grumbled but took his place in the kitchen with the women. Cecile went around the room checking out the lists, and the house fell quiet.

Life at the farm was about to change...again.

Chapter Thirty Four

It was as if the people, and even the house, was holding their collective breath. It was clear to everyone at the farm that something momentous was going on. Rosa and Louise looked around at the others uneasily. Rosa seemed on the verge of saying something but seemed to be holding back until after everyone had eaten. Cecile expected that she wanted to leave this strange house. Outside snow had begun to fall thick, fast, and silently, hushing the world. Perhaps that snow influenced the decision that Rosa ultimately made.

As they ate breakfast, Henry presented the idea for Rosa and her daughter to remain at the house with the Montgomery/Winston family until spring, along with lists of possible chores they would be required to do to earn their room and board.

"We'll consolidate these lists into one list and that way you will know exactly what we expect. Right now the whole idea is a work in progress. You might not have to do all these things and there might be something not on the list we'll ask you to do later."

Louise looked at her mother. "I vote 'No'."

"Look out the window," Rosa commanded. "Where we going in that?"

Henry stood up. "I think we should all go away and let Rosa and Louise talk about this while they are cleaning up the dishes," he said.

Everyone put on coats and headed out to the barn where they helped Henry with feeding and other barn chores for the next forty-five minutes. Cecile did not go with them. She remained in the house to see what Rosa and Louise would decide.

"See...they want us to be slave labor for them. Look who's doing the dishes," Louise said.

"It's only right that we earn our way. I don't want to be beholden to anyone anyway," Rosa said.

"This place is scary."

"They say its Elton up to his no good tricks. After what he's done, I believe it," Rosa said.

"So you believe in ghosts?" Louise swiveled her head toward her mother throwing soap suds onto the floor with her sudden moves.

"Don't believe in ghosts...don't believe their imaginary either. I'll just wait and see."

"If he's here; he could hurt us. He could hurt me. Do you want that?"

Rosa gave her only child a weary look. "Of course not, but what do you think might happen to us on the road. This would only be for three or four months. It's got to be better than homeless in the winter."

Louise slapped the dishrag down angrily, throwing soapy suds around again. Rosa looked at her pointedly. "You know you have to clean that up before these folks get back don't you?"

"What if I don't? I don't plan to be anyone's slave even for three or four months."

"You will do what I decide," Rosa said firmly. "It's my job to keep us safe. It's not my job to keep everything so you can lay around and eat bonbons. You need to do your part; you know that."

Louise huffed but didn't say anything more for a while.

Finally Rosa said. "I'm going to agree to this. At least we are going to have full bellies and we will be warm. Every night we'll know where we're going to sleep. That's the best I can do for us right now."

Apparently Louise knew her mother was right but she chose not to agree. She was silent.

"You'll also have a chance to get to know your real grandparents, the Montgomery's. They'll be moving in here the first of the year for three months while Henry goes home and does work at his house and store," Rosa told Louise.

Louise grunted.

All the women owned was in the bags on their backs so there wasn't as much of a storage problem as there would have been otherwise. Vanessa wasn't happy with the newcomers in her bedroom. When the roof was fixed where the tree branch had penetrated it, she noticed the attic space up above the room and confiscated it for her own. Harrison helped her to build a ladder that allowed her to climb up and down from the loft. Although she was actually in the same room, she had some privacy up there to put some of her favorite things and to sleep. She didn't have a bed but she made a nice bed roll and managed pretty well with that.

She was coldly friendly to Louise and Rosa.

Harrison was nicer to his new sister, not having been displaced by another boy as Vanessa had been by another girl. Still neither of them invited Louise to go with them to Reuben's house or included her in the things they had always done together.

"When am I going to meet the new girl and her Mama," Reuben asked.

Harrison had told him about the situation and how his grandparents had decided to let the two women stay during the winter.

"I guess you can come to dinner before Grandpa Henry leaves," Harrison said.

Reuben showed up a few days later with a brace of five squirrels he'd shot and a big pot to cook them in. He and Harrison cleaned and cooked the wild game outside at the stone grill Elton had made long before. Once the feast was finished they took the food inside as an offering for dinner. Rosa had made chicken and dumplings and they added squirrel to the menu.

Cecile noticed Elton had made an appearance at the meal staying carefully across the room from where she stood watching over her family. Her Dad was leaving and the Montgomery family was moving in. She was going to miss him. In an effort to stop thinking about her father's departure, she tuned back in to the residents of the house and their conversation. Surprised she noticed that Reuben had suddenly become the life of the party telling stories and actively wooing and entertaining the ladies. Cecile had never seen this side of him before.

Elton was glaring blue fury at him.

She should have expected it but even Cecile jumped when Elton sent the pie safe, which held two apple pies, made from apples canned during the summer, crashing onto its face shooting apple pie all over the floor. Although she went after her malicious husband, he was gone before she could get to him.

Everyone in the room stared.

When Rosa got up to clean up the mess caused by the pies, Reuben gallantly helped her.

Chapter Thirty Five

Vanessa took up painting pictures in early December and some color began to creep back into her world. Eventually she was once again wearing items that had escaped the black dye bath. Cecile wished she could buy or make some clothes for her daughter...could somehow make her happy again but she resigned herself to being glad for the small steps and progress Vanessa was making. Reuben got a dog and named him Parker. He brought Parker over to the farm house to show to the family, but most of his comments were directed to Rosa. Clearly he liked the woman. Cecile laughed to herself when she saw Elton glaring from a window behind Reuben, but moved between the two, just in case, and Reuben survived his fury. Elton once again vanished, avoiding her.

Infuriated at Elton's violent jealousy over Rosa, Cecile did anything she could to remove barriers to a romance between Reuben and Rosa. She spent a long time ruminating endlessly over the injustices she'd suffered because of Elton Montgomery. Served him right if his little sugar plum found another sugar daddy.

Elton took me for granted; he didn't show jealousy of me.

Here he was running around like a hound-dog in heat while I took care of him, his house, and kids. He never showed respect for me; and then he killed me.

That dog will have his day...just wait.

Her anger heated and simmered under the surface of her ethereal body and Cecile smoldered with a desire to punish her husband. Funny that she was angrier over his affair with Rosa than about the fact that he had murdered her!!!! Strangely she didn't have any hatred for Rosa although she tried to come up with some fury 'just because'. Rosa seemed a little naïve sometimes and it was easy to believe that Elton had hoodwinked her.

Cecile was sitting on the other side of a campfire Reuben had constructed in the clearing outside his shack watching Vanessa paint a not so good landscape and listening to Reuben and Harrison talk about the dog, which he had named Parker, one morning. Parker was running around the clearing licking at everything and everyone near him.

"That dog's a licker," Reuben said.

"He's a nipper too...just nipped at my hand," Harrison said. "I'd get a dog, but they're too expensive. My grandparents wouldn't let me because we can't afford to feed it."

"Not even a good hunting dog?"

"No; they're not wild about me hunting all that much. Don't like me to be out in the woods with a gun...afraid I'll have an accident or something."

"I think you need a dog."

"Can't afford it." Harrison shrugged and stared at the melting ice around the fire-pit.

"Think about it... if you fish and hunt and give the dog the spare parts for its food then it earns its own keep and you have food to share with your family. I know where there's a good blue tick hound if you want it. Owner had a heart attack. It needs a good home."

Cecile saw the temptation in Harrison's eyes but then he said "No...I can't ask my grandparents to take on another mouth to feed."

"Get the dog." Cecile's words shocked everyone to stillness.

Vanessa put down the paint brush and looked toward Cecile as if she could see her.

"Mom?"

"Harrison needs a dog." Cecile's words ratcheted up the tension.

Reuben stood up turning in circles not knowing what to do. He seemed dumfounded that this ethereal voice had entered his clearing to haunt him and his friends. He tried to say something but it came out as a cough instead. Harrison cleared his throat which seemed dry from the sound of it.

"Why do you want me to have a dog, Mom?"

"Need it... keep you company."

All at once Cecile felt herself losing power as if something was draining her. She had never had this exact feeling before. She sank to a log and sat staring at the scene in front of her while her world swirled and whirled around her. She managed a small smile when she heard Harrison say to Reuben,

"Let's go see about that blue-tick hound then."

Later, after she had recovered from 'the spell' that had afflicted her, Cecile checked in on the Montgomery's who were newly installed in the house with their three grandchildren. She resented them because of her sure knowledge that if the child had been hers rather than Elton's, they would have fought strongly to keep Louise from living under this roof which they considered Elton's not Cecile's.

There's always a double standard.

Dad was, and is, such a nice man; so compassionate to all.

The Montgomery family is selfish; they didn't even want their own granddaughter to stay here because it would force them to do something.

Cecile had found more and more bitterness creeping into her being. Having Elton's mistress living here wasn't easy in spite of her best efforts.

"Louise...well...let's say she's a lot different from Vanessa and full of teenage rebellion."

Clearly Louise resented that she had to help around the house but understood that she had no choice. It made her surly and ungrateful for the benefits Cecile's father had offered her. Now George and Ethel were back at the farm and they hadn't warmed up very much toward their new granddaughter either.

Maybe she's just more proof of their son's low nature and they don't like facing it.

George was sitting at the kitchen table with a newspaper. Ethel was wiping up after lunch. The kids and Rosa were all out of the house doing something. Cecile was listening in to the conversation.

"What are we going to do about Christmas this year," Ethel asked, wiping her hands on a dishtowel.

"What's to do? We fix a meal, give a few gifts and go into the New Year," George said.

"I mean we have two more people this year. Are we buying a gift for them?"

George put the paper down and clumped his elbows down on it. "I guess we should," he said after a little thought.

"Louise is our grandchild too."

"Huh"

"You don't have doubts about her belonging to Elton, do you?"

"Can't say... all I'm saying is our boy knew how to pick em."

"What's wrong with Rosa...except she had an affair with a married man, I mean."

"How many others did she have an affair with?"

"Cecile was a good woman except she didn't appreciate Elton enough. Elton didn't choose loose women; he went to see Louise and claimed her, so it's probably true that she's his."

"That's what they're telling us."

"Why would they lie?"

"To get a place in out of the cold with food and shelter for the winter."

Ethel considered that. "Wish I could ask Elton if she was his. Why is it that Cecile's ghost does all the talking? If Elton's around, why doesn't he say so?"

"Might be mad at us for some reason," George said as he got up and headed out to check on the cows.

Cecile thought "Because there is nothing he can say for himself after all he's done."

Chapter Thirty Six

The grandparents decided that they would have a jointly celebrated Christmas season at the farm. George would kill some chickens, Henry would bring goodies from the store and everyone would work together to make it a nice holiday. There was tension between Henry and the Montgomery couple but he worked hard to put aside the fact that their son had cheated on and murdered his daughter. After all the grandchildren loved both sides of the family and it should be made as easy for them as possible. Rosa and Louise added a new wrinkle to the family mosaic.

"And what is Elton doing," Cecile wondered. He had been conspicuously absent for several days.

She had caught him one night watching his daughters as they were getting ready for bed. Although at the time both were fully dressed, Cecile was suspicious and wondered how long Elton had been hovering around the young ladies. The minute he saw her he shot upward moving through the ceiling at maximum speed. Although she was fast when needed, by the time Cecile broke through the ceiling after him, Elton had vanished.

"Maybe he's finally ashamed of himself and that's why he's staying away," Cecile hoped.

Sticking closer to the girls, Cecile found herself monitoring the relationship between them. Louise didn't seem to like Vanessa much and Vanessa was hardly gracious in the way she treated the younger girl. They held short conversations sometime but mostly it was just to share information, not friendship. That is what was happening on this evening. Louise was looking critically at a painting of a landscape that Vanessa was working on.

"Why are there no people in your paintings," Louise asked.

"Because people mess everything up," Vanessa said.

"You mean people like your Dad?"

"He's your Dad too, I hear."

"I wish I'd never met him."

"Why...what did he ever do to you? It's me who lost everything. You're better off that he left you alone."

Cecile saw that Vanessa was not going to give up her major claim to self- pity to Louise. Too bad...self-pity was making Vanessa's life pitiful.

Louise turned and stalked out of the room, seemingly unwilling to continue the conversation. Outside the room came a crash. Zipping ahead of Vanessa, Cecile got to Louise first. Louise was sitting on the floor rubbing a huge lump that was swelling across her forehead. A large vase lay unbroken beside her. Vanessa arrived and offered a hand to Louise.

"What happened?"

"That vase just jumped off the shelf and hit me in the head," Louise accused, daring Vanessa to deny it.

"Must be your dad's ghost," Vanessa said.

"Of course...it's dear old Dad; at least that's what everyone says, but maybe it's your mother who doesn't want me here." Louise jerked her hand away from Vanessa and stood up by herself. "I wish my Mom would leave this freaky place," she said.

"You just don't appreciate anything folks do for you," Vanessa retaliated.

The girls ignored each other the rest of the day even when they had to wash and dry dishes together at lunch time. Reuben was coming to dinner again tonight. He had promised that he would bring along three fat groundhogs for the icebox. The Montgomery's had groundhog from time to time and the family liked the dark meat which is mild flavored and tender. They prepared it in a similar way to chicken or rabbit. Cecile wondered how Elton was going to take to this visit. Obviously Reuben liked Rosa and she liked him. Elton was jealous.

Cecile thought a romance between the two single people might be a good idea. Both were probably lonely. It was true that Reuben had few prospects. He lived in a shack using his wits and primitive means to get by. He probably couldn't take care of Rosa and Louise, but he had a right to his dreams didn't he? Anyway, Rosa didn't have anything either so maybe working together they could both prosper. At least they'd be better off together than they would be apart.

Snow was on the ground and Ethel had convinced George to hook up the horses to the spring wagon so they could take a drive around the farm in the snowy twilight. Ethel had put hot water bottles and blankets in the wagon to keep them warm. Cecile perched on the wagon tongue and laughed silently when the horses sensed her presence and snorted large gulps of air into the frosty snow. Reuben sat beside Rosa while George and Ethel rode on the front seat. Vanessa, Harrison, and Louise huddled in their blankets across from Reuben and Rosa.

Vanessa was staring moodily into the distance while Harrison was talking to Louise about

Reuben's dog. They had been too late to get the blue tick hound Reuben had told him about. The owner had already given it away. Cecile thought that Reuben might be holding Rosa's hand under the blanket. The family had left the food to keep warm in the oven while they went off on this jaunt through the snow. Afterwards they'd eat a late supper. No doubt it would be romantic if you were in the mood for it.

Elton suddenly appeared and although he was in a mood...it wasn't a romantic mood.

Cecile watched as Elton breathed his coldest draft down the back of Reuben's shirt. Reuben moved closer to Rosa as if to get warm. Taking a handful of hay from the wagon bed, Elton threw it directly into Rosa's face. She screamed, alerting everyone to trouble. Cecile banished Elton with her presence, swooping toward him so fast that he barely got away. She had no idea why she had this sudden power over her vindictive husband, but she certainly did like it. Elton could not seem to tolerate her to be within a few feet of him. Without exception, he had run away.

Rosa was trembling but not with cold; Louise had moved over beside her mother.

"Are you okay," Louise asked.

"What's going on back there," George asked for the second time.

Hay blew into Rosa's face and eyes," Vanessa said.

"Don't be playing any games back there. We're trying to have a nice little sleigh ride tonight. Don't spoil it." Ethel seemed to think the kids were at fault.

Later when everyone was eating and talking happily, immersed in a holiday spirit, Elton returned. He blew so much smoke down the chimney that they had to open windows to the cold air to get the room cleared. Cecile was again too late to anticipate him but she did help with clearing the air in the room. Bitterness toward Elton was eating at her. Elton as always the person in opposition to everyone else... the spoilsport. She wanted to force him to go away and stay away...but how? She berated herself because she didn't think like Elton, and so found it very hard to anticipate what he'd do. Cecile had been neglecting to pray but suddenly she decided that would be a good thing to do during the holidays. Lord knew the family needed help so they could move on.

Please give me wisdom to know how to cope with Elton and to keep him away from my family so I can leave here knowing they are safe from him,

Cecile prayed. She opened her eyes to see Elton glaring at her from a window.

He's not going to go away willingly.

How can I harness an evil spirit and make it do what I want?

Only you can do that Father...unless of course you show me how.

Chapter Thirty Seven

Christmas Eve was snowy and cold. The families had gathered to eat dinner and then to exchange gifts. They would listen to Christmas music on the radio and tell tales about Christmas' past. It was to be an old fashioned Christmas. Things went well during the meal and they had fun opening the meager gifts they had been able to afford. Right after the gifts were opened, the electric lights went out. Peering out the window they could see objects reflected in the white snow but inside the house it was nearly pitch dark except in the room with the fireplace which thankfully had a fire in it. They also lit a candle but since they only had a limited supply of candles and no way to know how long they would be without electricity, they only lit the one.

Cecile wondered if Elton had anything to do with the lights going out but she hadn't seen him around. Making the most of the situation the family sat around the fireplace sipping hot cocoa and telling stories about past Christmas Eves.

Dad came to see me one Christmas Eve," Louise said.

Cecile bolted up from her warm place on the hearth. "When? When could he have done that?" And then she remembered a Christmas Eve about six years back when Elton had claimed he was stuck in town and couldn't get home because of a snow storm. Apparently he had been with his other daughter and her mother instead. Hatred for her husband flared anew; Cecile burned with it, her senses inflamed.

"How could he?"

"You shouldn't have mentioned that," Rosa told her daughter.

"Why not? At least he cared enough about me to come to see me and bring me a gift. It was one of the only good memories." Louise was angry and defensive. Rosa let it go.

"Did you have any special Christmas traditions," Henry asked Rosa, changing the subject.

"No...not really. We used to fix a special Christmas Eve meal and if we could afford it we had nuts, oranges, and hard tack candy for Christmas."

"Did you go to church," Ethel asked.

"No."

"Mom used to take us to church," Harrison said.

Cecile spotted a tear hovering in the corner of his eye.

"Her Mom and I always took Cecile when she was little. That is what we did on Christmas Eve.," Henry said,

"Dad never went with us," Vanessa mumbled. "He didn't like church. Maybe if he had gone to church..." She left the idea hanging in the cool air.

"We don't do much for the holidays usually. We just fix a nice Christmas dinner and lots of good deserts. On Christmas we usually just lay around and eat," George said. "Since your parents have been dead, we've changed things around some for you kids," he told Vanessa and Harrison.

After a few minutes of silence, Rosa spoke to Harrison.

"What's Reuben doing for Christmas?"

'I expect he'll be over later. He had some squirrels he wanted to fry up and I think he bought some moonshine from old Jeremiah down the road. If he don't go to sleep after eating, he'll probably come over to see us." Harrison got up and went to look out the window into the darkness.

Rosa screamed out suddenly. "Ouch!"

"What happened?"

Everyone looked her direction in the dim light from the fireplace.

"Something or someone pinched me real hard." Rosa's face looked red and inflamed in the firelight.

"We need to get out of this place; I told you so," Louise said, running over to stand beside her mother.

"I'm all right," Rosa told her, patting her hand.

"It's Dad because he's jealous of Reuben," Louise said. "I'm afraid of him. Can't we go someplace else? Please."

Rosa turned to the others. "I'm sorry. We really do appreciate what you're doing by letting us stay here. It's just a little scary around here sometimes."

"I know. It's all right," Henry said.

George and Ethel didn't say anything.

Is it because they don't want to criticize their precious Elton or are they afraid of him?

They never say anything bad about him and he doesn't do anything to them.

But he tries to burn my father with hot soup and he hits Harrison in the face.

If we were both alive I might be the one to kill him next time around!

Cecile was boiling inside, hissing and steaming from all the injuries her husband had done to her and her children. She looked around hoping to find the culprit but Elton wasn't visible. It suddenly occurred to her that Elton might have a way to make himself invisible to her. That could be why she wasn't able to see him at times. She leaned back against the mantle contemplating that idea.

Maybe he's here right now but has made himself invisible? Can that be?

But no...she saw Elton at last hiding behind the buffet in the dining room, staring out at his family...staring at her defiantly. She had no doubt that he had pinched Rosa because she had dared to ask about Reuben.

"We could put the radio on. It operates on batteries," Henry suggested.

"There probably isn't anything on but Amos and Andy," Ethel complained.

"Might be some Christmas music," Henry suggested.

Vanessa got up and went to the radio and turned it on. A song about a silent night flooded out of it and everyone relaxed back into their seats to listen.

"What are we going to do with that Christmas tree when Christmas is over," Harrison asked. He was pointing to a small cedar tree in the corner that had been decorated with strings of popcorn and dried cranberries. There were also a few paper decorations that he and Vanessa had made sometime during their childhood.

"It's a tree for the birds," Ethel said. "On New Year's Day we'll take it out and put it where the birds can eat the popcorn and cranberries. They'll celebrate Christmas too."

"That's nice," Louise said. "Why didn't we ever do that," she asked her mother.

"Never thought of it," Rosa said, shrugging.

"Jack Benny might be on the radio," George suggested.

"I don't like him," Ethel said. "Let's stay with the music."

Since no one argued, the music continued, segueing into 'Little town of Bethlehem'.

Cecile felt lost and sad. Life was going on without her. Her children had not even mentioned the years when she was with them. It was as if she had been forgotten. Louise had remembered a time when Elton had left Cecile and their children behind to spend Christmas Eve with her and Rosa. That made Cecile angry and hurt. She felt so wronged by Elton and all the nastiness he had done to her, Vanessa, and Harrison. Sparks of fury roiled out of her, coiling into a snake shaped mass, it raced across the room toward Elton's hiding spot. It was as if flecks of red lava had burst out of her and flashed across the room toward him...unearthly fire.

Surprised at this new display of her power, Cecile saw that Elton was hit with her fury and was battling to get away from the swirling mass that was attacking him. Smoke tendrils wafted upward and there was a smell of burning material in the air. He surged upward toward the roof, trailing a smoky mist behind him. Cecile sat amazed as the people in the room noted some kind of disturbance and looked around to see where the burnt odor was coming from.

"What is that smell," Louise asked her mother.

"Smells like a cat got too close to the stove, but since we don't have a cat around here, I guess someone must have dropped something too close to the fireplace," Rosa said.

Cecile grinned at this explanation as she basked in her new found skills.

Chapter Thirty Eight

Christmas day Cecile managed to slip a small gift into Vanessa's pocket. She waited impatiently for Vanessa to find it, anxious to see how her daughter would react. Hoping the gift would make her happy. During her time wandering the farmhouse following her demise, Cecile had found her mother's ring which had been lost for two years prior to her death. It was tucked into a corner of her bedroom nearly underneath the molding. Taking it up, realizing that she had no desire for it...ghosts don't need rings, and feeling that Vanessa should have this family heirloom, she determined to give it to her daughter for Christmas. She wanted to give Harrison something too, but finding a gift to give Harrison was more difficult. Watching Vanessa move around the room, never putting her hand near the pocket that held the treasure was agony. Finally Vanessa seemed to notice something was in her pocket and stuck her hand inside. When she pulled out the ring she looked shocked.

"Mom?"

"I'm here honey."

"Is this Grandma's ring."

"Yes."

Vanessa eyed the ring in awe.

"Who you talking to girl?" Ethel was standing with her hands on her hips watching Vanessa as she turned in circles scanning the room. Apparently Ethel had not heard Cecile's voice.

"Myself I guess," Vanessa muttered sticking the ring back into her pocket and beginning to wipe down the table.

Rosa and Louise were outside talking to Reuben who had brought over a chicken for Christmas dinner. George and Henry were in the barn doing something. Harrison was with Reuben and the girls. Just Vanessa and Ethel were in the house...other than Cecile, of course.

For Harrison, Cecile had uncovered a small secret cache of money that Elton had apparently hidden from his family. It wasn't much but she planned to give a little to her son with instructions to buy himself something nice. She had even managed to write a simple note to him. She signed the note Mom. The money and the note were hidden in his underwear drawer. Harrison hadn't found the money this morning but she hoped he would look more carefully the next time he opened the drawer.

It felt good to be able to give something, however small, to her children. Who would have thought that she would still be able to watch over and sometimes help her children more than two years after her death? Although a strong believer in God, Cecile would not have expected things to work out this way. Before she died she had thought of death as a long sleep that would end when Jesus returned to earth to wake the faithful and take them to heaven. She had visions of a resurrection morning when Jesus would come and the graves would open to allow the faithful to be reunited with him and his father. It hadn't happened that way. Hearing the others re-entering the house, Cecile slid behind a cabinet to watch the tableau. Reuben was carrying a large bowl in which he had a cut-up chicken which he presented to Ethel.

"Here's something for Christmas dinner," he said.

"Thanks. I see you have it all ready for cooking," Ethel told him.

"Anything I can do to please, Ma'am."

Cecile giggled behind her hand. She knew Ethel would not like being addressed as Ma'am. Ethel was a bit vane sometimes and the term would probably make her feel old. Still, it was a sign of respect, so good for Reuben. Outside she could see that the snow was falling hard, Large fluffy flakes were filling the yard and lane rapidly with a soft chasteness. It was a white Christmas. The falling flakes reminded her of what her own mother had told her when she was little. The short rhyme went:

> Old Ms. Reece
> Is picking her geese,
> And old Ms. Brown
> Is throwing the feathers down.

That was how Cecile's mother had explained the falling snow.

Thinking about her mother made Cecile sad. Her mother wasn't around any longer. Apparently all people who die do not get stuck in the same nether world that she and Elton were in. Remembering the beaconing light she had seen and the choice she had been given, Cecile wondered if she had made the right decision. Thinking about it, she decided that she had no real choice. If she wanted to protect her children from their father, she had to stay here since he had stayed.

Why did Elton choose to stay? That was the eternal question.

Is he trying to spy on his children? Does he want to control them?

Does he want to protect himself from secrets that might come to light in his absence?

As the family sat, at the mid-day Christmas meal, Cecile gazed at them fondly...even her husband's mistress and illegitimate daughter. They had all become her little family now, Reuben also. She noticed that Reuben had been sprucing himself up a lot lately. She was sure it was to win Rosa's approval. Although Reuben wasn't a handsome man, his efforts helped. Once you knew him you didn't see or care about his appearance. He had a good heart.

"Thanks again for sharing your home and you food with us," Rosa said.

George, Ethel, and Henry nodded telling her that she was welcome.

"I know it's a lot...especially for you, Henry," Rosa said. "I hope you get a gold star in heaven for your kindness."

Across the room, Elton had appeared and to her confusion and surprise, Cecile noticed him wiping an ectoplasm tear from his eyes. She was startled and amazed to see that he cared about anything. Apparently he was glad his mistress and child had a warm place to stay after all.

But if he'd had his way they'd be out sleeping in a boxcar somewhere in zero weather.

Why this change of heart?

Reuben was chatting happily with Rosa who was beaming his direction. Even Louise seemed captivated by the neighbor. Elton was eyeing the couple who were sitting side by side with an angry glint in his eye now. He had no more tears. Flashing up behind Reuben and Rosa, Elton smacked their two heads together with a sudden movement that scared everyone in the room. Rosa stood up and turned toward where she thought Elton was standing.

"Get your good for nothing self out of here and let us enjoy Christmas," she yelled.

To Cecile's surprise, Elton vanished through the floor.

"I think I should be getting along home now," Reuben said, rubbing his ear where it had collided with Rosa's skull. "Things are too crazy around here for me."

Rosa looked crushed as Reuben put on his hat and gloves, nodded at her, and then headed out into the snow.

Chapter Thirty Nine

Rosa sat in the bedroom chair crying her heart out. Vanessa and Louise sat on each side of her holding her hands. Ethel had come into the room but seemed to not know what to do; she turned and walked back out of the bedroom.

"He has ruined my life," Rosa blubbered. "And he's still ruining it."

"Who," Vanessa asked.

"Elton Montgomery, that's who. He didn't want me but he never wanted anyone else to have me either."

"He scared Reuben away, didn't he?" Louise asked.

"Reuben is afraid of him. He knows Elton's ghost is around here and it scares him to death."

"What happened out there," Vanessa asked.

"I felt his hands on my head and suddenly he shoved my head and Reuben's head together. It hurt!"

"I wonder why my Mom didn't stop him," Vanessa said.

"He probably did it so fast she didn't know what he was up to," Louise speculated. "Anyway we all know what kind of man he was so it's no surprise." Louise sniffled in disgust.

Vanessa stared at her half-sister. "I thought you got along with him."

"I did when I was little...and then he turned into a jerk."

"What did he do to you?"

Rosa looked up and shook her head "No" as her daughter went on talking anyway.

"He touched me in bad places. I told Mom and she yelled at him. He never came back after that."

Bile bubbled up into Cecile's throat. She felt like she could throw up, though what would come up she had no idea since she hadn't eaten in years. Regardless the feeling was the same. Her husband literally made her sick!

He's no husband of mine...

He lost that title when he killed me, not to mention what he did before that.

Everyone was staring at Louise now. Vanessa was swallowing and swallowing as if she couldn't get air into her system. Rosa's look was one of silent dread, knowing that another secret was out of the bag now. Cecile felt like running out and finding the worthless father of her children and throwing the lightning bolts, the snake of fire, she had found so useful recently, at him. If only she was sure how she'd done it, she would, but next time it might not work. Still, in all this time since her death, Elton had not hurt her, except mentally.

But why would God let him hit Harrison, pinch Rosa, and knock Rosa and Reuben's heads together?

It doesn't make sense that he can't hurt me but can hurt living people...unless...unless God has given me special protection so I can stay here and battle his evil intentions. Maybe that's it.

Rosa was crying again and Louise was blubbering too. Vanessa didn't seem to know how to react. Cecile put a comforting hand on her daughter's shoulder. Vanessa hadn't been the only victim of Elton's lust it seemed. His other daughter was a victim also, and Louise had been much younger. Even knowing Elton's character, Cecile had a hard time believing that he was so depraved. Rosa had done the right thing by protecting her daughter; fortunately Elton had not killed her for her efforts, as he had done with Cecile.

The thoughts were underlined in her mind. In the same situation Elton had not resorted to murder. Cecile wanted to talk to the people in the room, especially to Rosa and Louise. There were so many questions she'd like to ask but she shied away from using her voice. So far she had only spoken to Vanessa, Henry, Reuben, and Harrison, although she had said something aloud a time or two when others were present. Elton had never announced his presence by speech, not to her usually and not to others. He had preferred to strike others in rage or beat the house with tree branches to express his anger. Suddenly she wondered why. He had the ability to speak...to say 'please' when he wanted her to go away and not listen to what Rosa and Louise said. Was it that he just had nothing to say to her having said it all with a bullet? The tumult of thoughts that raged in her mind blanked out the conversation around her until she heard Rosa say,

"He attacked me when I confronted him about Louise. I guess I'm very lucky he didn't kill me like he did your mother."

Vanessa was staring at Rosa, stunned.

So he had reacted violently when Rosa accused him of wrongdoing. That made Cecile feel strange. She wasn't sure what she was thinking. Apparently Elton didn't care who confronted him. He reacted the same. The situation that resulted in her own death had not been an anomaly but just his standard behavior. He had also attempted to molest both his daughters.

What a terrible man he was; at least he did the world a favor by taking his own life!

"I cried for days," Louise said. "Mom was hurt and my Dad wasn't ever coming back. I felt like it was my fault. I shouldn't have told her."

"The worst thing of all is he offered his daughter money as if she was a tramp. He tried to bribe his little girl into letting him do things to her. I'm so proud of her that she said 'No' and came and told me," Rosa said. "She was just a baby at the time."

Cecile thought about the little cache of money that Elton had hidden and she had found. Was that money meant for bribing little girls to do his bidding? What other little girls did he know? Perhaps he has other daughters somewhere that no one knows about. She sniffed in disgust.

"But you were coming here to get his help...why?" Vanessa looked from mother to daughter. "You knew what he was like."

"Yes," Rosa said, "We knew but we also had learned that he had a wife. We thought she'd keep him under control. We had no idea that he had murdered her and killed himself."

"I'm sorry this happened to you Louise," Vanessa turned and impulsively hugged her younger sister. "I'm glad you are with us now."

"But Dad's still around and he's still trying to hurt us," Louise said.

"Don't worry about that. My mom will keep him from getting too far out of control."

Cecile gazed at Vanessa. How was she going to live up that promise? She hadn't done too well at it so far.

Chapter Forty

After the confidences that Rosa and Louise had shared in the bedroom the women became quiet. The evening was spent with the girls playing checkers while George and Ethel listened to the radio. Harrison was over at Reuben's house, having left right after Reuben so he could see that his friend was okay. Cecile stayed in the bedroom after the others had left. She lay on her daughter's bed thinking.

I've got to do a better job of protecting everyone against Elton's antics. I should have known he'd do something to Rosa and Reuben. He's jealous. That's clear to everyone. I have to be here every time when the girls are getting dressed or bathing to be sure he's not spying on them. Poor Harrison...he's not getting much of my attention but I can't be everywhere at once.

Feeling that she was letting her son down, Cecile got up and headed over to Reuben's house. She didn't expect the girls to be in any jeopardy until another two or three hours when they got ready for bed. Reuben and Harrison were sitting in front of a bonfire that had been built in the bottom of a cut off barrel. The fire was in front of them with their backs to his shack to block the wind. In spite of the cold and the snow they appeared to be warm enough. Cecile settled down close to Harrison and listened in to their conversation.

"I like Rosa a lot but I can't deal with things I can't see. It's too spooky."

"I understand but I don't think Rosa does. Her feelings are hurt because you left."

"I don't know how your mother put up with that man; if he was like he is now she must have been a saint."

"She would have protected you and Rosa if she knew what Dad was up to."

"Maybe… but she can't be too happy about Rosa having an affair with her husband and all…even having a kid with him."

Harrison sat quiet for a time absorbing that. Finally he offered his opinion.

"Mom is probably hurt by all Dad did…things she knew about and things she didn't. Still if Rosa is telling the truth about not knowing he was married and that she stopped the affair once she did, Mom would forgive her I think. Mom is a very fair person."

"Rosa is a good woman but I don't know what she thought was going to happen when she got here and met up with Elton again. Was she going to blackmail him into giving her and Louise money? She could threaten to tell his wife what he'd been up to. And then there is the fact that they'd been together before…was she going to prostitute herself with him in order to get help for herself and their daughter? I like Rosa a lot but I'm just not sure. I'm not sure enough to risk dealing with a jealous ghost who might hurt me."

Harrison was silent again. Cecile thought her son might be wondering the same things Reuben was. She gave her own attention to the matter. What did Rosa expect to happen when she got to the farm and talked to Elton? Louise was Elton's daughter and he should help her which would also help her mother. Rosa must have been desperate to go to see him in the first place. How much was she willing to give up in exchange for the help she needed.

"Ask her," Cecile said to the silent men.

Reuben jumped and pulled his coat tight around him while he looked furtively around the clearing, seeing nothing.

"Mom?" Harrison asked.

"Ask Rosa what she thought would happen,"

Cecile said aloud, then she drifted away from the clearing, her son, and his friend. She left them to speculate as they would on her advice. She returned to the farmhouse where she had lived so long, wondering about Rosa's intentions herself. For the next two hours she focused on Rosa, watching her every move and listening to her every word. She was trying to assess the personality of the other woman. Had she been telling the truth or was she just so desperate for a means of survival that she would have done anything Elton wanted in order to provide for herself and Louise?

And what if Elton and I were both alive when Rosa and Louise got here...what would she have done? Elton didn't hesitate to kill me when he thought I was going to leave. Would he have killed Rosa to keep her from telling? What about Louise? Would he have killed her too? But those are questions that Rosa can't answer. Only Elton can. It was much better for Rosa and Louise that Elton and I were no longer living, although Elton still doesn't want to allow Rosa to have her own life.

I wonder if I can make Elton talk to me.

How can I do that?

The fast and angry thoughts poured through Cecile's head as she pondered the 'what if's 'of the situation. As Rosa, Louise, and Vanessa finished a game they were playing and headed to the

~ 219 ~

bedroom, Cecile tagged along behind them. Sleeping in the same area had caused some degree of bonding of the women although Vanessa had made herself a space in the loft of the room to get away from the others. Like a spirit guard, Cecile patrolled the areas of the room as everyone got ready to go to bed. Elton was not around.

I've got to find Elton and ask him some questions. Where is he?

When everyone is asleep I'll go look for him.

Where does he go when he disappears?

Cecile thought about these things in depth as she maintained her vigil over the other women. She wondered if Reuben would ask Rosa the questions he had voiced to Harrison. Would Harrison ask any questions of either Rosa or Louise?

She hoped he would ask. If Rosa was what she claimed to be she would be an asset to Reuben should they marry, and he would be around to help fend for the mother and daughter. That would be a good solution to their current problems. Reuben was poor but he could provide for their basic needs. He hunted and fished so there would likely be food to eat. Rosa could decorate the old shack and bring color and light into Reuben's life. She could even help him make baskets to sell in town.

Feeling like a matchmaker, Cecile settled down to wait for sleep to overtake her charges.

Chapter Forty One

Dwelling on all she knew about Elton Montgomery, Cecile considered where he would go to get away. What had been his favorite spots when he was alive? Funny but she couldn't remember. He had spent a lot of time out in the fields and woods. Who knows what he'd been doing out there. She hadn't wondered at the time but now she did. The night was bright because of a nearly full moon and the whiteness of the snow. However, Elton seemed to have a way to make himself invisible even to her. After she had searched and searched, in frustration, Cecile stood in the middle of the barnyard and yelled out to the empty fields and trees, to the barn and its inhabitants; to all who might hear.

"Elton Montgomery. I need to talk to you!"

Turning in a slow circle she looked out toward the place where she and Elton had been buried. The ghostly old tree stood silhouetted against a winter sky, its one arm uplifted, its other branch pointing down. A mist seemed to be rising from one side of the tree...Elton's side.

Horrified, Cecile was shocked to find that Elton had gone to his grave to rest, or to hide from his sins. She had never considered going back to her body which must be decayed by now. How could Elton even think about doing that? Elton seemed reluctant as he sidled around the area, partially hiding himself from her behind the barn door. It was as if her command had obliged him to come to her against his will.

Interesting!

"I want to talk to you," Cecile said firmly, then wondered what she wanted to say. Suddenly the words she'd rehearsed seemed to be gone.

Elton peered around the door, staring her down but saying nothing.

"Why did you cheat on me? "

Elton didn't move, nor did he speak.

Why did you abuse your own daughters?"

Elton stared intently at her but remained silent.

"Why did you kill me? Didn't you care about me at all?"

Cecile was appalled at the last question she had uttered which was given in a plaintive and self-pitying way as if she was begging him to love her. Hastily she added...

"I mean, I'm the mother of your children. If you love them you have to know they needed me."

Elton put his hands over his ears and did not utter a word.

"If Rosa and Louise had showed up while we were still living, what would you have done? Would you have told me the truth? Would you have made them leave? Would you have hurt them?"

Elton stamped his foot and turned his back on her.

"What's wrong with you? Cat got your tongue?" Cecile taunted, fury coming to claim her.

Elton's refusal to speak to her fueled anger that had lain dormant like banked coals in the fireplace, just ready to burst into flame. Looking down she saw that the snow was melting around her as if the flame of her anger was heating the spot where she stood.

Still Elton stood where he was, saying nothing.

"Can't you speak?"

No reply.

Cecile tapped her foot on the ground. She was still hesitant to approach Elton and suspected that if she did he would disappear again. How was she going to get answers to her questions if he refused to speak to her?

"Why do you hurt your own children," she asked. "You've hit Harrison and you've abused Vanessa and even Louise. Don't you love them?"

Elton had turned around to face her again but now he looked at the ground. He did not speak.

Cecile wondered if she should give up. She still had a lot of questions but asking Elton was getting her nowhere. Finally she asked,

"Why are you still here? Why didn't you go on to wherever you're supposed to go? Afraid of the penalty for your sins?"

From where she stood Cecile could see Elton wince at her words but he did not reply to her charges. From his reaction though she was pretty sure she had hit on a truth.

"Well I'm here to tell you to leave **my** family alone. I don't consider you a part of the family anymore because I think you've forfeited that right with what you've done. There will be consequences if you hurt anyone else, I'm telling you that. As for you and me...it was till death do us part and you parted us for good."

Elton turned to leave.

"Come back here you coward and face up to what you've done," Cecile screamed.

To her surprise Elton turned around and stopped moving away. He stood statue like gazing at her, still saying nothing. Later she would reflect that he didn't seem to have a choice. He was compelled to come when she called. Right now she covered her surprise with another ultimatum.

"If you hurt anyone else, I'll make you pay. Go on back to your grave."

She watched in fascination as Elton drifted back toward the cemetery.

Feeling empowered, Cecile made her rounds of the farm and then settled into a nook beside her daughter to rest. Vanessa seemed to be sleeping a little better these days. In spite of the awkwardness she had endured by having to share her space with the two women, Vanessa had gained from the experience. It was much harder to withdraw into yourself in a crowded room. Also she was slowly getting to know her half-sister and they seemed to be bonding a little.

Thinking of the threats she had made toward Elton, Cecile wondered what she was going to do if Elton did hurt anyone else. The threat had come easy but how was she going to enforce it? Would Elton fear it or challenge it?

Overcome with worry about the future and what it would hold, Cecile got up and wandered around the house, looking for something to distract her. She found George and Ethel still awake although it was quite late. Ethel was saying,

"If I had any doubts about whether Elton and Rosa were actually together in the past, I wouldn't now. From that stunt he pulled tonight, smacking her and Reuben's heads together, I know he thinks Rosa belongs to him and he resents Reuben."

"So? Rosa doesn't have any right to be romancing another man in Elton's own house."

"Our son is dead if only he'd accept it. He needs to go on and leave the living folks alone."

"So you're buying into all this ghost stuff the others are talking about. I haven't seen Elton and

I'm sure that if he was around he'd find a way to let me know."

"He ploughed the field and did chores for you."

"Someone did; might not be him.'

Suddenly the pillow slid out from under George's head, rose above him and smacked itself down on his face. From her spot by the door, Cecile could see Elton smiling at his Dad as he walloped him. Wondering if this was meant to be a challenge to her or just a way to let his Dad know he was still around, Cecile hesitated to act. After all a pillow in the face didn't really hurt George. She found herself smiling too as Elton faded from sight. George's expression was a funny mixture of surprise, awe, and confusion.

Chapter Forty Two

On New Year's Eve the family was together again to celebrate the coming year. It would soon be 1929 and everyone was hoping the economy would be better. Rosa had mentioned her concerns about what she and Louise would do in April or May when the winter was gone and they would be on their own again. To be fair she had only mentioned this to Louise and had not said anything to the rest of the family. Cecile had heard her tell Louise that she didn't want to impose on the family any longer than they had to. Times were hard in the country and there was no sign things would be better in the New Year, but she was hopeful.

Reuben hadn't been around much and that grieved Rosa. "I know he's afraid of your father," she told Louise. "That's too bad because I liked that man."

"He's not very good looking," Louise said.

"Maybe not but he's beautiful inside."

Rosa and Ethel cooked a dinner for everyone and then to finish it off, Ethel started to make homemade eggnog. Using heavy cream and vanilla beans with sugar, nutmeg, and cinnamon,

Ethel added egg yolks, warm milk and stirred. Finally she added some bourbon after cautioning the kids that they were not to have any of her creation.

"Where'd you get the bourbon," Rosa asked. "Not much of that available with prohibition."

"We've had this around for years," Ethel said. "Never really found a use for it until now."

"I'm going to sneak some eggnog," Louise whispered to Vanessa. "You and Harrison creep quietly out to the barn after a while and I'll give you a cup. We'll need to wait until the old folks are tipsy and then they won't notice what we're doing."

Cecile wasn't sure what to do, so for the moment she did nothing. Ethel took the warm eggnog and put it in a pie safe on the back porch to cool. A little later Louise brought a clean glass canning jar and filled it with some of the mixture, which she spirited out to the barn, and hid under the hay in the hayloft. After a glass of eggnog each of the adults began to liven up. It was extremely rare for any of them to imbibe in alcohol, so a little affected them a lot. The kids sat back and watched the adults waiting for the time when they thought their absence would go unnoticed.

The radio was on and playing waltz music. Henry asked Rosa to dance and they whirled around the small living room with abandon. Cecile saw Elton emerge from the shadows. He was no doubt angry that Henry was enjoying the dance with Rosa so much. Cecile got ready to intervene. However, in the most civilized way, just as a gentleman might act, Elton tapped Henry on the shoulder, apparently asking for the dance. Henry looked up but ignored the tap. Cecile moved toward the three people. Elton tapped again, and then again. Henry ignored him. Cecile approached to within a few feet and Elton faded away.

Only after the dance was over did Henry tell Rosa what had happened.

"I wondered," she said. "It was like you stopped dancing for a moment and then started up again."

Harrison was listening to what his grandfather said. "I don't think Dad would be that polite," he murmured.

"Maybe he's turned over a new leaf," Rosa suggested.

"Not likely...nothing's going to change him," Harrison said as he rubbed his jaw unconsciously.

Cecile knew he was thinking of the times his father had hit him. She put an arm around Harrison to comfort him but when it seemed to disturb him instead, she withdrew her arm and moved away a little.

"Everything is okay," she whispered in his ear.

She had been noticing that Harrison seemed to be disturbed a lot lately. Cecile was no longer so concerned about Vanessa. Her attention had shifted to her son. He didn't seem to have any friends at school. Reuben was his only friend. The small amount of bonding that had been occurring between Louise and Vanessa seemed to leave Harrison out and he was no longer as close to his sister as he had once been. However, Cecile was at a loss as to what she could do to help him. A tiny terror licked at her soul. Was Harrison going to be okay?

When she saw Louise sneak out of the house and go to the barn, Cecile had followed her and watched where she hid the eggnog. After Louise returned to the house, Cecile searched the barn, wondering if Elton had hidden anything of interest out here. After having found things he'd stashed in the house, she had begun to wonder what else he might have hidden away. Still it was a surprise when she found several jars of moonshine hidden under a bale of hay and a tarpaulin.

Elton's moonshine she had poured out long ago, afraid it might tempt one of the kids to drink it. Of course she knew that Elton drank...especially on the day he had killed her and himself, but how long had this liquor been here? This had not been in the barn when she had last searched it. One jar was almost gone, but held about a tenth of the liquid. It was as if someone had just drank from it. Would Elton still be drinking? No...he wouldn't, Cecile believed. He should have no need to eat or drink anything in his current state.

Reuben had been getting moonshine from someone in the neighborhood. She had seen him drink it and had worried about Harrison following suit but Reuben had told him he was too young to drink. She applauded Reuben for that. She was also glad that Harrison hadn't objected to being denied alcohol. Of course that was several months ago. Had Reuben brought liquor over to the barn and hidden it so he could imbibe when he came to visit her son? Had Harrison been drinking it? Harrison hadn't been himself lately. Was he drinking alcohol when no one was around? That might explain the changes in him. Cecile had a new crusade. She was going to watch and see who was partaking of the moonshine in the barn. Carefully she put everything back the way it was.

A little later she watched as the children entered the barn and sat on bales of straw while Louise poured eggnog into three purloined cups. She had considered throwing the jar of eggnog away or dumping the contents out, but finally she had decided to watch and see what happened instead. A cup of the drink wouldn't harm anyone permanently. She'd rather know where the children were coming from than to block them and never know.

Louise raised her cup and said, "A toast to 1929...cheers everyone."

Chapter Forty Three

Cecile was amazed at the sophisticated way with which Louise raised her cup to toast the New Year. Where had she learned that? Harrison sipped the drink from his cup and then set it down. Vanessa did the same after wrinkling her nose at the taste.

"Good, she doesn't like it," Cecile thought.

She watched Harrison who was looking into his cup sadly as if the world was sitting heavily on his head. He didn't seem anxious to drink the eggnog although he had sipped a little of it. Maybe he didn't like it either. However, Louise was busy drinking her share hungrily. When the cup was empty she poured the little that remained in the jar into her own cup and drank that as well.

"What's wrong with you two? Drink your eggnog," she said.

Obediently the brother and sister took another sip of the mixture.

Louise asked them," Don't you like it?"

"Not really," Vanessa said.

"Drink up and you'll like how it makes you feel."

"What are you; some kind of drunk," Harrison asked.

Louise tossed her head. "You just don't appreciate what I did for you. That is good stuff and you'll like it if you give it a chance."

"Alcohol is illegal; we have prohibition."

"Your grandparents are drinking it. Lots of people do. The dry crusaders just want everyone to live the way they do. Well I won't." Louise drained the cup of liquid, then licked the rim.

Harrison took another sip. Cecile wondered what he was thinking. The expression on his face was dark and unhappy. "This makes me feel worse, not better," he told Louise.

Vanessa was sitting still watching the two of them. "We'll all be in trouble if our grandparents find us," she said.

"So what? All they want to do is stop us from having fun," Louise countered.

"I've seen drunks before and they aren't happy. All they want to do is cry in their beer," Vanessa said.

"You two are dreary dopes," Louise said. "Go on back into the house and I'll stay here and finish up your drinks. Can't let a good eggnog go to waste."

The brother and sister looked relieved. They stood and made their way out of the barn.

As the others left Cecile watched Louise do what she had promised, finish up the eggnog in the other cups. Louise sat looking into space then. Cecile wondered if the alcohol was making her sleepy. After a bit, Louise got up and to Cecile's surprise she went to the spot where the moonshine was hidden and dug out a jar of it. She poured some of it into her cup and went back to sit on the straw.

That girl has a problem.

Where did she get all that moonshine; she doesn't have any money.

She must have stolen it, but from who?

Curious as to what Louise was up to, Cecile continued to watch her as she drank some of the moonshine and then cuddled up in an old horse blanket underneath the hay. Cold as it was, she supposed Louise would be warm enough wrapped in the blanket. Cecile had known of a few people, drunkards all, who had frozen to death in winter weather because the alcohol had put them so deep asleep that they did not awaken to the cold. She watched for a while and then decided she had to get one of the adults to take Louise inside. She was afraid for the girl.

Why hasn't someone missed her and come looking for her?

I should tell Rosa; she's Louise's mother after all.

Going to the house, Cecile found everyone in a merry mood, full of food and drink, glad to shine a ray of light into the depressing cold winter. She hesitated to approach Rosa. What would she do if Cecile suddenly whispered in her ear that Louise was in trouble? Instead of saying anything to Rosa, Cecile decided to go back to the barn and check on Louise herself. She got there just in time to interrupt Elton who was bent over his daughter pulling her upright. Not knowing what he planned, Cecile stayed hidden and watched.

Elton pulled Louise to a sitting position but she was groggy and kept falling over. He reached down and picked her up, threw her over his shoulder and began to carry her out of the barn. So far he wasn't hurting Louise so Cecile just followed him as he went to the house. At the door, he knocked loudly on the door and then dumped Louise on the porch like a sack of potatoes. From a pocket somewhere, Elton pulled out an empty jar of corn mash (moonshine) and laid it beside the comatose girl so there would be little doubt as to what her condition was.

No one answered the door. Elton knocked again, even louder. George Montgomery came to see what was up and stared in surprise at Louise lying unconscious on the porch. He glared around wide eyed but appeared to see no one although both Elton and Cecile were right there.

"Rosa," George bellowed out as he tried to get Louise to stand on her feet. She wouldn't.

Rosa and everyone else in the house ran to the door. Harrison and Vanessa stared at Louise and the empty jar of home squeezing that lay beside her. They didn't know where Louise had found the liquor but they knew what it was.

Rosa saw the empty jar and almost collapsed saying "Oh no."

"Let's get her inside," Henry told George and together the two men carried Louise into the house and lay her on a davenport beside the fire.

"Make some strong black coffee," George told his wife who ran to do his bidding.

Henry was rubbing Louise's hands trying to get circulation back into them. "She's mighty cold," he mentioned.

When the coffee was made, George and Rosa held Louise upright forcing the hot coffee into her mouth. Louise chocked on the drink and vomited all over the area causing Ethel to almost lose her own dinner. Louise kept trying to go back to sleep but George wouldn't let her and finally she seemed to be partially aroused.

"What are you doing," she asked.

"You're sick; what have you been drinking," Rosa accused.

Louise seemed to get it that she had been found out. She became defensive. "Leave me alone," she roared.

Henry took her hand. "Little girl, you almost froze to death. The stuff you drank put you to sleep and if you hadn't made it to the porch somehow and knocked on the door, you'd be dead by now."

Louise stiffened and shook her head. "I didn't leave the barn. I'm sure of it: and I sure didn't knock on the door."

Everyone looked at everyone else. Cecile knew they were asking themselves if a ghost had saved Louise's life and if a ghost had, which ghost. She was willing to bet that the truth would not be the answer they arrived at. Who would think Elton would even care?

Chapter Forty Four

Louise stayed in a surly mood and George carried her to her bed where her mother tucked her in for the night. It was already ten o'clock. The mood of the celebration had become sober now and Cecile heard Vanessa and Harrison whispering about Louise and her close call. Cecile berated herself for not realizing how cold it was and how impaired Louise had been. At first she thought the teenager would be warm enough with the blanket and the layer of hay she'd put over herself. She was glad that Elton had acted when he did or there might have been another tragedy at the farm. At least this time Elton had saved the day; she wondered why.

"Does he love his daughter in his own way?"

Elton appeared to have left as soon as he'd found help for Louise. If he'd stayed around he must have hidden or made himself invisible in some way. Cecile wasn't sure if he could make himself invisible to her but at times it seemed as if he had. She thought about the other jars of moonshine lying in the barn just waiting for Louise to go drink them. She was the only one who knew about those. Considering what she should do, Cecile went back to the barn to look more closely at the home brew.

Where did it come from?
How did Louise get it?
She would have had to steal it because she has no money.

Cecile realized that Louise had some major problems that needed to be dealt with right away. Most likely, drinking and stealing were two of her problems; did Louise have more? Cecile was concerned that Vanessa and Harrison might copy her behavior.

There were six jars of moonshine in Louise's hiding spot. There were two empty jars as well. Cecile wondered how long this had been going on. On the outside Louise seemed to be fine but the way she'd reacted earlier, greedily consuming the alcohol and alcoholic drinks, showed that she had some kind of problem with alcohol already, or if not yet, she wasn't far from it.

Elton was smart to take the empty jar of shine with him so the family could see what was wrong with her. If nothing else the smell would give away what had been in the jar.

Cecile wasn't happy to give Elton praise but she always believed in giving credit where credit was due. Elton deserved praise for the way he'd handled this emergency. Sometimes Cecile felt it was a curse to have a 'fairness' gene that made her see the other side of issues she'd rather not acknowledge.

Thinking of how Elton had refused to speak to her when she'd tried to ask him questions made Cecile livid. "How dare he? Why wouldn't he speak? Questions revolved through her mind but even though she was a ghost herself she didn't understand all the workings of the in-between world. For example she didn't know why Elton would not tolerate her getting physically close to him...why he always ran away. She didn't know where he went or what he did for long stretches of time. She didn't know how he could hurt her and the kids even though he had supposedly loved them. Much of life...and death... was an unknowable mystery.

Cecile picked up the jars of moonshine and went to the door of the garage where she poured all of them on the ground. Louise certainly didn't need access to them and she didn't consider them useful to anyone in the house.

Now I'll watch to see what Louise does and where she goes to get more liquor.

She has a taste for it so I know she'll try to go back to her source.

The next morning George sat Rosa and Louise down for a chat. Louise was grumpy and resistant but Rosa told her she had no choice. She had behaved badly.

"I didn't do anything you guys didn't do," Louise countered.

"We drank a little spiked eggnog. We didn't add a quart of moonshine to it," Rosa said.

George took the initiative when all were seated. "You," he said pointing to Louise, "Are out of control. Why were you drunk and passed out last night? Where did you get the shine anyway?"

"None of your business."

Rosa frowned at her daughter. "Keep a civil tongue," she said to Louise, then to George she said. "She won't do that again."

Louise sat silent, although she looked ready to contradict her mother, to the watching Cecile.

"You know alcohol is illegal. Whoever made that moonshine is a bootlegger and the revenuers will arrest him sooner or later. How did you get it? Do you have any more?"

Louise looked down and shook her head 'No'.

"You've got to do something with this girl. She's trouble the way she's acting now and she's only thirteen. What do you think she'll be like in a couple of years?" George asked Rosa.

"I know she has a problem. I'll deal with it."

"You'd better or you'll have to leave here. We don't need any more trouble. Louise could have died out there in the cold, as drunk as she was last night. I don't know how she managed to stumble up on the porch and knock on the door. She was passed out when I got there."

"It's a good thing she brought the moonshine jar with her or we wouldn't have known what was wrong with her," Ethel said, directing her remark to Rosa.

"I know. We'll work on it." Rosa said.

"I didn't bring a jar of moonshine up on the porch. I didn't even walk up there. The last I knew I got under a blanket in the barn and went to sleep. Someone must have carried me to the porch." Louise sounded stubborn and resistant to George's comments.

"But she's right...Elton carried her. She would never have brought the moonshine jar herself. She didn't want anyone to know what she'd done," Cecile thought.

George looked sternly at Louise. "You'd better shape up girl," he said. "If not you've got to leave here and fend for yourself. We don't want any drunks or liars around here. Granddaughter or not, I don't want you here if you're going to act like that."

Louise stood and ran out of the room, crying.

Chapter Forty Five

Ethel attempted to intervene with Louise while they were fixing lunch. Vanessa and Harrison were doing work in the barn, George was off somewhere in the fields and Ethel was alone with her newly found granddaughter. Cecile didn't know where Rosa was; she began to wonder.

"You know alcohol isn't really good for anyone," Ethel said. "We had a little just to celebrate but we shouldn't have because of prohibition. It's illegal to make it, have it, or drink it."

"Didn't hurt me a bit," Louise said defiantly.

"You could have woke up dead out in the cold like that. I've known more than one person to drink themselves into a stupor and not wake up when they started to freeze. My own uncle died that way."

"I had a blanket around me and hay on top of me."

"Not enough on a night that cold."

Louise stomped her foot, dropping the potato she was peeling. "I don't know what all the fuss is about. I'm fine."

"You'd better realize that you had a close call. You could have died and we wouldn't have even known where you were until it was too late. You are lucky to be alive to argue with me today."

Louise turned away but Cecile saw a frustrated tear in her eye. Maybe she was starting to suspect that she had been in actual danger. If so, that was a good thing.

Ethel turned back to her work, frowning over the chicken she was frying. Cecile watched her methodically turn each piece of the breaded chicken in the huge iron skillet. Clearly trouble was on Ethel's mind. Cecile had kept a close eye on Louise but so far she had not gone to the barn to check on her stash of liquor. That was probably because everyone else was watching her too. Louise would likely wait for the heat to die down and then go for the liquor. Her reaction when she found it missing would be interesting and probably very telling as to what her true nature was.

Cecile drifted out to the barn where Vanessa was helping Harrison clean out a stall. She glanced at the spot where Louise's empty jars were stored, placed back where she'd found them, but empty of contents; she didn't see any sign of disturbance. Harrison was leaning on a rake with which he'd been mucking out the stall. "Thanks for helping me," he told his sister.

"It's nothing. Gets me out of the house. I don't like Grandma hovering over me all the time."

"Yeah, it's better out here."

"What do you think about Louise; she could have died," Vanessa said.

"Stupid."

Harrison didn't elaborate.

"Well I hope she's not going to keep trying to get us in trouble too like with the eggnog," Vanessa said. "Why'd she need eggnog anyway? She had moonshine."

"I guess she just wanted to try it to see how it tasted."

Harrison picked up the pitchfork and threw some dirty hay into a wheelbarrow to haul it away. The day had turned clear and although cold there was a sunny presence in the sky.

"Are you and Reuben doing anything this afternoon," Vanessa asked after a while.

"No...he's busy."

Vanessa stopped working and looked questioning at her brother. "Rosa?"

Harrison shrugged. "I didn't ask."

Cecile's curiosity was aroused. She decided to find out. Swiftly she left the barn and headed down the path toward Reuben's shack. Sure enough there was Reuben and Rosa sitting cozily in front of a fire he had built. They were holding hands.

On the other side of the fire, Elton arose just as Cecile got there, his eyes flaming, the firelight dancing crazily in them. Cecile felt instant danger in the pit of her stomach and she launched herself to block Elton's rage. Never would she have done this when she was alive because she was afraid of her unpredictable husband, although she strove to never let him know it. Now she acted without thought, believing that he'd run away from her as he had been doing.

Elton held his ground, glaring past her at Rosa and Reuben. Suddenly he made an evasive maneuver and circumvented Cecile to get to Reuben and Rosa. He smacked Reuben in the back of his head with his fist then rapidly faded into the weathered boards of Reuben's shack where Cecile could no longer see him.

Cecile whirled to see if Reuben was hurt. He was lying on the ground blinking; his eyes were tear filled. His face was red and worried. Rosa was sitting there stunned; finding her courage, she knelt beside Reuben to help him up.

"What happened," she asked.

"Someone hit me," Reuben mumbled.

Cecile hovered helplessly, not knowing what she could do in this situation. Rosa was surveying the back of Reuben's head and Cecile could see that a bump was forming where Elton had hit him. She was mad at herself because she had not been fast enough to prevent Elton from getting to Reuben. She felt she should have predicted his behavior, but she hadn't.

I could say something to them, but that would scare them more.

What can I do?

Cecile sat on a log beside the fire and hung her head. She had failed. Elton had done his dirty work in spite of her being right here. She had not been able to stop him, although he had run away afterward. He was still hurting people and that wasn't right. Cecile knew she needed to stop Elton and to somehow make him leave this place, but she had no clue how. Elton's mean spirit had now hurt Reuben, and Reuben didn't deserve it. As for Rosa, if what she said was true, she had ended her affair with Elton years before his death. He had no right to be jealous of her.

He had no right to ever have an affair with her in the first place. He was married to me!

Cecile felt the anger rising in her again Although a part of her believed she needed to let go and let God deal with Elton, another part of her believed that God had allowed her to stay here to keep Elton in check. If so, what did he want her to do? She shook her head wearily.

Across the clearing Rosa was crying. "I need to go away," she said. "I'm bad for you. I got you hurt."

Reuben appeared to be collecting his strength. He got to his feet slowly and glared around the clearing as if daring Elton to attack him again. Maybe he was putting on a show for Rosa but his act looked good to Cecile.

"It's hard to fight what you can't see; come on back here and let me see you, you coward," he yelled to the absent ghost. "Come on back and fight fair!"

Chapter Forty Six

It was evening before Louise ventured out to the barn. She had dutifully washed the dishes and put them away, so as to arouse no suspicion, and then she had said she was going off to take a nap. Instead she slipped out the side door and tramped through the snowy dark night to the barn. She didn't light a lantern until she was inside the barn.

Cecile watched as Louise peeked out the barn door looking toward the house just to be sure she was alone. Apparently she was convinced that she was, because she then headed to her stash of moonshine. When she pulled up the first empty jar, she looked surprised but reached again to pull up another one. She became frantic when all the jars turned out to be empty. Racing around the barn, Louise looked behind everything as if her moonshine had run away and hid from her. It was almost comical if it hadn't been so sad, Cecile thought. Finally Louise sat on a bale of hay and began to sob.

Such grief over lost liquor shows she's in trouble. What should I do?

Lifting her face to God, Cecile asked him again, "What should I do?"

She didn't get an immediate answer.

Well then; I guess I'll keep on doing what I've been doing. I'll watch over her.

After she had cried for a while, Louise wiped her eyes, washed her face in the cold water from a bucket and dried it with a rag she found in the horse stall. Then she returned to the house sneaking back in through the side door. She went to the room she'd been sharing with Vanessa and her mother first, then she peeked in the living room to see where everyone was. Finally she tiptoed into the master bedroom where George and Ethel now slept. She pulled a box of things Cecile had left behind when she died out of a drawer and selected a jeweled brooch. The box was carefully put back where she'd found it.

So she's stealing my jewelry. Why?

Cecile dogged Louise's footsteps as she left the house by the same side door and headed down the lane. A clock in the house had chimed 8:00pm as she exited. Cecile wondered where Louise was going with a stolen brooch at this time of night. That mystery didn't take long to solve. Louise headed for the Branham farm which was about a mile away on the left. When she got there she tossed snow balls at an upper window until a boy looked out and waved to her.

James Branham!

I should have suspected that no good boy was involved but how does Louise even know him?

In a few minutes a slender seventeen year old boy in tattered denims came out of the house through a back door. He walked up to Louise and put his arm around her as if they were old friends.

"I got another piece of jewelry; can I get some more moonshine," Louise asked as she sidled out of the arm James had placed around her.

"What's your hurry? I want to socialize a bit," James said. "You're not being friendly."

Louise pulled her coat around her and tightened the belt around it. "I've got to get back before they miss me," she said.

"I don't have a use for any more jewelry," James said with a leer. "What else you got for me?"

"Look at it. It's pretty. You can sell it for more than moonshine is worth." Louise held the jewelry up where a bit of light from inside the house was falling.

"The shine is hidden out in the barn. We buried it deep but I don't think it will freeze anyhow. They say the water in it will freeze but not the alcohol. Since we don't know for sure we keep it wrapped up and buried deep in straw and hay. Come on out and see what we got."

Louise didn't look happy but followed along behind James.

"I've put it in the barn and it never froze; I kept it covered up too though."

They entered the barn and James went to a spot beside a cow stall with a restless cow in it; the cow was snorting a grey mist into the cold air. James began to move things and to dig down into the straw and hay. The cow stomped and grunted above his head while he worked on the other side of her fenced in area.

Louise stood back a little, letting James do what he was trying to do. James held up a jar of the shine finally and smiled at her.

"I got what you want."

Louise tried to hand him the brooch but James stood and pushed her hand away. "I told you. Don't need no more jewelry. I need a little friendly loving if you want this." He held up the jar of home brew to entice her.

Louise was shaking her head 'No' and backing away from James who steadily moved toward her, leering at her discomfort.

Anger bubbled up swiftly inside Cecile nearly chocking her with its red hot substance. She cast her eyes about angrily to see what she could do to dissuade James from what he apparently intended to do. Seeing nothing handy, she rushed outside and wrenched a large switch from a tree. Zipping back inside she saw that James had backed Louise into a wall and was trying to pull up her dress. Using his body and left hand to hold her, James undid his belt buckle with the other and let his pants fall. That gave Cecile just the opportunity she'd longed for.

Whack!

"Shame on you James Branham!"

Cecile's voice echoed eerily in the dim light of the barn.

The switch caught James on his bare behind and it was comical to see him lurch forward in surprise, pain, and fury. He let go of Louise in the process. Stunned for only a minute, Louise grabbed the jar of moonshine and ran for the door.

"Shame on you!"

Whack, another welt rose as Cecile connected again with James' bare skin.

James was staggering in circles trying to pull up his pants with one hand while searching for his attacker with the other. His eyes were wild and he was whimpering like a kicked dog. Cecile reflected that he was just like any bully. He couldn't take it when the shoe was on the other foot. She whacked him again causing his pants to fall back down to his ankles.

"Shame, shame, shame!"

Before she finally let him pull the pants up, James had welts all over his behind and even his lower back, as well as some on his hands where he'd tried to fend off her blows. Finally she allowed him to dress and leave the barn, but before he was fully away, she called after him,

"Leave Louise alone. Don't give her alcohol. Don't touch her or you'll be sorry."

Chapter Forty Seven

Cecile was conflicted. On her way back to the farm house she was overcome with such a bevy of discordant thoughts and emotions she didn't know what to do.

Am I as bad as Elton by resorting to violence?

James deserved it if anyone ever did.

Louise is to blame too, stealing and sneaking out at night to get moonshine, and drinking.

Why do I care what happens to my husband's illegitimate daughter anyway?

Oh God; have I let you down or did I do what you put me here to do?

The whirling thoughts made Cecile dizzy and tired. She felt like she needed to sleep although previously she had not needed to do that. Maybe she had expended all her emotional energy and that was a part of it. She had used her voice repeatedly to shave James and that always seemed to tire her as well.

I can't rest yet. Louise is out there drinking that moonshine right now, I'll bet.

Going straight to the barn, she was just in time to see Louise take a drink and then furtively hide the jar in a new location. She had only drank about a fourth of the alcohol. Cecile debated whether she should confront Louise about this now or wait to see what happened. Louise had had a fright as had James. Already she seemed to have decided to pace herself and only drink a small amount of the brew instead of the whole thing.

I can always pour it out again but this time I don't think I will.

I want to see what she'll do next.

What Louise did next was go to the house and go to bed.

As Cecile settled down on a soft spot near her daughter Vanessa, she surveyed the others in the room. All were asleep now. Vanessa was resting comfortably it seemed. Louise was sleeping the deep sleep of the drugged and Rosa was tossing and turning in her sleep. Cecile then closed her own eyes hoping to give her mind and emotions a rest if not her body.

Ethel and George were up early the next morning. They sat in the kitchen over a cup of coffee, biscuits, and gravy. George was looking at a piece of paper he'd found beside his plate.

"What is this?"

Ethel looked his way. "What does it say?"

George cleared his throat. "It says 'send this to the sheriff'."

"Send what to the sheriff?" Ethel was frowning his way.

"I'm getting to it...there's another piece of paper. It says: "Moonshine being sold on Branham farm. Do your job and arrest them."

Ethel snorted. "Someone's having fun with us. Who signed the note?"

"Nobody signed it." George hesitated a second. "You won't believe me but it looks like Elton's writing."

Ethel swallowed and chocked; clearing her throat she said, "Let me see."

She took the paper and looked at it, swallowed and coughed again. "Where did you find it?"

"Right here."

"I think that might be where Louise got that moonshine." Ethel surmised after a bit.

"Probably."

"Are you taking it to the sheriff?"

"Yeah...think I got to."

After he'd eaten his breakfast George went off to town. The others straggled into the kitchen slowly. Louise was last. She had a bruise sliding down the right side of her face.

"What happened to you," Harrison asked.

"I tripped and fell down." Vanessa tossed her head daring him to contradict her. She looked around furtively though, wondering if anyone would challenge her version of events, no doubt, Cecile thought.

"You look like someone walloped you," Harrison said.

Louise ignored him, her shoulder cold and distant, showing him that she didn't care what he thought.

"Are you feeling okay," Rosa asked her daughter.

"I'm fine."

"You still look tired; maybe you should lay back down," Rosa advised.

Louise grabbed a biscuit and ran out of the room. Cecile followed and saw that she sat on her bed eating the biscuit which she had put honey on. Gobbling the bread down, dripping honey all over, Louise slid under the covers, clothes and all and pulled the comforter over her head.

She's ashamed and well she should be; that's why she's hiding from everyone.

Cecile left the room and went back to the kitchen where the rest of the family was having their breakfast.

"Where's Grandpa," Harrison asked.

"Had to go to town," Ethel replied.

"Wish he'd taken me with him."

Harrison sounded grumpy but Cecile couldn't blame him. He spent most of his life on the farm. It would have been a nice outing for him if he could have gone to town.

"What are you doing today? Maybe you and I can go fishing after we do our chores," Vanessa said. She gave Harrison a special look which Cecile thought might mean that Vanessa had something to discuss with him. No one asked why they'd want to go fishing in this cold and snowy weather.

"Okay." Harrison stood up… "I'll get started on feeding and watering the animals."

Cecile followed Harrison to the barn. After he was finished she planned to go with him and Vanessa when they left the farm. She didn't want to miss whatever her daughter had to say. Later as the brother and sister walked into the drifted woods carrying fishing poles in spite of the weather, Vanessa said, "Let's sit down on this log a minute. I want to tell you something.

They sat.

"Louise told me something this morning that I think you should know about."

"Yeah…what's up with her?"

"I think she's been getting her liquor from James Branham Junior. She said she went over there last night and he attacked her. That's where she got the bruise."

"Why didn't his parents stop him?"

"Oh… to hear her tell it someone stopped him all right but it wasn't his parents. They're moonshiners and for all I know they're as bad as their son. He's always been nasty. I know him from school."

"Yeah, he's a corker all right."

"She says James tried to rape her and she got the bruise fighting him off."

"Why was she there anyhow?"

"To get the moonshine. She's like an alcoholic I think. She sure does like that liquor."

"We got us a peach of a sister didn't we?" Harrison's voice was bitter.

"She is our sister though and we can't let the likes of James Branham hurt her."

"So who does she say came to her rescue? How did she get away?"

"She says...swears this is true...she says that James hit her in the face, shoved her against a wall, had his left hand on her throat, and was blocking her from moving with his body. His pants were down and he was trying to pull up her dress. According to Louise he was about to rape her when out of the blue something or someone attacked him with a switch. She saw the switch hitting his bare behind but she was so scared she couldn't do much to help herself. She says that he screamed when he got hit and let go of her. She told me a woman's voice said 'James Branham, shame on you. Shame, Shame, Shame.' That has to be Mom. Who else would protect her husband's bastard that way? Mom just can't stop being a mom even if it's Louise who's in trouble."

Chapter Forty Eight

Vanessa and Harrison were both looking around them cautiously. They were in agreement that their mom had intervened to help Louise who kept getting herself into trouble. Rosa wasn't an overly strict parent such as theirs had been. It was hard for the Montgomery children to understand their half-sister's lawlessness.

"How did Louise get the moonshine? I'm sure James didn't give it to her for free," Harrison said.

"I know. I forgot to ask her about that."

"I guess he was trying to get payment last night."

"I suppose so." Vanessa stood up. "This log is wet and cold. I don't want to sit on it anymore. Let's walk over and see what Reuben's doing."

Glancing at his sister with surprise, Harrison stood up too and brushed loose snow off his pants. "Reuben might be out hunting," he said.

"Too snowy today for that."

Reuben wasn't hunting. He had an old chair leaned up against his shack with a fire in front of him and a cup of coffee in his hand when they arrived. The fire had melted the snow around his house but the ground was wet and soggy.

"Let me get a couple of kitchen chairs so you can sit down," he said and bolted for the house. He was back right away with two chairs which he placed beside his own in a semi-circle with the fire in the middle.

"Want coffee," he asked.

Harrison said 'yes' and Vanessa said 'no'.

"How about some hot cocoa," Reuben asked her.

"Okay."

Reuben made another trip to the house coming back with a container of cocoa and some milk. He poured this into a sauce pan and set it on a grate over the fire.

"Be ready in a jiffy."

He headed back into the house and returned with two cups, one he filled with coffee for Harrison and one he set aside for Vanessa's cocoa.

"What brings you guys out today," he asked as he sat down and leaned his chair against the house propped up on its back legs.

"Cabin fever I guess," Harrison said.

"Probably glad to get out of that spooky house," Reuben allowed.

"Has anything else happened to you," Harrison asked giving his friend a curious look.

"Not lately but watch out tonight; I'm coming courting."

"Really...you like Rosa a lot don't you," Harrison asked.

Reuben glanced at Vanessa who was sitting silent. "I like her, and more important than that, no ghost is going to tell me who I can and can't see."

"Better watch out. Dad can get mean." Harrison looked at Reuben with concern in his eyes.

"I know that; I've felt his temper. But, he's not here on earth anymore, and when he was here he was married to your mother and so, had no right to Rosa. Since he has no claim on her, I'll claim her if I want to."

"You don't have to convince me. My mom is a good woman and he had no right to see someone else...to cheat on her."

"Why don't your mom stop him from the things he's doing?"

"I wonder that all the time, but she can't do it all. Dad is fast and she'd have to have eyes in the back of her head to predict everything he might be up to. She'd keep him in line if she could."

Thanks for the vote of confidence Harrison.

Cecile got up from the soggy log on which she'd been resting and floated over beside Vanessa. She didn't like it that her daughter was so silent today. What was on her mind?

"Well Cecile Montgomery, if you're here today, get ready for tonight because I'm bringing Rosa some candy that I got in town. I'm going to smooch her right there in the house. I'll do it right in front of her daughter and everyone else and if Elton Montgomery don't like it, he can lump it. I might even marry that woman before it's all over."

Cecile was amazed at Reuben's defiant attitude; she guessed that is what love can do to some people. Reuben was looking around the clearing as if waiting for a blow to land on him. However, Cecile didn't see Elton right now. He must be off somewhere dreaming up a devilish plan of some sort.

What can I do to stop Elton?

At least Reuben gave me warning and I know to be on guard.

I don't know what it is about Rosa; Elton never worried about me.

Of course he never had to. I was a good hardworking wife who never looked at anyone else.

"Don't make my Dad mad," Vanessa spoke up. "He'll hurt you."

"Yeah...he's hit me often enough," Harrison said.

"It's not fair for him to still be causing trouble for the living after he's already passed on and left this world. I can't let him mess up my life that way."

~ 261 ~

Reuben absently rubbed at eyes that were red and irritated by the smoke and fire.

"People who don't know, those people who haven't seen what we've seen, would think we're crazy to be talking about a ghost this way. They wouldn't believe us," Vanessa said.

"That's just all they know. I've been attacked by your father's ghost and I know he's real. He's mean too!"

As if his ears had been burning because they were talking about him, Elton Montgomery arrived at the clearing with a whoosh that only Cecile could hear. He stood aggressively looking at the scene, staring at Reuben. Cecile knew he was looking for something to do to Reuben but she couldn't figure out what he'd do.

Elton stared at the woodpile and Cecile circled to it.

Elton circled away.

He eyed the fire itself; Cecile moved in front of him.

Elton turned his attention to the chair on which Reuben was balanced.

He's going to jerk the chair out from under Reuben and make him fall.

As fast as she realized this, Cecile ran toward Reuben but Elton was already moving the chair legs and Reuben was in midair falling. The only thing she could think to do was to catch Reuben, so Cecile grabbed for him, strained and strained to hold him, then fell to the ground underneath her children's friend. Wiggling free as fast as she could, Cecile surveyed the stunned man who was lying on the wet ground. Above him Harrison and Vanessa stood reaching for his arms to pull him upright.

"I think I just met your mother close up," Reuben wheezed through lungs that had had the air knocked out of them.

Chapter Forty Nine

"What do you mean," Harrison demanded as he set Reuben on his feet. "How did you meet my mother?"

Harrison puffed air into his lungs and out again. "That wasn't a fall. Someone jerked the chair out from under me; but someone else grabbed me and broke my fall. In fact I fell right on her I think."

Vanessa was standing with her hands on her hips frowning at Reuben. Cecile supposed that she doubted what Reuben was saying and why he was saying it. She looked around. As usual Elton had vanished from the scene. Cecile was starting to believe that Reuben was right when he called him a coward.

"How do you know it was my mom who grabbed you," Vanessa asked.

"Who else would it be? Your Dad pulled the chair out from under me. Why would he then grab me to break my fall? Anyway...she was all soft and womanly, not like a man."

"I guess you are right."

Vanessa turned away and stared out into the woods that surrounded Reuben's property. Reuben swiped at mud that had stuck to his clothes with his right hand.

"I'm not going to back down. I have a right to court Rosa and I will court Rosa."

Harrison half nodded Reuben's way, but said, "I'm worried about you. My mom can't save you all the time. She has no way to know ahead of time what Dad will do."

"He might hurt Rosa. Have you thought about that," Vanessa asked.

Reuben scowled. "Well, maybe, but she's the mother of his child so he wouldn't want to hurt her enough to cause her not to be able to help Louise. If he does anything to her I think it will be something small and not serious."

"You don't' know that for sure," Vanessa said stubbornly. "We needed Mom but he took her away from us."

Reuben made a shushing motion and turned around sitting on the same chair he'd been on before but this time with all the legs solidly on the ground.

"We'd better get home," Vanessa told Harrison. "Thanks for the cocoa," she said to Reuben.

"I'm going to hang around a little longer. I'll see you at the house," Harrison said.

Vanessa strode off onto the path a little testily, Cecile thought. Vanessa didn't seem to like it that her brother had opted to stay with his friend instead of walking home with her. Cecile decided to walk with Vanessa so she wouldn't be alone. After all if James Branham had tried to rape one girl, he might go after another one if he found her alone. Vanessa walked along, her eyes on the ground. Rounded shoulders made her appear to be carrying a heavy weight. Cecile wanted to put her arm around her daughter.

Vanessa stopped and gazed around her. Hesitantly she said, "Mom are you here?"

Cecile's heart soared. Her daughter wanted her and she wasn't afraid of her.

"I'm right here honey."

Vanessa jumped in spite of her brave invitation to her mother to speak. She looked toward where her mother's voice had come from then said. "I miss you Mom."

"I know but I'm okay."

"You seem almost alive again when I hear your voice."

"I can't explain it. I'm here but I'm not exactly here. I still love you and I'm proud of you."

"Did you save Louise?"

"Yes I did, but she didn't deserve it. She was asking for trouble."

"How did she get the moonshine?"

"She's been trading pieces of my jewelry for it."

Vanessa was startled into verbal action. "That little hussy! That jewelry is mine now. She had no right to steal it. Of course, it's still yours Mom if you want it, "Vanessa backpedaled. " I won't let her steal from you either."

Cecile went to Vanessa and put a hand on her shoulder. "Just take the jewelry and hide it in a good place where she can't find it. I don't want or need it anymore. It's yours. In fact, I'm going to try to get back the jewelry she stole and I'll give that to you too."

"Louise shouldn't get off Scott free."

"She won't; she needs a consequence or she'll be a thief all her life. I'll take care of it."

Cecile patted her daughter on the shoulder. "Mom's here and I'll watch over things. You go on home and let me figure out what to do."

"I love you, Mom."

"I love you Sweetheart."

Cecile parted from her daughter and floated to the farmhouse alone, moving more rapidly than Vanessa. She checked to see where everyone was and then settled down to watch what was happening. She felt tired. Although she'd managed to grab Reuben and break his fall, the physical impact had had an effect on her. Soon she was drifting away in a sleeplike stupor.

Later Cecile followed Louise when she crept out of the house and headed for the barn. She went straight to the spot where she had hidden the moonshine and nervously tipped it up to take a drink. That's when Cecile spoke to her, just as the jar was tipped.

"You traded my jewelry for alcohol. You are at thief. Shame on you."

Louise jumped and dropped the jar. Devastated the girl stared at the precious liquid running into the straw of the barn floor. She looked around her helplessly, shaking a bit, but from fear or the cold, Cecile couldn't figure out.

"You stole my jewelry." Cecile had made her voice into a plaintive high pitched wail.

"I- I- I'm sorry."

Louise had tears running down her face and freezing on her pale skin. Cecile thought that was a good thing. She planned to scare Louise straight if possible.

"Don't you ever do that again or you'll be really sorry. I mean it."

Cecile pushed Louise who fell onto the cold wet straw. "I mean what I say. You stole my jewelry and you traded it for liquor. As a result you nearly froze to death and were almost raped. You can thank me you weren't. I'll take the switch to you next time."

Her words sounded eerie to herself and she hoped Louise was convinced.

"I'll be good," Louise whispered as she bent into a position suggestive of prayer. "Don't hurt me."

"R E M EM B E R...." Cecile said, dragging her syllables out in a long loud ominous lament.

Louise nodded, jumped to her feet and bolted for the house.

Chapter Fifty

Cecile waited a while, thinking about how she would approach James Branham and the problem of getting back jewelry that Louise had traded for moonshine. James might not even have the jewelry now. He may have traded it for something else or sold it to someone.

Since people can't see me I can search an empty room without anyone knowing.

Maybe I can watch James and he'll lead me to it.

I wonder if his parents know about the trade he made

The whole family is probably involved in the moonshine business though.

Cecile decided there is no time like the present and headed for the Branham farm. She went to the barn first thinking that might be where James spent his time. She was right and James was busy washing up jars to put the illegal liquid in. He had a large washtub over a fire and was boiling water in the tub. Using tongs he was slowly dipping each canning jar into the boiling water, holding it there for a minute or so and then setting it on a rickety table.

Well at least he's trying to sterilize the jars so he doesn't kill anyone.

Cecile didn't know why but she was surprised that James seemed to be taking precautions to sterilize his equipment. As she watched the son, James Branham Sr. walked up to the area where James Junior was working.

"Glad you're getting those jars ready because I have a batch finishing up," he said to his son.

Cecile had never liked James Senior and now that she'd seen his son in action, she disliked both of them. Father and son were both dark haired with dark brown eyes and weathered complexions. The father was a little hefty but James Junior was of slighter build. Both had a coldly intense look in their eyes.

Carefully the son packed the sterilized jars into a box and the two men carried the jars to a shed on the outskirts of the property. Cecile followed along. They had set up a still complete with a lot of pipes and other intricate equipment. That impressed her in spite of herself because it was all so complicated and also because it was clean. Cecile didn't expect much in organization and cleanliness from men, especially bootleggers. She found it surprising that these particular men were so neat. As she watched them work she noticed a vehicle was coming down the lane. The men were busy and didn't seem to hear it. When it got closer she saw it was the Sherriff.

When the men noticed they panicked. Running about aimlessly, hands in the air, James Jr. was asking

"What are we going to do? What are we going to do?"

"You stay here and hide as much as you can but keep an eye out. If I rub the tip of my cap, you come running because we don't want them to search for you." The father hurried away to see what the sheriff wanted. Cecile followed the father because she thought it would be more interesting than watching the son hide liquor.

"Can I help you," James Sr. was congenial in his tone.

"I came to see your son this time," the sheriff said.

"What you want with my son?"

"I have some questions for him."

"What's it about."

"I'd rather talk to him about it first if you don't mind. Where is he?"

"Oh he's around here somewhere," James said, fingering the tip of his cap. "I expect to see him anytime now because it's almost time to eat and that boy likes to eat."

"Recon I'll wait."

The men stood eying each other

"Cold," James said.

"Yep."

"How's your family?"

"Great."

James Jr. was heading across a field toward them now. He paused when he arrived in their midst and said, "Sheriff...what brings you here?"

"Got some questions for you."

"For me?" James tried to look innocent.

Yes."

The sheriff motioned to James Sr. "You can go on back to work now. We've got it."

Reluctantly James Sr. turned and walked toward the barn. The sheriff was silent until the father was out of earshot and then he calmly told James Jr. that he was arresting him for attempted rape.

Cecile smiled. She had sent a little note to the sheriff using Ethel's stationery. James played dumb.

"Who am I supposed to have tried to rape?"

"The little girl on the Montgomery farm. That girls only thirteen years old. Why would you try to rape a baby?"

~ 273 ~

James was silent and then apparently decided to go on the offensive. "That girl's crazy. She came over here in the middle of the night and attacked me out in the barn." He turned and pulled up his shirt showing bruises up and down his spine and backside. She had a big stick and she crept up behind me and kept whacking me with it. I'm lucky she didn't kill me. She don't have any bruises I'll bet."

"You can put all that in writing down at the station," the sheriff said.

Cecile didn't think the sheriff was impressed with James' story, but she had to admit it was a good one. He knew his attacker wasn't Louise but the marks on his back came in handy as evidence that he, not Louise, was a victim.

The sheriff put handcuffs on James and took him away. Cecile decided not to waste the opportunity to search the house that she'd been given...especially James' room. She headed toward the house where she saw James Sr. and his wife in a heated conversation. Slipping past them she made her way to the bedrooms and began her search. Finding the room she suspected was James' she began to go through everything but quietly. No need to disturb his parents at the moment. Under sox in his drawer she found one of her necklaces and confiscated that. There was no way to determine at this time just what pieces were missing. How long the 'trades' had been going on was anyone's guess. She would have to look at what jewelry remained and then she'd have a better idea.

Inside a pillowslip she found one of her treasures, but it wasn't a necklace. It was an old and decorative picture album that still held pictures of her mother and her mother's family.

Opening it, she found the old and irreplaceable pictures still inside. Dumbstruck, Cecile stood glaring angrily at the heirloom Louise had traded for alcohol.

"That girl may need another lesson," she decided." A good harsh one."

Chapter Fifty One

Everyone seemed edgy when Reuben came to dinner with candy and a handmade card for Rosa. He also brought a couple of rabbits for the icebox. The residents of the Montgomery house all knew they'd likely have an angry ghost to contend with, and that made everyone edgy and worried. Even George and Ethel were clearly waiting for trouble to start.

Rosa shyly accepted Reuben's courtship. She didn't seem to know how to respond given the circumstances and with Elton's parents standing on the other side of the room though. Cecile believed that she genuinely cared for Reuben from the way she looked at him.

"I made something for you," Rosa said when Reuben handed her the box of candy. "Just a minute."

Rosa went to her room and returned with a hand crocheted rag rug. She handed it to Reuben who didn't seem sure what he was holding.

"It's to put on your floor; maybe in front of your bed so your feet don't get cold when you get up in the night," Rosa said.

"It's great; that's just what I'll do with it," Reuben announced.

Cecile knew that Rosa had cut up old dresses that she and Louise no longer wore to get the material. To her it seemed one more token of Rosa's sincerity where Reuben was concerned.

Maybe they'll get married; she and Louise can't stay here forever. Spring is coming.

She glanced out the window and saw that there was no sign of spring yet. The weather was cold and ice held to the ground in many places. She hoped Louise straightened out soon or Rosa was in for a long, sad stint with her. In truth Louise had been a bit better since Cecile had berated her with scalding words meant to discipline her. Maybe hearing from a ghost who could monitor her every move had brought Louise in check.

But I still have to address the theft of my photo album and family pictures.

Obviously they meant nothing to Louise; she didn't care that this was family for her brother and sister. She used the value of my beautiful album as a pawn to get the moonshine she wanted. As for James...he didn't care where she got things. He wanted them to resell. Why didn't she at least take the pictures out of the album? I guess that was too much trouble.

Cecile snorted in disgust. A startled Rosa looked around fearfully but Harrison told her that the sound they'd heard was probably not made by his dad. With that she relaxed a little. Dinner was chicken and dumplings with homemade biscuits. At first everyone was wary but as the meal went on, most of the family relaxed. Cecile didn't see any sign of Elton and wondered. Was he hiding or had he declined to attend dinner tonight? He'd heard Reuben say he was going courting.

Anger licked at Cecile's mind. Talk about having been done wrong. Elton had certainly done her wrong and was still doing hurtful things. He seemed bent on showing her that Rosa was the one he cared for, not the wife he'd murdered.

Reuben sat beside Rosa and was giving her careful attention. The family was looking on, waiting to see what would transpire. All at once Elton was in the room. He had been absent and then in a heartbeat, he was right beside Reuben, a glass of water poised over his head. Rosa looked up and saw a glass of water standing above her and Reuben, suspended in mid-air, and screamed. Elton dropped the glass clunking Reuben in the head and spilling the water everywhere.

Elton moved to the far side of the room as Cecile practically flew toward him.

Harrison was on his feet.

"Come on Dad; can't you fight fair," he yelled. "You hit people and run. Reuben's right you are a coward."

The electric lights began to go on and off frantically then remained off. In the darkness, Cecile could see that Elton was advancing on his son. She ran to Harrison and draped her body around him, protecting him. Elton backed away from her. Beneath her arms, Harrison squirmed apparently uncomfortable at being held by invisible arms. She let go.

The electric came back on. Tension sat in the room as Cecile gazed at pale faces filled with worried frowns. Finally Cecile went back to the side of the room where she'd been originally standing. People began to eat again slowly.

"What happened," Reuben asked. "Why am I all wet?"

Rosa explained what had happened to him and what Harrison had said.

"Thanks pal," Reuben told Harrison. "But I'm surprised he didn't clobber you for it."

"I think he must have tried," Harrison said. "I felt arms wrap around me and then I was held tight. I think my Mom intervened and stopped him."

"Really?" Vanessa was staring at her brother.

"It's true. First time I've felt my mother's arms in a long time. It scared me at first but now that I think about it...it was nice."

George and Ethel were staring at their grandson and then at each other. "This is the craziest place I've ever been in my life," George said to his wife.

Ethel harrumphed, but said nothing; then she got up and began to clear the table, clearly upset. Rosa was helping Reuben to his feet when all at once she jerked her head back and screamed. As Cecile watched a large red splotch colored one side of Rosa's face. She let go of Reuben and put her hand to that area where a welt was now forming in the shape of a hand. Cecile had not seen Elton slap Rosa but he must have done so. The red patch on her face gave evidence to that.

Looking around she could not find her violent husband anywhere in the room. His parents were no help in this situation. They didn't seem to want to rile their son, the ghost. In fact even when he was alive they had been cautious of him if they would admit it. Only Cecile had stood up to him and look where that had landed her.

Well he seems to be afraid of me now and I intend to use that; he's a bully, but like most bullies, he's a coward at heart. I'm proud of our son for standing up to him. Even Reuben has had enough of his shenanigans.

Satisfied with the way the evening had gone over all, Cecile smiled as she watched Harrison and Vanessa wash dishes. Love warmed her to her core. God had given her special children.

Chapter Fifty Two

"I don't care what you think," Ethel said to George. "I've had it with this place for now, son or no son, grandchildren or no grandchildren. Henry can take a turn with the kids."

"He's not due to move in for another two weeks."

"Tell him it's some kind of emergency and we have to go back home."

George eyed his nearly hysterical wife disgustedly. She had not combed her hair this morning and her eyes were wild with fear. The black grey of her hair, standing on end as it was, emphasized her fear, and made her look like a wild woman. He rubbed his own bloodshot eyes and wondered if Henry would come two weeks early and let the two of them get away from all the stress. He hated to admit it, but Henry was a good sort and sensitive to other people's needs; he might do it.

"I'll talk with Henry," he said.

"And I hear that Louise was stealing jewelry that used to be Cecile's and trading it to that James Branham Jr. for moonshine. That's how she got the liquor. They arrested the boy, I hear. Lucky for Louise that she didn't get arrested too."

"Maybe you should talk to her," George said.

"From what the kids have told me, Cecile's ghost already has. Scared the girl out of her sox, I hear."

Cecile was tired of this conversation and drifted to the barn where Harrison and Vanessa were pitching hay down from the haymow to feed the cattle and horses.

"Louise had better get herself together or she's going to have to leave here," Harrison said.

"She's not all that bad." Vanessa heaved a bale of hay over the side of the loft.

"Stealing and drinking aren't exactly good things."

"She never had a dad around and her mother isn't very strict with her; she'll grow out of this," Vanessa said, crossing her fingers for a second.

"Do you like her then," Harrison looked at his sister curiously.

Vanessa stopped and stood tall to ease the cricks in her back. "I don't not like her. She's our sister so we should try to keep her out of trouble, I guess. We're older than she is; we need to set a good example. How about Rosa? Is Reuben going to marry her?"

"He hasn't told me."

Harrison lifted another bale of hay and positioned it to fall into a horse manger. "It would solve problems for everyone if he did. I guess Louise would live with him and Rosa and we wouldn't have to worry about the two of them."

"What if Louise didn't like for them to marry and wanted to stay here with us?"

"That won't happen. She don't like us that much."

Cecile wondered if Elton would give up and leave the couple alone if they were married. Maybe he was just trying to break them up before they got too close, but if that didn't work and they married, he'd stop his shenanigans and move on to something else.

Why has Elton stayed? He has a reason I know…a bad one.

Maybe he wants to control what happens in his family.

Maybe he wants to victimize the kids or to protect secrets...wish I knew.

If I did, maybe I could figure out how to make him go.

Cecile wondered if ghosts are at different levels just as living society is. If so how did the levels between her and Elton compare? Cecile had come to believe that she'd been given some kind of power or ascendency over Elton after death. She had chosen to believe that God had given her something to protect her, and that Elton was aware of it. That was why he ran away from her and would not allow her near him. Thoughts about this went through her mind constantly.

If that's so, I wonder what it is I don't understand it.

Her children had continued to work while she'd lost herself in thought. She had not even seen Elton when he'd entered the barn. Now she saw him standing over by a wall fingering a piece of leather tackle. He had his eyes on his kids. Cecile was afraid he'd held a grudge against Harrison for what Harrison had said about Elton being a coward. She started to move toward the father of her children, but Elton merely moved away without leaving the barn. Not wanting to speak aloud and scare the kids, Cecile kept silent but circled her husband like a wolf circling a calf. Elton just kept turning with her to keep her in sight and remained at a distance.

Unaware of the drama unfolding around them, Harrison and Vanessa finished the work they were doing, exited the barn, and returned to the house. That left Elton and his wife alone.

"Don't you go attacking our son for telling you the truth," Cecile shouted at Elton. "You do hit and run like he said. That is a cowardly thing to do."

Elton's face turned furious but he did not come after her.

"Why?"

"Just leave the kids alone and let them grow up in peace," Cecile said.

Elton remained silent glaring at her.

"I don't get it," Cecile said. "Why don't you move on and leave everyone alone?"

Elton turned his back and walked away.

Much later that day Elton returned in apparently an entirely different frame of mind. Cecile watched as he played games with his mother. Ethel had taken off her rings to do the dishes. They were laid carefully in a soap dish where she always put them. Elton swiped them and hid them elsewhere. He laughed and cut up as his mother searched high and low for the rings. She even went to find George to ask him if he'd seen her rings.

"Where'd you leave them," he asked, following her back to the kitchen.

"In the soap dish where I always leave them," Ethel pointed to the empty dish.

"Then they would be there."

"No they are not; you can see that for yourself."

She drug George to the counter and showed him the empty soap dish from close up.

"Well I don't know what you did with them," George grumbled.

"Help me find them," Ethel insisted.

Half-heartedly George searched the kitchen. Ethel searched also. Neither of them found the rings. Meanwhile, Elton sneaked the rings back to the soap dish where his mother had originally placed them. Both parents had seen the empty soap dish. Elton almost bounced up and down waiting for one of them to see that the rings were back in the dish now. Finally George walked over to the sink and glanced at the soap dish. He did a double take and his eyes flitted around the room as if looking for someone.

"Come here," he called to Ethel. "I found your rings."

"Where?"

"Right where you put them."

Both of them stood rigidly looking at the rings in the soap dish. When Ethel said again that she had to get away from this farm before it drove her crazy, George nodded his head, agreeing.

Chapter Fifty Three

Rosa was cuddled up with Reuben on his couch, watching the fire in his wood stove, and drinking hot cocoa. She snuggled closer and took his warm hand in hers.

"I like it here so much better than I do at the Montgomery farm," she said. "Elton doesn't seem to bother us as much over here. He thinks the farm is still his and that he has a right to control everything that goes on there."

"He's done things to me at my own house," Reuben protested.

"I know, but he doesn't seem to do quite as much."

The wood cracked in the stove and then hissed as sap got released into the fire. Both of them jumped at the sound. Reuben looked around carefully to be sure it was just the fire and not an unfriendly ghost.

There was a ghost in the room but this time it was Cecile; Elton was absent.

The shabby room was cozy and romantic tonight. Reuben had lit candles and there was also the light from the stove where the flames danced and pranced as if in some kind of ritual.

"I made some blackberry wine from last summer's berries. Would you like a glass?" Reuben asked.

Rosa hesitated. "I'm not a drinker," she said, and then, "Well maybe a glass won't hurt."

"I guess wine is illegal too since all alcohol is prohibited, but I can't see where the government has a right to tell me what I can and can't do with my own blackberries," Reuben said.

"Wine never hurt anyone unless they drank a ton of it," Rosa agreed.

Cecile drifted outside and stared at the surrounding woods, which were covered with an eerie mist. It made her feel bad to deny the lovers their privacy but she felt compelled to keep an eye on what was going on around and near the farm. Elton was unpredictable and he had it in for the couple. She could hear Rosa giggling inside the house and decided that maybe everything was okay here and she could return to the farmhouse.

Later after Rosa had returned to the farm and everyone was bedded down for the night, Cecile made her usual check on the women. Louise was deeply asleep and she wondered if the girl had found some other form of liquor to sedate herself with. Vanessa was asleep, but seemed troubled as she turned and fidgeted often. Rosa seemed to be sleeping well.

Cecile was about to leave the room when Elton was suddenly there standing beside Rosa's bed. She stopped where she was and watched to see what he was up to. For a time he just stood quietly staring down at his one-time mistress. Cecile felt herself getting angry; she saw this as an intentional slight to her. Of course Elton knew she was in the room.

Rosa turned uneasily but didn't waken.

Elton stayed where he was, although he glanced at his two daughters to see if they were still asleep. Rosa turned over so she was now facing the spot where Elton stood. Elton reached out a hand and touched her hair. Rosa's eyes snapped open and she seemed to see Elton for the first time...to actually see him. Cecile was fascinated because up until now both she and Elton had been invisible to the living.

Rosa stared and stared in apparent horror. Her mouth opened but words would not come.

She then closed her eyes tight and pulling the covers up around her head began reciting the Lord's Prayer aloud over and over. The covers around her were pulled tighter and tighter as she said the prayer. Cecile was frozen in place unable to act as she watched the tableau in front of her. Elton seemed stunned at Rosa's reaction and he stood stiffly one arm out toward her as he listened to the prayer and watched Rosa's trembling form under the covers. All at once it was as if a mighty hand reached down and snatched Elton. Cecile could almost see the hand and she had no doubt what was happening. Elton was jerked upward through the roof amid a rush of sound that awakened everyone in the room.

"What's going on," Vanessa asked the others from her spot in the attic. She was leaning over and staring down at the scene below.

Rosa slowly uncovered her head and looked around the room.

"Elton was standing right there. I saw him. He touched my hair."

"You were dreaming Mom," Louise said.

Rosa was sitting up in bed now, indignant. "I know what I saw."

"What made that rushing or swishing sound," Vanessa asked.

"I don't know," Rosa admitted. "I had my head covered up. I was saying the Lord's Prayer and all at once I heard that sound and Elton was gone."

Louise stared at her mother. "Do you think God took him away because you said that prayer?"

"I don't know but I hope he took him away for good."

Cecile was wondering some of the same things. She felt sure that God had intervened this time but why this time and not the other times when Elton was behaving badly?

It must be because of the prayer.

That's the only thing that was different.

"What was he doing Mom?" Louise looked scared to death.

"Just standing there...well he reached out and touched my hair."

"Why didn't you scream," Vanessa asked. "I'd have screamed if I'd seen him."

"I tried. I couldn't make any sounds. My mouth was dry and nothing would work. My vocal cords must have dried up."

"Should we tell the rest of the family?" Vanessa seemed uncertain what to do now.

"Your grandma is already scared to death, even if Elton is her own son. They're leaving tomorrow and Henry is coming here to stay. Maybe we should just keep it to ourselves until they make the switch," Rosa suggested.

"I'm going to tell Harrison and maybe Grandpa Henry when he gets here," Vanessa said.

"I told you we need to leave this place," Louise told her mother.

"And go where? It will be warm soon. You need to hold your horses and wait until we can make a plan," Rosa said.

Vanessa was looking very thoughtful. "We have had a lot more trouble since you two have been around," she said. "Dad is jealous and that's making him act worse than ever."

Rosa seemed upset. She sniffed a little and fluffed her pillow before saying, "Well, we'll be out of your hair soon enough." She flopped over onto her side facing the wall and pulled the covers back up over her face. She didn't respond to Vanessa's,

"Sorry."

Chapter Fifty Four

When everyone went back to sleep, Cecile headed outside to find Elton. He needed to answer some questions, she thought. She searched through the house and barn, but no Elton. She skimmed the fields in the cold moonlight and still no Elton. Finally she went to Reuben's shack to check on him. It had occurred to her that Elton might go and take out his frustration on poor Reuben. Sure enough Elton was hovering, a malignant spirit, watching his rival. He wasn't doing anything, and when he saw Cecile, his displeasure was evident on his face. Clearly he wanted his wife to go away and leave him to his malicious intentions.

Cecile wasn't going anywhere!

He eyed her, glanced at Reuben, shook his head in disgust and walked through the wall of Reuben's cabin. Reuben did not appear to have noticed that he had a visitor. He was energetically putting wood into his heating stove. That done, he set a pot of water on the top of the stove and added cocoa and sugar to it. He picked up a newspaper and sat in the light of a kerosene lamp to read it while waiting for the chocolate to brew.

Cecile stayed for a while just in case Elton returned but he didn't.

The girls.

Is he using my absence to harass the girls?

She sped back to the farmhouse. Sure enough Elton was in the bedroom where Rosa, Vanessa, and Louise were asleep. He wasn't doing anything, just watching them as they slept. However, the women seemed to be aware something was wrong as they were all tossing and turning in their sleep.

Cecile headed toward Elton and he exited the room. She alternated between watching the women, her father, who had moved back to the farmhouse the day before, and Harrison, all night. She was exhausted by morning, more from worry than lack of rest. She wished she could understand what Elton's intent was for remaining here. She also fretted because she had no idea what she could do to make him go away permanently. Sure...she could make him leave an area using some unknown power she seemed to possess these days. She didn't know how that worked either. Sighing she lay down in a corner of the kitchen as the family assembled for breakfast. Her inability to sleep was unsettling to her but she could go into a sort of daydream that was almost like being asleep sometimes. She did this now.

Around her no one was saying much.

Eventually Rosa started to talk, telling stories of Elton that the family had not heard before. She explained how he'd reacted when she ended their affair once she knew he had a wife. At first he had sworn he would leave his wife and marry her. Rosa had not bought that. Then he'd said...

"Well, I can't leave Cecile until the kids are grown but then I'll leave her and marry you."

After all his cajoling had not worked, he'd thrown a fit and spent one long night prancing around the house screaming bad things about her, and to her. Rosa said that she locked all doors and weathered the storm of his wrath until finally he gave up and left in the cold morning light.

Cecile came fully alert as she heard this. She wondered when this had happened if it had. When had Elton stayed away all night? Upon reflection, she realized that he had done this more than once using various excuses such as weather or broken wheels on a wagon. It could have happened as Rosa said. It did sound like the way Elton acted when he was angry.

"He also said he had a stash of money set aside with which he would disappear one day. He said we could disappear together using that money."

Everyone's ears perked up at that.

Cecile wondered if he could have meant the small stash she had found, some of which she had given to Harrison one Christmas. It hadn't been that much money. "No...that wasn't enough money to go somewhere and start over. Does he have more money hidden around here somewhere? If he does, the kids need it. It belongs to them."

She decided that she would be doing a thorough search starting today. Eventually she had to find it didn't she?

"But you let him come back to see me," Louise put in.

"I did that for your sake but I told him one more episode of violence and I wouldn't let him come to see you...and then...well you know what he did, so I made him stay away."

"I think Dad is very mad at me," Vanessa said. "I can feel it. I'm surrounded by a coldness that seeps into my bones sometimes and I know it's coming from him."

"Why is he mad at you?" Harrison looked at his sister intently.

"Because I told on him and in his mind it's my fault that he and Mom had a fight and that he killed her and himself. I don't think he'll stop until he's humiliated and punished me. He thinks I'm to blame; maybe I am."

"No you are not! Henry's voice boomed loudly in the sudden stillness. "He's responsible for everything he did. If he hadn't done wrong things to you, there would have been nothing to tell. He started it and he ended it. It's all on his soul, not yours!"

Henry had risen from his seat and was standing defiantly staring around the room as if expecting Elton to strike him. Cecile sighed and stood so she'd be ready if Elton attempted an attack on her father. Her eyes skimmed the enclosure looking for her husband. Elton was in the room. He was floating up near the ceiling this time, looking down on them all. He began to float toward her father; Cecile intercepted him. As she hoped, he sidled away from her. Again she wondered why he seemed to be afraid of her. He must know something she didn't.

Henry slowly sat down at the table again. "I wish we knew where his stash was then," He said. "His children could use it; he can't."

Cecile wondered if there was any way to persuade Elton to give what money he might have hidden from her and the kids in the past to the children now, since he had no way to use it.

"Probably not," she decided. "But I can try."

Chapter Fifty Five

She found Elton in the barn a few days later. He had been watching Harrison but Harrison had finished his chores and returned to the house. Now Elton and Cecile were squared off on different sides of the barn, staring at each other.

"If you have a hidden stash of money you need to give it to the kids," Cecile said.

Elton turned his back on her, but she could see he was watching her in an old dirty pane of glass in the window.

Must be afraid I'll sneak up and get him.

"Do you hear me? Those are your kids. They just barely get by working this farm the best they can, but they need an education. They need to get trained so they can make something of themselves."

Elton shook his head and gazed at the straw under his feet. He had turned back around and was keeping an eye on her while pretending to study the ground.

"You can't use the money. What do you need money for now," Cecile persisted. "Give it to them. Give some to Louise too if you want; well don't trust her with money... give it to Rosa. They don't have anything and they can't stay here forever. It's rough living the life of a hobo...especially for two women."

Elton snorted loudly but didn't say a word. In fact, in spite of her best endeavors, during her entire spiel which went on for nearly an hour longer, Elton never said a word to his wife. Finally he just turned and walked through the wall of the barn and disappeared from her sight.

During the next week Cecile noticed that when Elton as around, he wasn't himself. He was angry and brooding, true, but there was an undercurrent of electricity that permeated his presence. She could feel the tension building but had no idea what to do...except try to stay prepared for anything. Still Elton didn't do anything to anyone and the family didn't seem to notice when he was around.

Maybe they're coping with everything by denial, and blocking out the fact that a malevolent spirit is around.

She lamented anew that her association with Elton Montgomery was endless and even death didn't seem to separate them.

"I only made a vow to stay with him until death us do part," she cried out to God when she was in her worst depression. "Why must I deal with him endlessly?"

God chose not to respond at that particular time and Cecile felt alone and frustrated. She had no one to talk to...not really. Of course she could speak to the living and maybe get some interaction but what could she say and what stress was she putting her loved ones under by speaking across the veil to the world of the living. She knew she scared her children even though she also gave them some comfort to know that she was still with them.

She debated her options over and over. Convinced that Elton was gearing up for a major explosion, she wondered if she should alert her family to be extra cautious. Finally she decided to approach her father when she could find him alone. He would know what to do.

Henry was working in the barn, temporarily alone as Harrison had gone over to check on

Reuben who had been absent for a couple of days. Sometimes Vanessa helped him in the barn but Louise and Rosa were assigned to kitchen duties when Henry was living at the house. They didn't know much about running a farm, he reasoned, and he didn't know all that much about cooking and cleaning although he'd been doing it for a long time.

"Best to let people do what they are good at," he'd told them.

He had encouraged Vanessa to work harder on her homework, excusing her from some of the kitchen duties to do so. Sometimes she came to help him in the barn when she had everything caught up, wanted to talk to him, or when she chose to share time with Harrison. Her grades had improved dramatically and she had begun to talk about the possibility of taking additional classes when school was out. He thought that was a very good sign.

He almost jumped into the haymow when Cecile spoke to him.

"How are you Dad?"

"Cecile?"

"Don't be scared; I just want to talk to you."

"Where are you?"

"Over here by the milking stool."

Henry gazed her way and took his time getting his equilibrium back.

"Is everything all right," he asked her.

"I'm good, but Elton is up to something."

"What?"

"Don't know; he's brooding and building up steam over something."

"Probably Rosa again."

"Probably."

"Are the kids in danger do you think?"

"Anyone could be...you too. He's got a grudge against Vanessa."

"Elton doesn't like me but he respects me a little. Will he hurt you," Henry asked his daughter.

"I don't know... he seems afraid of me."

"Maybe he was afraid all along and that's why he shot you, the coward." Henry's face twisted in agony as he remembered his daughter's death at the hands of his son in law.

"Be careful Dad; he's a dangerous man. He's building up a grudge against the family, I think, and it's hard to tell what he'll do. Vanessa thinks he blames her for telling me what he did to her. She's afraid of him and I don't blame her."

"He hit Harrison in the face... what kind of father does these things?"

Cecile was beginning to feel so weary she might faint if that was possible in her state. Communication with the living seemed to take every bit of her energy, draining her. Maybe that's why Elton never spoke to the family. She knew she had to wrap up this conversation soon. What could she say to make her warning clear? She felt her way through her foggy brain trying to reason it out. She didn't know what her father could do to prepare but she was desperate to give him warning as to how to prepare himself and the kids for what was sure to come.

"Pray," she said in a weak voice. "Rosa prayed and I saw him yanked up through the ceiling. I think God intervened. Pray!"

She felt herself fading away.

Chapter Fifty Six

The winter weather hung over the farmhouse like a shroud, depressing Cecile along with the living members of the household. She looked out a window where a fine snow was falling again. The ground was already covered and the temperature was bitterly cold. Rosa had complained that the stores of food in the pantry were getting low and Reuben had gone hunting. He arrived at the Montgomery house with a pheasant and two squirrels over his shoulder just before dark. He also had some field corn which he had gleaned from a nearby field.

"We can grind this up and make cornmeal," he said. "It won't be the best but it will keep everyone alive until the weather breaks."

He used the food grinder to grind the corn. Although the corn was still coarse and difficult to work with, he said it made pretty good corncakes. "I make my corncakes in a skillet on top of the stove," he told Rosa with a laugh.

"Thanks for helping out," she gave him a peck on the cheek.

Rolling up his sleeves, baring his arms, and using a dish pan to clean the squirrels, he began that job as Rosa started working with the corn meal.

"You are so good to help me this way," she said.

"It's just work. We all got to work to eat," Reuben said.

Cecile, who was watching the two of them, thanked God for Reuben because he had helped the family through this difficult winter by providing food and assistance. Maybe some of it was to impress Rosa but still, she remembered that he had brought food to the family before Rosa was on the scene. She blessed him in her heart and asked God to protect him from Elton in her prayers. Elton was still brooding and silent. He hadn't taken any adverse actions toward the family though and as usual, he avoided Cecile.

If only I knew why he runs away from me.
Of course, he doesn't have a gun now.
He hid behind the gun before.

Louise had been keeping a low profile since the episode with James Branham and his attempt to rape her. Cecile heard her tell Vanessa that he scared her about to death, but even worse was the sudden appearance of a switch coming out of thin air and being wielded by a ghost. She didn't think the ghost was her father. She had heard a woman's voice shaming James.

"Why did you fool around with that guy anyhow," Vanessa asked, showing little sympathy for the fix Louise had gotten herself into.

"He had moonshine and I wanted it."

"Well I heard that his father and mother have been arrested for making moonshine. James Junior is in jail for trying to rape you and for helping his parents make moonshine and selling it. I guess you won't be getting any more of that stuff, thank goodness."

"Don't knock what you haven't tried." Louise's voice was angry and petulant.

"Don't you knock the benefits of keeping your nose clean and doing what's right! You could have ended up in jail with the Branhams."

Cecile beamed with pride in her daughter.

Louise stalked out of the room and went looking for Harrison and Reuben who were playing cards in the barn. She carried some hot coffee in a pot along with cups to serve to the men. Having had words with Vanessa, Cecile figured Louise was trying to find a friendly face where ever she could. The hot coffee would insure her welcome.

The men had pulled milking stools up to a bale of hay and were using it as a table to lay their cards on. They had built a fire in the old coal stove and were cuddled beside its welcome heat. Reuben smiled when he saw Louise and smelled the coffee.

"Is that for us," he asked.

"Yep," Louise said..."And for me too."

"You don't drink coffee," Harrison told her.

"Yes I do when I want to," Louise told him.

Harrison didn't argue. He shrugged his shoulders as if to say, 'It's your stomach" and looked at his cards.

"What are you playing," Louise asked.

"Five hundred Rum," Reuben said, pouring himself a cup of coffee from the coffee pot.

"Why are you playing cards out here in the cold?"

"It's not cold. We have a good fire going."

"I guess it's okay but you have to sit almost on top of the stove. There's too many drafts out here."

"You're right," Reuben said and laid down a set of cards. "Do you want to play next hand?"

Louise considered. "No...I'm going back to the house where it's warm."

After Louise took the empty coffee pot and left, the men finished the game. Harrison paused and took a drink of coffee, made a face, and spit it out.

"Cold," he mouthed.

"Yeah it cools down fast out here."

"Can I ask you a question Reuben?"

"I guess so."

"Are you going to marry Rosa?"

"Why do you ask?"

"Spring is coming and Rosa and Louise are supposed to move on when the weather breaks. That's the deal my grandparents made with them. I suppose they might let them stay longer but what if they don't?"

"I don't know," Reuben said. "I'm not in much of a position to provide for a family."

"Once I'm grown and take over the farm, you can work for me," Harrison said.

"I've been thinking about a job in town. I could get a horse and buggy to go back and forth...maybe someday get one of those automobiles and learn how to drive it."

"That would be great! I'd like to have an automobile myself. You watch; I'll get one of them 'machines' one of these days."

"Do you think Rosa will have me?"

"It's better than going out there and riding the rails," Harrison said and punched Reuben on the shoulder laughing.

Reuben laughed too, but then turned serious. "I'd like to have some prospects before I ask Rosa to marry me She could do a lot better than me. I know it."

"I don't know," Harrison said. "You love her. I can tell. That might make all the difference to a woman." He sighed. "I wonder if my Dad ever loved my Mom. He sure didn't act like it."

"It sounds like your Dad was just a selfish man. He seems to have saved all his love for himself, Reuben said.

He looked around hastily ready to duck as he said it. However, Elton wasn't present to hear his words.

Chapter Fifty Seven

The snow continued to fall. The family made a pallet for Reuben behind the stove so he wouldn't have to climb through the snow drifts to get back to his shack. The fine snow of earlier in the day had now morphed into large feathery drops that built up fast leaving the land buried underneath. Wandering out to the graves where her body and Elton's had been laid, Cecile could hardly tell it was even a cemetery, the snow had drifted so badly. Above her the old tree stood its branches still making a snowy statement as it pointed up on one side and down on the other. It looked ominous against a winter sky. At the time of her funeral it had seemed like an omen, she had felt vindicated, but both she and Elton were still here so now the old tree seemed to have lost its significance. She had not gone to heaven and he had not gone to the other place.

Cecile seldom thought about the bodies lying under the tree. She wasn't there...just a shell of what she used to be was hidden under all that earth and snow. As for Elton, he was still around the farm causing trouble...although not so much trouble lately. It was the calm before the storm no doubt. Around her the world was all black, white, and pale gray. The sky was a very light gray...almost white with the snow falling from its misty depths. Today she felt more strongly that she was a ghost in a ghostly world than she ever had.

"Snow has a way of muffling the normal sounds of the world and giving you an isolated feeling," she thought, saying this aloud. She liked the sound of her own voice.

She was lonely; why was her spirit and Elton's the only ones still here in this limbo between worlds? Where had the other people in the family plot gone? Was it because of the way she and Elton had died; the emotional as well as physical trauma she had suffered and Elton's rage that they remained here? Of course she had been given a choice to go into the light and hadn't done so because of Elton and her need to protect her children from him. She prayed to God that she'd have another chance to go to the light someday. Around and around she thought the same old things and never found any answers.

What would it be like to be here watching my children age and eventually die?

I don't think I could stand it.

I might have grandchildren and I'd see them grow up...at least I would if they stayed here on the farm. But even Vanessa and Harrison might move away from this farm someday soon. I'd be really lonely then.

Cecile felt a heaviness in her heart that pulled her down into a heap on the ground beside her grave. She wondered if she could choose to just sink into that grave and join her body. The thought was repugnant to her and she arose and went back to the house. Inside everyone was sitting around the fire, too cold to move it seemed. The cold snowy winter had made everyone depressed. Cecile flitted around the house checking everything out before settling down with the others to stare at the fire.

Harrison was playing with a yoyo trying to get it to climb back up to his hand once he extended it. At least he'd found something to occupy his time. Vanessa was holding a book up to the firelight, struggling to read it in the dim light. Rosa had pieces of a quilt that she was sewing together beside her. She was sewing two pieces of material together while chatting with Reuben about how he should decorate his house. Reuben seemed to like her attention but not the subject so much. Cecile glanced at her Dad. Henry was working on a piece of harness. He had set himself up at a table in the corner of the room close to the fire and was drilling a hole in the leather with a bit and augur. Louise wasn't in the room. Cecile had not seen her when she searched the house, where was the girl? She made another circuit of the house but didn't see the teenager.

If she's not inside, she must be out in the barn.
But why be out there in the cold?
I hope she didn't find more moonshine.
Should have learned her lesson the last time; but I'll bet she didn't.

Cecile headed through the wall and toward the barn. The cold didn't really bother Cecile any more except to depress her with its chill. However, she knew that Louise could freeze to death rapidly in this weather. Inside the garage she found that someone, probably Louise, had built a fire in the stove. It had started to die down though. She didn't see Louise right away so she decided to search every cranny. As she moved away from the fire, the temperature in the garage dropped several degrees. If Louise was in here, why wasn't she by the fire? Zooming up to the hayloft, almost flying through the wood frame, Cecile finally found Louise...and Elton.

Elton had a hand over Louise's mouth. The girl was laid back on the straw of the haymow, her mouth constricted, and abject fear in her eyes, petrified, as she stared at the spot where her invisible attacker hunkered as he undressed her. Fury greater than any she had felt toward Elton before catapulted Cecile into action.

"You dirty skunk," she shouted as she ran toward Elton. "Louise is your own daughter. What kind of animal are you?"

Elton let go of Louise and morphed through the wall of the barn, landing on his feet heavily on the ground below.

"Get your clothes on and get into the house, and stay there!" Cecile yelled at Louise before going after Elton.

She exited the barn in the same way her husband had and landed in the snow and mud beside the barn wall. Looking around she tried to see where Elton had gone but he hadn't left a trace. There were no footprints to track, no scent to follow.

"What would he do," she asked herself.

She stood watching as Louise exited the barn and raced for the house as if pursued by a devil.

"Run girl, run," Cecile said. "You are pursued by a devil all right."

Chapter Fifty Eight

Louise ran into the house and then into the bedroom. Climbing up to the attic where Vanessa had been sleeping, she curled herself into a ball and began to weep softly trying to muffle the sound so no one would hear. Cecile followed her and watched as the girl cried bitter tears into Vanessa's pillow. She felt like reprimanding her for being on Vanessa's bed but didn't have the heart for it.

I never saw a person who was such a lightning rod for trouble as this girl is.

But no wonder she's really traumatized this time; her father's ghost tried to rape her.

How could anyone deal with that?

Cecile was at a loss. It was up to her to stop Elton right now because he was going to seriously hurt someone...maybe Vanessa next time...or even Harrison. He seemed to be having some kind of break down. In desperation she began to pray for help to deal with him.

"Please show me what to do Lord because I don't know how to make him go away."

After she's said her own prayer she began to say The Lord's Prayer over and over again remembering how that prayer seemed to have protected Rosa. She prayed for the safety of the entire family and for the ability to protect them from any danger Elton could inflict.

Would Elton have raped Louise?

Could a ghost actually rape a living person?

Was he just testing his abilities, or trying to scare Louise; to punish her?

What on earth could he have been thinking?

She wondered again how she could have been so blind to the depths of depravity Elton had sunk to while alive. Why hadn't she realized what he was capable of?

Because I was just a perfect little housewife and mother. I had blinders on. I was stupid!

The bitterness in her own heart stunned Cecile. She didn't want to think like that but Elton had done her and her entire family wrong and he was still getting away Scott-free. It wasn't fair.

Her thoughts turned to God and her unanswered prayers. She knew her own heart wasn't pure because she was harboring hatred.

Please help me to let go and let you take care of Elton.

Help me not to hate him but pity what he's become.

Leaving Louise, who had cried herself to sleep, Cecile headed to the living room where the rest of the family still congregated.

"This is the winter that won't end," Henry was saying.

"Food stores are lower every day," Rosa agreed. "If not for Reuben's help..." She took Reuben's hand in hers.

"I'll go hunting again tomorrow if the snow lets up a little," Reuben said. "There's more corn in the field too, but it's buried under three feet of snow. It's not the best but we can live on it. The Indians did."

"Too bad we don't have that money Elton told me he was saving so he could disappear. We could keep the wolf from the door with that," Rosa commented.

"Tell me more about the money," Henry directed Rosa." Did he give you any clue as to where he stashed it?"

"Just that it was hidden away where no one would find it and someday he and I could use it to leave Ohio and start over."

"Did he say how much money it was," Harrison asked.

"Nope...but he seemed to think he had a good nest egg saved."

Cecile was thinking about how Elton had left her to scrimp and save every penny, to wear old clothes and dress her kids in ragged, patched, clothes just so he could stash away money with which to desert his family. She had meant to search for that hidden treasure but somehow she had forgotten to do it in the midst of other problems. Her anger rumbled inside her seeking an outlet. Someone should give Elton what he had coming.

"Vengeance is mine sayeth the Lord."

The words popped into her head so fast she startled. Was it a message from God or just a memory of words she'd once read in the Bible? Maybe it was an answer to her prayer. She brooded on this as the family began to get ready for bed. Reuben was going to spend the night in a bedroll beside the fireplace again. The family seemed glad to have him around and he'd been a big help with food and his assistance with chores.

"It's your job to keep the fire going tonight," Henry said.

"I will," Reuben promised.

"Get out of my bed!" Vanessa's loud voice echoed through the house. She had apparently found Louise.

Cecile went into the women's room to watch as Louise got to her feet and stumbled down the ladder and onto the bed she was supposed to sleep in. She covered her head and appeared to go back to sleep. Vanessa grumbled to herself as she remade her bed and crawled into it. She turned restlessly several times and then got up to go to the kitchen. Cecile followed her. She watched as her daughter warmed milk, poured it into a cup, and drank it. Vanessa had always had trouble sleeping and Cecile used to make warm milk for her to encourage sleep to come. It was kind of nice to see that Vanessa had carried on the tradition that her mother had set.

The house had fallen quiet by now with everyone asleep or almost asleep except for Vanessa. Vanessa sat in a kitchen chair leaning her head on one hand, sipping milk with the other. She looked tired and depressed. Cecile could understand why. She decided to speak to her daughter.

"Don't be afraid," she whispered. Cecile had slipped onto a chair across from her daughter.

"Mom?" Vanessa had gotten used to her mother's voice and knew she meant no harm to her.

"I need to tell you something," Cecile said. "It's about your father. He tried to rape Louise tonight. He might have hurt her badly if I hadn't stopped him. Don't go anywhere alone. Louise was out messing around in the barn and that's where he found her. There's some safety in numbers so stay with the others."

Vanessa was aghast. She stared at the place where she heard her mother's voice coming from.

"Can he actually rape someone?"

"I don't know. I stopped him but he was holding her and taking off her clothes. That was his intent. I think he's mad because you and Louise both told on him when he was alive. This is his way of punishing you. Be very careful. Stay with Grandpa Henry or with Harrison as much as you can. They'll help you."

Vanessa sat crying into her hands. "Why would you do these things to us Dad," she asked the empty walls.

Cecile moved away leaving Vanessa to her sorrow. She was once again exhausted, as she usually was when she interacted with the living in any way.

Chapter Fifty Nine

Cecile left her daughter sitting in the kitchen talking to the walls and went looking for Elton again. She had a piece of her mind to give that low life animal. She searched the barn from top to bottom but he wasn't there. He wasn't in any of the outbuildings either and when she stood at the grave where his body had been laid to rest and yelled at him, there was no response. Cecile went back to the house, and just in time.

She heard a muffled scream from the kitchen as she entered through the living room. Although she didn't need to use doors, old habits die hard, and she usually entered through doors anyway, although she usually entered without opening them. Heading through to the kitchen where she had left Vanessa, she stopped and screamed herself when she saw what was going on. Elton had Vanessa by the throat and he was squeezing as he used his other hand to rip at her clothes. She heard mumbled words coming from his mouth. The words were hard to make out but it sounded like.

"You tell your mother I abused you. Let me show you what abuse is."

Across the table Cecile saw a wad of money scattered hap-hazardly as if it had been thrown there. Where had it come from. Was this Elton's stash? She remembered that Rosa said he had tried to bribe Louise with money. Would he try to bribe Vanessa?

Cecile's body was rigid in shock; she was unable to think what to do. Her thoughts seemed trapped in a vicious circle that she could not process. The screams had awakened everyone and people started to enter the kitchen. Seeing an approximation of what was happening, her father headed toward Elton and Vanessa, only to be thrown halfway across the room by an out of control Elton. Reuben rushed in to help but he too was thrown back against a wall violently.

Beginning to get herself together, Cecile advanced on Elton but in his fury he didn't seem to notice her. Cecile grabbed his shoulder which actually felt substantial under her hand. Elton roared at her touch. Surprised, Cecile noticed smoke arising from the shoulder where her hand had touched him. In spite of apparent pain from her touch, Elton struck out at her tossing her backward. He then began to choke Vanessa with both hands.

Harrison entered the fight screaming "Leave my sister alone. You are a coward, attacking women."

"You want some of this," Elton raged, finding his voice at last, and hit Harrison in the mouth causing him to fall to the floor.

Cecile went icy cold again and her body became paralyzed with fear for her daughter and her son. It took agonizing minutes, it seemed, but she pulled herself free of the paralysis, she attacked Elton again, a ball of lava like fire streaking across the room in front of her as she reached him and grabbed at his face. All this caused further roars of pain from Elton but he didn't let go of Vanessa. He seemed determined to kill her.

By now Henry was striking out blindly trying to hit an invisible adversary and Reuben had staggered back into the fight. Elton struck out at both of them sending them tumbling but he had to let go of Vanessa to do it. Vanessa wasn't moving though. Her fear greater than any she'd known before, Cecile ran to help her daughter just as Elton turned back toward his victim.

Suddenly Cecile had had enough.

"You will not touch this girl again," she screamed at her husband, pointing lava spewing fingertips at Elton.

"What kind of father are you?

What kind of man?

Go away and stay gone. Don't ever come back here. I command you to leave for good."

She stretched herself to her tallest and was speaking with a voice she did not recognize. Her fury rushed out of her in a fiery stream striking Elton in the chest, propelling him backward.

"You will leave," she thundered. "Leave and never return to this place!"

At this point, Elton seemed to be whisked by some invisible force that carried him up through the ceiling and out into the cold winter night. Sighing loudly, trembling in fear, Cecile ran back to Vanessa and tried to revive her. Her father was there beside her.

"We need a doctor," Henry said.

"I'll go get Dr. Allen," Reuben said, "But what are we going to tell him?"

"I hadn't thought of that," Henry said. "He'll think one of us did this to Vanessa. He'd never believe what really happened. He'll call in the sheriff."

Cecile was rubbing Vanessa's hands and draping a wet cloth over her face. No one seemed to notice that the washcloth was moving itself.

"We could tell him she tried to hang herself," Louise said. "That would explain the marks on her throat."

Everyone looked at Louise. Rosa patted her daughter on the shoulder.

"That's really not a bad idea," Henry said. "You go get the doctor and we'll put a rope up somewhere to show him. Hopefully she'll revive before the doctor gets here and we'll tell her the story so she won't wake up and contradict us."

Reuben pulled on his clothes and headed out into the snow drifts, intent on his mission.

"You're in charge of getting a rope up over a rafter or something to show the doctor when he gets here," Henry told Harrison.

"How are we going to explain our bruises," Harrison asked. "You and I and Reuben all have shiners. Won't the doctor be suspicious?"

"Tell him that you found her hanging but she was still conscious," Louise said. "Tell him that she fought you when you tried to get her down and that she kicked you in your faces."

Again everyone looked at Louise who was apparently an accomplished liar.

Henry shrugged. "That's as good a story as any. If we tell him the truth he'll never believe it and will think we are covering up for one of us who did this to her, or that we all did it."

"We know the truth though don't we?" Rosa sounded bitter. Louise had just whispered in her ear the story of what had happened to her earlier in the barn.

Cecile who had been wrapped up in her daughter's situation, had never the less been aware of conversations going on in the room. With heightened senses, she had heard Louise's words to her mother.

But I don't know how Rosa can believe anything Louise says. She has a logical story for everything...just not the truth.

The doctor arrived and Henry and Harrison who had been beside Vanessa moved away so he could examine her. As unobtrusively as possible, Henry went to the table and picked up the dollar bills that had been scattered there.

"We'll have to ask Vanessa where these come from when she comes to," he whispered to Harrison.

"This almost looks like finger marks on her throat," the doctor said suspiciously.

"We were trying to pull the rope away from her throat. Maybe we left marks doing that," Harrison said.

The doctor looked at Vanessa again. "How long has she been unconscious?" he asked.

Cecile looked at the clock. The family had gone to bed about 11:00, she had left Vanessa in the kitchen about 12:00 and it was now 1:30 am.

Henry said, "It's been about an hour since we found her. Reuben had to go fetch you."

"Well, she's breathing but her brain lost a lot of oxygen I think. We'll just have to wait and see. Now...show me the rope she tried to hang herself from."

Harrison took the doctor to the bedroom where he'd put a rope around a joist in the ceiling and left it dangling with a noose in the bottom. The doctor looked it over, shook his head, but didn't say anything more.

Chapter Sixty

Cecile stayed with her daughter the rest of the night holding her hand and whispering to her. Vanessa had remained in her coma like state. Dr. Allen was supposed to return in the morning but that gave Cecile little comfort. He didn't seem to know how to help her daughter. Harrison had been around several times to sit with his sister, but he had finally gone to sleep in the living room by the fire. Cecile was exhausted from the night's events and had been in her own dream like state a part of the night. She tried to remain vigilant in case Elton came back. His behavior had been extreme tonight and she thought he had gone insane for sure. What he'd done had been so cruel and senseless.

"You'll be all right," she whispered to Vanessa; she hoped that was the truth.

Rosa and Louise checked on Vanessa early in the morning and Louise remained with her while Rosa went to cook breakfast. Louise stared at her half-sister with a look that Cecile thought was a combination of sorrow and concern. It could have been Louise lying unconscious in that bed and she knew it.

Cecile moved back as Louise took her sister's hand and began to speak to her.

"I know what you went through. He tried to do the same thing to me tonight. I think your mother saved me again. I want her to know how much I appreciate what she did. Especially since I'm the proof that her husband cheated on her."

Cecile was surprised to hear Louise voice appreciation for what she had done. It was even more surprising that Louise had enough empathy to see that the situation was painful for Cecile.

Vanessa lay passive as Louise held her hand. She seemed to be breathing easier this morning though, Cecile thought. As for Louise, maybe all the catastrophic happenings in this house were helping her to mature faster than she would have otherwise. She had been faced with some unpleasant and scary situations.

Vanessa stirred in her position on the bed. She whimpered a little.

Cecile jumped to her feet and hovered on the side of the bed away from Louise. She stroked her daughter's hand. Vanessa's eyelids fluttered, opened, and then closed again. Louise jumped up and ran to get her mother.

"Vanessa," Cecile whispered. "We had to call the doctor for you. He thinks you tried to hang yourself. We had to tell him something to explain the marks on your neck."

Vanessa's eyes opened and closed but there was no way to know if she knew or understood what Cecile had said. The rest of the family came running into the room. Henry went to Vanessa and hugged her gently. "Wake up little girl," he said. "We're all here and we all love you."

Vanessa opened tired eyes that barely focused and then slid closed again.

"You're doing good. Dr. Allen will be here soon to check on you, but you're going to be okay." Henry had tears in his eyes.

Cecile had tears dripping through the ectoplasm of her body as well. She had been so scared for her daughter.

Dr. Allen came around ten am and checked on Vanessa, who was still groggy but able to wake up for short times.

"It's a miracle," he said. "When I left here last night I didn't know if this girl was going to make it or not."

He looked down at Vanessa who was momentarily awake and said, "No more of that young lady. I want your promise that you won't ever do that again."

Vanessa looked perplexed. "What did I do?" she managed to whisper.

"You tried to hang yourself is what. Don't you dare ever try that again!" The doctor glared at her while Vanessa just stared at him a few moments and then succumbed to the lure of sleep.

"Keep a close eye on her and try to be extra nice to her when she wakes up," the doctor advised. "Call me if you need me. If not, I'll see her again in a few days."

"She's going to be all right?" Henry asked.

"I think so…yes."

Cecile couldn't rest even after she believed her daughter was going to be okay. Where had Elton gone and would he be back sometime soon to continue his campaign of violence?

She remembered how she had stood defiantly ordering him to go away and that he seemed to have no choice. The blast of her fury had propelled him backward as if she had shot fire and brimstone at him. Then it was if a mighty hand had jerked him away from the kitchen and the house. Somewhere she had heard that if you order a spirit to go away, it will have to go. Could that be true? Did I have the means to rid this house of Elton all the time and I was just too ignorant to use it? If so, how did I know to use it now?

Cecile remembered the prayers she had said on her own and The Lord's Prayer which she had repeated over and over just before Elton had morphed into a monster from her worst nightmares. She wondered if God had intervened to let her know what to do. He had saved her... but could Elton come back?

She had no idea.

Continuing to pray, Cecile asked that God would let her know if Elton was gone for good and if her children were safe now.

"Show me a sign that will let me know it's over," she prayed.

Meanwhile she was vigilant as she had never been before.

Vanessa began to heal and was soon back to her old self. She remembered much of what had happened and knew that her father's ghost had choked her. It made her cry when anyone mentioned it.

"It's so humiliating," she confided. "He had the nerve to try to pay me to let him do what he wanted to me. That's where all that money came from. I threw it at him."

"You're not responsible for what your parents do or don't do," Cecile advised her when they had a moment alone. "Your father will pay for his sins. I think he's gone and I don't believe he'll be back."

Vanessa cried some more, sobbing, "I hope so."

"Whatever happens, remember I will always love you," Cecile told her family at every opportunity. Even Henry and Harrison had become used to hearing her voice and were no longer afraid. She explained that she had seen the light coming for her but that she couldn't go at that time because of Elton.

"If the light comes back for me I will go with it this time, because it will mean that Elton is gone for good," she said. "Don't worry, I'll see you all later when it's your time."

It was a couple of weeks after Vanessa's near death, and miraculously the day had turned warm and sunny. Cecile was wandering in the fields of the farm looking for signs of the spring flowers that would soon be peeking out of the earth. She loved spring best of all the seasons.

The sky was a pastel blue with cotton puff clouds floating softly along its breezy pathways. She stared upward in delight. That's when she saw it. The light began to consolidate and make a beam of yellow white atoms that sought her out. Cecile thrilled at the sight. The light had returned for her. Still she was hesitant to walk into it.

"Is it okay to leave? Will Elton be back," she asked.

In the upper reaches of the light she could see figures standing, beckoning to her. She was delighted as the figures came closer to see that one was her mother.

"Oh Mom," she breathed out in awe and delight.

"Elton is gone," her mother said, "Come to Mama. The kids will be all right."

Cecile smiled in joyful relief and went to her mother, who hugged her.

finis

Saundra Crum Akers was born in Urbana, Ohio but lived in rural Southern Ohio during most of her childhood. Her family roots all date back to the early 1800's in Ohio and merge into one of four adjacent counties, namely, Adams, Pike, Highland, and Brown. She now lives in Columbus, Ohio but visits her home territory often. Her novels are set in real towns and villages with some local history and landmarks involved in the overall plot. She believes this adds a new and unique dimension to her stories for those who live in the area, and does not diminish the storyline for those who do not. All books must be set somewhere and most seem to be in Los Angeles, New York, or the like. Rural America has its own culture; this culture is also valid and just as interesting and mysterious.

Novels by Saundra Crum Akers

Bite of the Serpent
Dream Buster
Endless
Fear Treads the Mountains
Ghost Hunter
Guilty!
Joe White and the Seven Ghosts
Manifesting Destiny
Roadrunner
Sins of the Mothers
Spooked
Tempest Rider
The Abandoned Ghost
The Smelly Man
The Wannabe Witch
Whispers on the Wind

The Questing Hart Series
Hopeful Hart
Shattered Hart
Spirited Hart

Made in the USA
Middletown, DE
25 August 2022

71299710R00203